HEIRS *of the* TIDE

LOST TALES OF SEPHARAD - BOOK TWO

· MICHELLE FOGLE ·

Enjoy other great books by Michelle Fogle

City of Liars

Book One in the Lost Tales of Sepharad Series

Heirs of the Tide

This is a work of fiction. Names, characters, organizations, places, and events are either products of the author's imagination or are used fictionally. Any resemblance to actual persons, living or dead, or actual events are coincidental.
Text copyright © 2023 by Michelle Fogle
All rights reserved

No part of this book may be reproduced, or stored in a retrieval system, or transmitted in any form or by any means, electronic, mechanical, photocopying, recording, or otherwise without express written permission of the publisher.

Published by Legacy Imprints
Distributed by Amazon Publishing
ISBN (e-book) 978-1-7379534-4-9
ISBN (paperback) 978-1-7379534-3-2
Cover design by Damonza
First edition

*This book is dedicated to
Adam, Alex, and Brendan*

PROLOGUE

June 23, 1488, la Oració

Aularia Bautista

I STARE OUT over the gunwale of the pilgrimage ship, la Oració. Wiping the slaver from my lips, I draw a halting breath, trying to hold back the inevitable. At any moment, my belly could heave violently again. Twice this morning, I emptied my insides over the side. Could there be anything left but bile?

Joachim leaves his navigational duties at the binnacle and stands elbow to elbow with me. "Everyone goes through this when first at sea," he says. "I thought you'd adjust after a few days. But you seem to have a worse bout than most."

"Small comfort," I reply. My seasickness has lasted long after the other pilgrims' malady subsided. But the sea has been calm these four days, and the weather is clear and balmy. What if it's not seasickness at all?

Joachim strokes my arm. "I'll order the *despensero* to prepare an infusion to settle your stomach." He pulls away and walks toward the hatch.

I gaze back toward the sea and relish the breeze on my face. We're not even midway through our journey to the Holy Land. How will I cope if this biliousness doesn't stop? But we can only build a new life when we're far from the Inquisition's threat. Through all my misfortunes in Barcelona, I discovered strengths I didn't realize I had. Now I'm about to enter a foreign world. I don't know the language, the customs, or the dangers. Will those strengths sustain me?

Another wave of nausea makes me dry heave. I brace myself. From across the deck, the *despensero* Señyor Caro approaches me. Bearded and wearing a black apothecary coif, he offers me a steaming earthenware cup.

"Maestro Déulocresca asked me to make this for you, Sister."

I take a deep breath. "Bless you," I say. It seemed prudent to remain in the guise of a sister of St. Claire, at least until we reach Sicily.

"It's a blend of fennel, ginger, and peppermint, known to offer temporary relief from spells of seasickness," Señyor Caro says. "But I suggest you seek the advice of a physician when we land, if it continues."

I take the cup in both hands. The herbal ingredients have collected at the bottom. Señyor Caro smiles, bows, and returns below deck. The hot liquid has a pleasant fragrance. I take a few sips and the warm tonic seems to soothe my urge to vomit. All smells seem more pungent than usual, especially when first arising in the morning. The stench below deck is more than I can bear. The slop bucket and that horrid *alquitrán* surely must be what hell smells like. But even the cook pot and wood fire make me retch. There's a spot on the weather deck near the mainmast where a steady breeze purifies the air. That's where I prefer to spend my time. By midday, I might tolerate *galleta* and broth, but not much more. Joachim keeps assuring me we will soon arrive at the port city of Messina. Hopefully, I'll feel better once I plant my feet on solid ground again.

However, other things in my constitution trouble me besides this nausea. Despite eating very little, my belly has become bloated and there's a constant urge to urinate. From folklore and the wisdom of women, I've learned enough to recognize the sum of these signs. Please,

God, let it not be true. The thought makes me shudder. After my arrest by the Inquisition in April, I lost all track of time. I didn't count the days, but my expected menses have never come. I keep waiting, hoping my flow will begin.

Joachim knows I was raped, but I have not yet revealed the possibility I might be pregnant. The two of us have never been intimate. We planned to wait until we can marry. Friar Cirera's nightly assaults during my captivity make him the most likely father. I'm certain Joachim will accept and love such a child as his own. But what worries me more is whether *I* can love and accept this child. Will he or she be "the blessing from the curse" as Joachim refers to his own tragic origin? Or will the child be a painful, inescapable reminder of my rapist and the suffering he inflicted on me? I thought I had destroyed him and escaped his treachery. Does he haunt me still, inside my own flesh? I take another swallow of the drink to soothe my twisting gut. Right now, I need answers.

❧

Joachim Déulocresca

The port of Messina comes into view, with Reggio de Calabria also visible on the north side of the channel. The late afternoon sun is behind us, casting a golden glow onto the water. I turn to my young apprentice, Dâvi Salmonis.

"The main current through this strait shifts every six hours," I tell him. "With the level of the tide and rocky shoreline, it can take all your skills to bring the ship safely to port. But today we are fortunate. The current and the wind go our direction." I relay my landing instructions to the boatswain, who orders the crew to begin preparations for docking.

I glance at Aularia, standing at the leeward gunwale. She gazes at the terraced green hillside with tiered buildings crowned with terracotta roof tiles. Their plastered facades have turned rosy in the edge-wise sunlight. We are only a day and a half by sail from Girgente and the island where I hid her father's estate in a sea cave. I'm certain that my fisherman friend, Niccolo, would help me recover it. The money would help immensely to get established in Jerusalem and assure our future. But would Aularia and my young page be safe here without me, while I reclaim it? Separating probably isn't wise. If something happened to me, I hate to think what would become of them? Despite the peaceful vista, my palms are moist and my belly churns. Dâvi and I walk over to join her.

"This island is still in the realm of the Spanish sovereigns," I tell Dâvi. "The Inquisition cannot be far away. But like the people I met in Girgente, the locals view the Spanish as useless occupiers who provide neither protection nor benefit, and only levy taxes. Most make their livelihood on the goodwill of traders, merchants, and travelers."

"No one here knows us or any of the fugitives," Aularia says.

"That's right. As long as we don't draw attention to ourselves, we should be safe until we book passage to the Holy Land," I say.

"We need secure lodging for ourselves and the other pilgrims," she says.

"There's a large hostel right here at the water's edge in the Giudecca, the Jewish Quarter," I say. "Let's gather our belongings."

I escort our band of refugees ashore and use my fluency in Italian to arrange their lodging at the Ostello del Pellegrino. When I return to the ship, Aularia has removed the nun's habit, and replaced it with her grey velvet hooded cloak. We bring our possessions to the weather deck. As we prepare to depart, I collect my wages and say farewell to my trusted employer, Commander Fransèc Bonto, and his rescue ship, la Oració.

"You saved these people's lives," I say, "and our lives. I will never forget your kindness." We embrace and he gives me a firm pat on the shoulder. "I pray there will be no reprisal for your act of decency."

"Transporting pilgrims? Unlikely," he says. "I hate to lose you, Joachim. I hope smoother sailing lies ahead for you."

We slog our way to the Giudecca carrying our bags and locate the inn where Lluc Pascal and I stayed several months before. The innkeeper provides a room for Dâvi and me to share. Aularia will have her own. Since she continues to feel queasy, I ask the innkeeper for the name of a nearby physician. He points me to Dr. Moses Vitali and gives directions to find him.

Dâvi stays back at the inn with the door to our room bolted, while Aularia and I traverse the narrow, cobbled lanes to locate the doctor. With the help of locals, we arrive at the infirmary before dark. A placard beside the lintel bears Dr. Moses Vitali's name. We enter a large room with archways. Benches stand against the walls. An old man with a festering wound on his arm, and a mother and young girl wait for the physician.

A young woman greets us. Her head is covered in white linen and she has a white apron gathered at the collarbone over a blue gown after the manner of a midwife.

"*Buona sera*. I am Mira, the daughter of Dr. Vitali, and I assist him in the infirmary," she says in Italian. "How might I be of service?"

"I'm Signore Déulocresca and this is Aularia. We just arrived from Barcelona on our way to Jerusalem," I tell her.

She raises her brows. "Jerusalem. I see."

"Aularia developed what we thought was seasickness during the voyage. But her symptoms have continued."

"Are any of the other passengers still ill?"

"No."

She eyes Aularia with an agreeable smile. "Come this way." She leads us into a side room through a curtained portal. Shelving and a credenza display glass jars and bottles with various herbs and liquids, tools and basins. A low table commands the center of the room.

"We've had a steady stream of travelers from Spain in recent months. She studies my face. "Many head for Jerusalem like you. Some continue their journey to other cities of refuge, such as Salonica or Constantinople."

"Then you appreciate our need for discretion," I say.

"Absolutely. They captured a woman refugee from Zaragoza in Palermo last month. You must be very cautious."

A flush of heat spreads over my face and neck.

Mira turns to Aularia. "If you will, Signora, please lie down."

Signora? She assumes we are married. My stomach flutters as I translate her request. Aularia stretches out atop the table and I stand beside her. The signorina puts a pillow under her head. "Tell me what you have been experiencing."

Aularia describes her nausea, aversion to strong odors, and bloating. As I convey her explanation and watch Mira's eyes brighten, I realize what the likely cause of her malady might be. A rush of sanguine humor floods my veins and my smile goes stiff. Mira palpates Aularia's abdomen. Then she gestures to her breasts.

"And do you have tenderness here?"

Aularia seems to understand without translation and nods.

The signorina pats her lower belly. "Do you frequently need to urinate?"

My beloved looks at me to interpret, which I do. Her brows knot and she again nods.

"When was your last time of *niddah*?" she asks.

Aularia rubs her temple.

"It will be alright, my love," I say. "She asks when your last menses were."

A pained sigh escapes her lips, and she closes her eyes. "April," she whispers.

Signorina Vitali folds her arms, smiles at me and then at Aularia. She offers her hand to pull Aularia to a sitting position. "I can make an herbal remedy to help your nausea. However, I don't think you have an illness or need the services of a physician," she says.

I translate for my love and see her face cloud with dread.

Mira tips her head to one side. "You have reason to celebrate. As a midwife, I believe you are with child, Aularia. *Beshaah tova.*"

My eyes water, and my throat grows thick. I sit beside Aularia on the examining table and put one arm around her. "We are going to have a child." I stroke the back of her hand.

She leans into the hollow of my shoulder, drops her chin to her chest, and covers her mouth to stifle a whimper.

"Wonderful news," I say, though inside I'm bewildered. "You have been very helpful and kind, Signorina. We'll take those herbs."

Signorina Vitali turns to the shelves and removes several containers, carrying them to the credenza, where she formulates the medicine in a mortar and pestle. I caress Aularia's shoulder, and gently rock. The air feels dense with all the words we cannot say just now. Further conversation must wait until we're alone. After a few minutes, Signorina Vitali comes over and hands me a packet tied with string.

"Steep two pinches in a cup of boiling water. Drink this tonic each morning on arising. Try to eat a little something. Get fresh air. It should help."

As I translate, she notices Aularia's melancholia.

"It's not an ideal situation in which to bring a child. Have hope. You will be free and your child will be born in Jerusalem." Then she opens her hand and displays a *kame'ah*, a small Hebrew inscription on parchment. Aularia gapes with her head atilt.

"It's a protective amulet that bears the names of angels who guard expectant mothers from the forces of evil," I tell her.

From her apron pocket, Signorina Vitali pulls a lacy pomander attached to a long ribbon. "I filled this with rue for added protection," she says. "Wear it under your garments." She carefully folds the charm into a triangle and tucks the parchment inside the pomander. Then she ties the ribbon around Aularia's neck. Aularia lifts the pomander to her nose to inhale the fragrance and then drops it inside the neck of her gown with the hint of a smile.

I release a deep breath with a slight moan.

"Thank you for this," Aularia says and puts her palm to her chest.

"My father and I are here to help. Tell us if you have any further needs."

After paying for her services, we bid farewell and begin our walk back toward the inn. My mouth grows dry as I consider the thorny topic ahead.

"I should have told you what I suspected," Aularia says. "Forgive me."

"There's nothing to forgive. You weren't certain you were pregnant until now. Be assured, I will protect you and your honor. The child will have my name, even though he or she is not my blood. But they must never know otherwise. More than ever, it's essential that we marry as soon as we can arrange it."

"I have no hesitation about marrying you, Joachim. I love you."

"But I must tell you, there are some obstacles we must overcome."

She pauses and turns to me. "Obstacles?"

I take her hand and squeeze softly. We stand beside a large fountain surrounded by stone benches. Couples and families stroll nearby. I gesture for her to sit and we huddle together. The rush and splash of water masks our words from other's ears.

"You were raised outside the Jewish faith. Although your parents continued to practice it in secret and died for it, you are considered a Christian. It goes against Jewish law for me to marry you. I let the signorina think we were already married to shield you from disgrace. But I don't want to live a lie. I want to do this right."

"I agree. I am proud of my heritage and want to be accepted. What must we do?"

"The steps are simple, but weighty. There are rituals and ceremonies necessary to reclaim you as a Jew. You must stand before a Rabbinic court, a Bet Din. They will question both your knowledge and sincerity. Then you make a vow to embrace Jewish law and practices. You must go through a ritual purification in the cleansing waters of the *mikveh*. And you will also take a Hebrew name. Your parents likely gave you one at birth. Did they ever reveal such a name to you?"

"A Hebrew name? I don't believe so. Although, when I was very young, my mother used to call me Oralee or Oralita."

"Sounds like Aularia. Oralee, means, my light, or my little light in Hebrew."

"I never knew that. Most of what I've learned about the Jewish faith, I was taught by my murderous confessor, when he tutored me to gather his damning evidence."

I shake my head. "What ironic justice," I say.

"But could I hold up under the questioning of a court of rabbis?"

"They simply want to be assured that you do this of your own free volition, unlike the impossible decision your parents had to make. No one would ever force you. The opposite. They may try to talk you out of it."

"But we could not marry otherwise."

"Indeed. However, that can't be your primary reason. You must want it for yourself. We can go to the synagogue tomorrow and inquire. But honestly, we may have to wait until we're in Jerusalem."

"Why is that?"

"The Inquisition has spying eyes on the Jews of Messina, just as they did on Montjuic. It would place the community in great peril to reclaim any *converso*."

"They murdered your friend Aaron, his family, many in the community, or forced them from their homes."

"The same thing could happen here. So, I doubt they will risk it."

I survey the water spilling over the lip of the fountain and splashing into the pool. Its tranquil melody washes over me as I try to compose my thoughts. "There is another decision we must make together. And the choices are both undesirable. Every day we remain in Messina, we increase our risk of being discovered, arrested, and dragged back to Barcelona for trial."

"Signorina Vitali made that all too clear," she says.

"However, this is the closest we will be to the island where I hid your family assets. The longer we wait to reclaim them, the greater the likelihood they'll be stolen. Without that inheritance, we will arrive in Jerusalem with no means of support. There are no friends or relatives on whom we can rely. We could face unimaginable hardships."

She folds her arms and looks down. "I've pondered these things myself. Getting to safety takes precedence over searching for riches. I have the skills of a bookkeeper and you are a mapmaker and navigator. Surely, we can find ways to earn our keep or start our own endeavor. Once we're established, you can come back here to reclaim it. It may already be gone."

"I'd wager not. I watched the Janissaries walk up and down that strand, combing the beach and collecting cargo for hours. They never discovered it."

"Then, we can wait until the time is right. If it's that well-hidden, it should still be there."

"Let us hope."

CHAPTER 1

1515, Ramla, Filastin District

Yonatan Déulocresca

The urge to wager nettles me like an itch I cannot scratch; a worm burrowing deep inside my gut without relief. Sweat drizzles down my temples and beads on my upper lip. I study three contenders on horseback, who stand ready on the weather-beaten sod of the caravanserai. They shoulder variously colored pennants that flap in the dusty breeze. The Mameluke cavalrymen have erected tall masts for a game of Qabaq, gourd shooting on horseback. From the coffeehouse arcade in the northwest corner, I have a select view. The riders' course will pass directly in front of me. After sizing up their abilities, I'm certain who is most likely to win.

A Mameluke lieutenant sidles between tables, urging patrons to place their bets, noting their wagers on a beeswax tablet with his stylus. I wrestle to rein in my impulses. I promised. What good is my word if I go back on it now? But luck is in my favor. I just know it. One last time, and then I'll quit for good. I yield to the worm in my gut. My hand shoots skyward and I blurt out.

"Here, I'll wager!"

Patrons at nearby tables look up from the backgammon boards to smirk with amusement. The Mameluke lieutenant's steely eyes land on me. He swaggers over. The white turbaned officer looks down his bearded cheeks.

"Well?"

"Thirty *hatichot* on…" I tip my head, straining to read the Arabic moniker on the leather shield of my chosen rider. But reading has always been hard for me. "The master with the green pennant," I finally say.

The officer sneers. "You speak of the honorable Abdul al-Misri." His eyes narrow and he tugs at his thick moustache. "You're just a donkey herder. That equals more than a gold Sultani. Show your coin."

The last guilty prompt inside my head drifts away like a cloud on the *khamsin*. I pull out the drawstring pouch from my waistband and pour its contents onto the table. The money I'm about to gamble belongs to my father. He gave it to me to keep the donkeys well supplied until spring travelers arrive with full purses. This is the largest sum I've ever bet. My heart races and every muscle in my body pulses with the thrill.

The lieutenant stirs through the pieces of silver with his short sword. "Your currency is good, ass-boy." When he says that dual-meaning label, laughter echoes through the colonnade. I fume inside, glaring. If there is one thing that vexes me more than any other, it's when someone suggests that I'm stupid, just because I train animals. They'll soon learn how clever a donkey breeder can be. I've made a study of animal behavior. That's how I will win this gamble. They'll see.

"Who else will wager?" the officer shouts. "Who will lay odds on Master Ibn Faraj or Master Ibn Amir-Aziz?"

Olive-skinned hands adorned with elaborate henna filigree set a brass tray with a small cup onto my table next to the array of coins. The aroma of coffee tinged with cardamom wafts into my senses, eclipsing the stink of camels.

"Have you lost all reason, Yoni?" she whispers, leaning close to my ear. "Your father will disown you."

I turn to peer over my shoulder at the beauty in the marigold-colored veil, with kohl outlining her dark eyes. "I can win this, Shuli. You'll see," I say, more determined than ever.

With scorn knotting her brow, she releases an exasperated huff and disappears into the horde of coffeehouse patrons.

I began sizing up the abilities of these three challengers as soon as they appeared. They're from a company of the Halqa, a corps of free Mameluke cavalry that arrived three days ago from Egypt on their way north. Rumors whisper of an Ottoman invasion. This caravan station is at a strategic crossroad on the Via Maris, the highway between Cairo and Damascus, Jaffa and Jerusalem. Two sons of gentry, the *awlād an-nās*, are among them. If any are masters of *Furusiyya*, it would be those two. The centuries old tradition of Arabian horse mastery is something I've admired since I was a child. My earliest dream was to become a *faris*.

Regrettably, I can only appreciate it from a distance. They relegate Jews like me to *dhimmi* status in Muslim society, an inferior class. At no time can I ride a horse or camel, placing my head above that of a Muslim. The single time I tried it, I was sentenced to a public beating and my father had to pay a hefty fine. But my longing remains. Over the years, I've had many opportunities to observe a true horse master's wordless dialogue with his horse. They read messages from the swish of a tail, the angle of an ear; the velocity of a snort. They speak with a touch, a murmur, a bearing. This mystical dance can mean survival or death on the battlefield.

I turn toward the adjacent bay where a noisy band of tribesmen has assembled. Their gestures and facial expressions tell me I'm a target of their mockery. It confirms my hunch when I hear their competing bid for the crimson rider. They're betting on Master Razin Ibn Faraj from Alexandria.

But these are not ordinary tribesmen who herd sheep and goats in the hills between Ramla and Jerusalem. By the chevron pattern of their *keffiyot* and the curved dagger in the belt of the man who leads them; I can tell they are *Urbān*. The *Urbān* view all Mamelukes as exploitive colonizers, and Jews as worms in the dirt. I've heard they rob pilgrims and raid caravans en route to the Holy City. Their sheik has visited the *khan* before. With his ugly, toothy grin, he's earned the name al-Dabaa, the Hyaena. He leads a cabal of thugs and assassins who demand *baksheesh* from business owners, and traffic in stolen goods and prostitution. But as far as the owners of shops and eateries at the caravanserai are concerned, all paying customers are welcome as long as they honor the desert code of hospitality.

I also notice that the other cavalrymen placed their bets on the third rider, announced as Master Nasser ibn Amir-Aziz. Do they know something about his abilities that I don't? Have I bet on the wrong man? My stomach begins to churn. I hope they are simply loyalists.

The riders turn their horses and amble toward the south gate of the caravanserai. From several furlongs away, they can reach a full gallop by the time they come through the archway. A handful of soldiers urge travelers and merchants to move their camels and pack animals to the side, well beyond the course of the riders. Curious bystanders line the lower arcade and shopkeepers pause in their dealings to watch the competition from the shady portico.

With the high-pitched blast of a trumpet, the first horseman comes hurtling through the opening. The furious hooves raise a dust cloud. His blue riding tack flutters in the wind. It is the cavalrymen's favorite, Amir-Aziz. He rises in the stirrups, poised to shoot. One horse's length before the pole, he releases the arrow. But it merely grazes the gourd, lodging in the post. A chorus of groans spreads through the crowd.

The rider reaches the far end of the enclosure. He turns and doubles-back for the second shot. As he gallops past, he pivots in the saddle for a rear shot. But the arrow misses entirely. It plummets toward the spectators, who dive out of its path. The colonnade echoes with a blend of horror and hilarity. Master Amir-Aziz has likely disqualified himself. My estimation of him as unskilled has proved correct. He must be a ringer.

Next, the crimson rider comes streaming through the breezeway at full speed. I shade my eyes from the glare of the sun. Ibn Faraj balances in the stirrups, arching back and upward. He draws his bow. When he reaches the post, he releases the arrow. A straight shot. The gourd flails and bobs on the rope tether. The Urbān tribesmen break into a cheer and throw their fists in the air. Some glower at me. I lean forward, shrugging to loosen the knots in my shoulders.

Ibn Faraj reaches the northeast gate and swings his stallion around. He picks up speed as he gallops back toward the target. Raising his bow, the archer draws back on the string and releases. The shaft flies so fast; it seems invisible. But the tip deflects off the gourd and wedges in the mast itself. Tumult breaks out in the crowd. Nearby spectators debate the relative merit of this performance. Still, it will be difficult to beat.

I drum my fingers on the table, and my palms become moist. Al-Dabaa looks over, tosses his head back with taunting pride. He contorts his ugly mouth into a sneer. Two of his men raise their hands, swiveling their bodies in a premature victory dance. I take a sip of my coffee, wipe my mouth, and turn my eyes toward the gate.

The last marksman, Al-Misri, pounds into the enclosure with rolling thunder. I rise to my feet. Something brushes against my side. I glance over. Shuli stands beside me, watching the rider. She presses her fingers against her lips. My eyes shift back to Al-Misri. At three lengths out, the horseman raises his bow. Clenching my fists, I watch as the arrow arches. I hold my breath. A direct hit. The gourd swings violently. The force of the impact spins the rope around the pole.

I howl, pumping one fist. But before the gourd can fully unwind, the green rider shoots backward over the horse's tail. The second shaft pins the gourd to the post. What utter mastery. I shake my head in disbelief. Al-Misri has pegged the target with two shots in one pass. Onlookers gape, dumbstruck at first. Then a roar of amazement bursts the silence. Women in the upper arcade cut loose a laudatory trill with their tongues, ki-li-li-li-li… I leap into the air, flailing my arms and cheering. I won. I whirl around, gazing toward heaven. Then I throw my arms around Shuli.

"I knew it," I say. "I told you I'd win."

"And I say, God protects fools," she replies, resolute in her disapproval. She pulls away from my embrace and heads back inside the coffeehouse.

Al-Dabaa glares red-faced, curling his lips back like his namesake. His cohorts huddle around him, jabbering. A backlash is brewing. The Mameluke lieutenant saunters over to the *Urbān*, flanked by two other cavalrymen. Al-Dabaa continues his unflinching stare. The officer holds out his hand. The leader seems not to respond at first. Then he slides his hand toward his hip. He lifts the flap on the leather purse. Only then, as he counts the lost silver into the officer's hand, does he break the menacing gaze.

The officer takes his cut of the winnings and directs one of his escorts to deliver the rest to the victor. I gather my silver from the tabletop, feeding the coins back into the small leather sack. Then, I add my newly gained reward, cinch the sack, and tuck it into my waistband.

Al-Dabaa slumps onto his stool and several men sit down beside him. The tribesmen grumble, shifting aimlessly, all the while glaring at me. One man draws his flattened hand across his throat like a beheading. I stiffen. I don't want any trouble. All I want is a bottle of Arak and a good meal; fire roasted meat with *zhug*, the fiery dipping sauce Shuli's café owner mother Edna is famous for.

I push my way through the milling patrons and gaming tables into the café. My footfalls soften on the rugs covering a polished stone floor. Embroidered textiles adorn the walls, and enormous latticework oil lamps hang by chains from the ceiling. The air is infused with the aroma of coffee and sandalwood incense from braziers. Customers wearing multi-colored *ridas* recline on banquette seating with low tables. They dip wads of *lahoh*, a spongy flatbread into small saucers mounded with *ful* or mashed eggplant, garlic and peppers. My mouth waters. I seldom have the money or occasion to spoil myself here and feel a little out of place.

I notice an empty table, quickly weave a course between the diners, and sit down. Within moments Shuli appears holding a tray. She sets a small plate of pickled vegetables and olives in front of me.

"What can I serve you, Sayid?" she asks. Now inside her own place, she allows the gold hued veil to fall loosely about her shoulders.

"Sayid? So, you're going to call me sir; now that I have money?" I admire the perfect shape of her dainty mouth and the tiny birthmark at the margin of her upper lip. The bend in one brow and the flare of a nostril tell me she's still annoyed. But her voice remains polite. "We honor all our guests. Now- we have spit roasted mutton, stewed squab, or fire parched locust if you prefer."

I scowl, shuddering. "I've never understood why you like locust. That's not food."

"You don't know what you're missing." She strains a smile. "Well?"

I order the lamb I've been craving and a bottle of Arak. Shuli quickly returns with her tray, setting a bottle of licorice spirits, a carafe of spring water, and a glass on the table. I pour the potent liquor into the glass, and then add the cool water, turning the drink milky.

"Blessed is the Creator of all things," I say in Hebrew and tip my head back, throwing the contents down my throat. I'm pouring a second cup when I realize al-Dabaa and two of his men have entered the café and are snaking through the tables toward me.

"Dog piss," I whisper and gulp the liquor straight. Instinctively, I finger the handle of my mule whip, coiled at my side. A lot of good it will do in these close quarters. If they want a brawl, I'm ready, unless they draw blades. But there is no easy escape.

The three men tower over me, their hulking arms folded across their chests.

"The sheik wants his money, Jew," says a pock-marked tribesman.

"We're all honorable men, here. This was a fair wager. Sit. Let me buy you a drink." I strain to grin and motion to the unoccupied cushions.

Al-Dabaa bends down and sweeps the bottles and dishes from the table. The sound of smashing glass and pottery makes everything stop. Al-Dabaa leans in on one hand, coming eye to eye with me.

"We never drink with Jews, you cocky mule-fucker," he hisses. "Turn over my silver or I'll take your head off." The two thugs clasp their hands on the hilts of their knives, jostling them in a threatening manner. I grit my teeth, but no one moves.

At that instant, an object at high velocity flies between me and my enemy, wedging into the tabletop, a hair's breadth from al-Dabaa's hand. With a startled jump, the sheik's eyes bulge. A kitchen carving knife quivers in the wood. I gasp and rear back. We turn toward the source, which I know without even looking. Edna is known for more than her *zhug* recipe. As a maiden, she'd come to the caravanserai with a wandering troupe of acrobats and jugglers; one of the few professions permitted Jews in the southernmost part of Arabia where she was born.

"Get out!" she shouts in her deep voice. The petite, spry café owner stands behind the *Urbān*. Two Halqa soldiers flank her, wearing short-sleeved hauberks and white turbans, their swords drawn. Patrons rise from their tables, retreating out of the way. Al-Dabaa slowly stands upright, lifting his arms and hands away from his body as a sign of no contest. My gut tightens. I reach down and snatch the broken bottleneck from the floor. Al-Dabaa turns halfway toward Edna, keeping one eye on me. The men of the *Urbān* now draw their weapons, but then stop short when they judge their armored rivals. I grab the handle of the carving knife, yanking it out of the tabletop. Jumping to my feet, I hold the blade and jagged glass, ready to defend myself. Al-Dabaa glances over his shoulder at me. I flash a one-sided smirk. The sheik draws a tense, audible breath.

"You can't come in here and threaten my customers. It dishonors the code of hospitality," says Edna to the *Urbān*. "Make dust."

The sheik and his followers hesitate for a moment, and then turn their heads to survey their options.

"Keep your weapons sheathed and we'll allow you to depart in peace," says one of the Mamelukes. "We don't want bloodshed."

The tribesmen exchange glances. I study their furrowed brows and twitching frowns. Finally, al-Dabaa gives a subtle nod. The two marauders release their blades. I take a breath.

"Now go," says the soldier, gesturing with his scimitar.

The men bow toward their overlords, hedging toward the door. Al-Dabaa glares at me, hissing with venom in his breath. "You'll pay for this insult, donkey-boy. Tenfold."

The Halqa march them outside. Hopefully, they will force the *Urbān* to leave the caravanserai altogether. But will they be waiting for me when I depart? Do they know where I live? I will lie low for a while. The threat might pass with time, but I doubt it. Their kind hold grudges.

I meet Edna's stern gaze. She slowly shakes her head, extending her hand to retrieve the knife. "If I didn't have such fondness for your father…" She grimaces, inhaling deeply to withhold her usual burst of swearwords. "You're lucky I didn't have you thrown out with them."

"But…"

Edna thrusts out her hand. "Do not talk back to me!" She wags her finger. "You know very well not to bring such mayhem here. Had you not been gambling; this never would have happened. Your father taught you better. Shulamit!" she yells.

Shuli hurries over.

"Clean up this mess and bring our guest a fresh bottle of Arak."

Shuli gathers the broken glass and spilled food, shooting me fleeting glances. "Unbelievable," she mutters.

"Have your supper and go home, Yoni," Edna says and turns away.

I sink onto the cushion against the wall. I've earned their scorn – again. Edna and her daughter have been kind to me and my father for years. They are like family. I grew up with Shuli, and have always dreamed of one day marrying her. But she sees me as brash, impulsive, unlettered, and scruffy. There seems no way to redeem myself in her eyes. I cannot explain why trouble always seems to find me. Now, to make matters worse, a whole band of *Urbān* wants revenge.

I linger over my meal, but delay leaving until after sundown, playing a round of backgammon. Then I slip out of the back exit of the café. Stealing around the perimeter of the high stone wall to the opening, I survey the dark surroundings for attackers in wait. But I see no one. Still tethered to a post beside the water trough, my favorite jennet, Malka, neighs and leans into me. Her smooth neck feels warm to my palm. I can barely see the stirrup to place my foot, but climb into the saddle. With a soft click of the tongue and a shake of the reins, Malka saunters into the darkened almond grove at the edge of the village. If there are wild dogs or thugs hidden in the shadows, Malka's keen hearing and superior eyesight will notice. Donkeys don't advance if they sense danger. My shortcut through the grove is seldom traveled. It's the fastest way to our *gedayrah*, the stable and fenced paddock where we keep our drove of donkeys. They're the hardest working members of my father's enterprise, guiding pilgrims and travelers to the holy sites.

When we reach the enclosure, the herd clusters together in one corner. The moon is rising as I slide out of the saddle and open the gate. Malka trots past me, eager to reunite with her companion, Giboor. I hurriedly pile fodder into the feed troughs inside the gated bay beneath the upper story dwelling. The donkeys swarm inside, braying as they vie to be first at the mangers. I remove Malka's saddle and then swing the wood slat gate shut. Before ascending to the upper room where I stay, I scout the surrounding countryside. As I peer westward toward the coast, I notice it. There's a signal light from the *migdal-or*, one in a string of coastal watchtowers. When the first ships arrive each spring, they send out a beacon. That means a new season of commerce for all the local merchants, peddlers, and services like ours, who depend on the earnings they bring. As soon as the sun rises, I'll send word up to father in Jerusalem by carrier pigeon, and then make the donkey coffle ready for the journey to the port of Jaffa. With any luck, we'll be among the first to greet the visitors. I just hope we'll be safe, and al-Dabaa and his band of marauders don't cause us any trouble.

CHAPTER 2

Jaffa, Filastin District

Joachim Déulocresca

Sunrise reflects off the Mediterranean, glimmering in orange and rose, as I walk toward the sea through the crumbling remnants of what was once a Crusader fortress. I reach the steep footpath crisscrossing the incline to the shoreline. Three ships sit at anchor about a quarter parsang off shore. Below me on the ancient stone wharf stands my youngest son, Yonatan. He'd sent word by carrier pigeon up to Jerusalem when the vessels first arrived.

Now they've dropped anchor, the captains will dispatch their envoys to port, pay the tolls, and then wait. Passengers require travel permits before they can proceed inland. This can take a day or two, unless you know how to add a little *baksheesh* to speed the progress. Anytime now, the ships will lower their shore craft and begin ferrying groups of disagreeable, reeking Europeans in fancy velvet onto the sand. They come with impossible expectations and imperious demands, but have no idea what is in store for them. But we'll be ready with our coffle of mule-sized Qubressy donkeys to guide them to all the holy places in this ancient land they've envisioned. The Venetians, Dutch, and French are usually a decent sort. But I still harbor suspicion and bitterness toward the Spanish. However, all of them will be beholden to my expertise, and I have no qualms about making a fair profit from them.

Two Dominican friars near Yonatan also await the pilgrims. They compete with us to transport visitors to the holy sites. The black hooded capes they wear over their white wool habits flutter in the breeze. With them are two rough looking herders.

As I near the bottom of the incline, I hear Yonatan call over to them.

"Are those little Armenian black donkeys? They're just the right size for a child to ride."

The two herders stiffen and scowl. "What matter is it to you?" says one.

Why can't my son just address people with respect? Does he not grasp how others take offense to his jesting? He may have turned 21 this year, but I still find myself having to keep an eye on him like when he was a boy.

"No need to be hostile," says Yonatan.

"You shouldn't even be here," one priest says. "These are Christian pilgrims. They'll be under the supervision of the Brotherhood of Mount Zion."

"And so? That doesn't mean we can't transport them. You just want their ducats and livres."

Their faces twist and the friars grumble to each other and glare at him. But now one herder clasping a staff starts for our coffle. My guess is he intends to scatter them. Yonatan yanks his whip from his waistband and rushes to get between the herder and the animals.

"That wouldn't be wise," he says and lashes the whip to the side.

I clench my jaw. When I reach the sand, Yonatan is in a stare down with the man. He wavers, shifting side-to-side, appraising his options. But I come alongside my son and place a firm hand on his shoulder.

"Yonatan. Put the whip away," I say in a soothing voice. "Let me handle this." I walk calmly toward the herdsman with my palms turned outward. The wind flails back my amber woolen *mimtar*, revealing no weapon in my tunic's waistband. This seems to pacify them. Perhaps my graying temples and kind smile can persuade them I'm no threat.

"There is no contest here," I say. "There will be far more pilgrims than animals to bear them." I glance toward the ships, noticing the first boat starting the brief journey inland. I gesture toward the arrivals. "Please, you take the first group," I say to the friars. I doff my ochre tarbush with a bow and then place it back on my head.

The friars' disposition changes and they jump into action, setting out rope and olive wood stirrups. The herders strap crude saddles onto the little donkeys.

Then I turn and wrap my arm around my son and whisper. "Temperance, Yonatan, is an asset to cultivate, if you hope to have an enterprise of your own one day." He draws back and looks me in the eye.

"I know," he mutters.

It makes me cringe to watch him flounder so, from the time he was young. I couldn't teach him my navigation profession, because he could never learn to read very well. His eyes seemed to reverse the letters and numbers. Other boys made fun of him, called him *metumtam*. In response, he became prideful and denied any need for help. I saw in him an echo of my youth and the self-doubt I once had. But he always loved animals, caring for them, riding. So, that is why I decided to become a *Madrich*. It's like being a navigator on land. We acquired our own donkeys and I placed him in charge. Since then, our business conveying travelers throughout the land has prospered.

I pull a small parcel from my shoulder bag and hand it to Yonatan. "From Shuli," I say. Then I draw a hammered metal flask out of its wool-lined leather covering, offering it to him. He uncorks it and smells.

"Café? You even kept it warm for two hours?"

I give a little half-smile and nod. He grins and takes a sip. Opening the parcel, he finds fresh spongy bread spread with *kubbait*, made from ground carob and almond. He eagerly bites into it. I gaze off to the west, where a second craft is making its way toward land. I take out my spyglass and study the passengers and crew.

"Are we ready to do this?" I ask.

"If we must," he grumbles.

"The rear guard is vital to our safety," I remind him.

"Oh yeah, spending the morning staring at donkey butts. Really vital."

I shake my head. Yonatan's heart is not in this, and now he's complaining. Why can't he recognize the honor that comes with being an expert, trusted guide, and protector to strangers visiting this sacred place?

Raised voices erupt among the travelers with the Dominican friars. They're speaking in an unfamiliar tongue, Dutch perhaps. Their gestures imply they are far from satisfied with the form of transport. They shout orders at the herdsmen, who gape at them vacantly and dig in their heels. These travelers often assume there will be fine horses and carriages, lavish accommodations, and meals fit for kings. They bring their servants and chests of finery. No wonder they're disappointed and angry. So predictable, it's sometimes amusing.

A dinghy from an Italian ship carrying ten passengers plows into the sand. We stride down to the water's edge to meet them.

"*Saluto*," says the boatman, as he hops over the side onto the beach.

I clasp his hand. "*Benvenuto*. I'm glad to see you. How was your voyage?"

"I'm happy to see land. I am Giuseppe Ricci. We had an uneventful passage. Conflicts in the west are increasing. The Ottomans are trying to expand their control of the waterways. Privateers are taking more vessels. I've brought seven travelers with three servants, all from Spain and Italy."

"Well then, let's prepare our guests for what's ahead."

Yonatan remains with the livestock until I signal him to load.

Giuseppe assembles the passengers in a circle, away from the tide. I speak first in Spanish and he translates to Italian.

"Welcome to the Holy Land, gentlemen. This was once the port of entry for the cedars of Lebanon used to build Solomon's Temple. It's the place from which Jonah embarked. I am Maestro Déulocresca. During your travels here, I'll be your guide." I allow Giuseppe to translate.

I continue. "I arrived here from Spain 25 years ago. This land is a very singular place, with strange customs and rules you're unaccustomed to. To ensure your comfort and safe conduct in the holy places, I urge you to listen and take to heart what I'm about to tell you. I cannot protect you from the consequences if you do not heed my words."

Yonatan watches me from a distance, though he's heard this speech countless times. The men lean in, eyes pinned to me with grim faces.

"Whatever your status or class might be in your home country, it carries no weight here. If you have brought any weapons, swords, knives, even ceremonial ones, it is illegal and the authorities will imprison you. They must be returned to the ship. If you display your family crest or nation's flag, whether on your clothing or belongings, they consider it an affront, and it will bring flogging and fines to everyone in the company."

There is a round of groans and shifting glances.

"It is best you not flaunt your wealth, but dress in the manner of your servants, in order to avoid being a target for thieves and swindlers."

I take out a small stack of cards from my shoulder bag. "I have gained the permission from the Governor of Jerusalem to grant you legal status for the duration of your travels here. You must fill out this identity card with your name and sign it. I've brought a quill and ink." I take these from my bag, handing them to Giuseppe. "Carry it on your person at all times, as officials may ask you to show it. If you lose it, you can be fined. Now, do you have questions?"

One finely dressed man raises his hand. "I am Rodrigo de Soncino from Milan. This port city appears to be in ruins. Are we lodging here, or is there a decent place to stay and get an actual meal?"

I smile and nod my head. "We will not be lodging here in Jaffa. Two hours east, we'll lodge in the small city of Ramla. You may know it as Arimathea, the home of Joseph of Arimathea. According to Christian scripture, he entombed the crucified Jesus. During the time of King David, it was also the Philistine city of Gath."

Their eyes are filled with wonder. One man crosses himself. Another man steps forward and points to the donkeys.

"You don't expect us to ride those animals, do you?"

"Your name, sir?" I ask.

"This is Lord Enzo Bacardi," says Giuseppe.

"Lord Bacardi," I say and bow. "I acknowledge this may seem an indignity to you. However, in this land, no Christian or Jew may ride an animal or transport vehicle that places your head above that of a Muslim's. Horses or camels are not permitted to us."

He frowns and exchanges glances with the other travelers.

"Oh, and there's one other caution. Do not leave the group, no matter the reason. There have been reports of marauders or highwaymen between here and Jerusalem. We have safety in numbers."

The men offer their hand or pat me on the back. They seem reassured; unlike the floundering priests who are still bickering with their tourists. While Giuseppe distributes the identity cards, the servants unload the travelers' belongings. One collects the weapons from the owners to return them to the ship. Several of the men change into garments of their retainers.

I join Yonatan to assist in loading the pack animals. "Courtesy and respect always win their trust and cooperation," I whisper. He thinks I didn't notice him rolling his eyes. I know he feels disadvantaged; as I once did, being a Jew. It's probably what led him to start gambling, as a way to get ahead. That's gotten him in trouble several times. What kind of future can he have with these shortcomings?

In an orderly fashion, we ensure each traveler is prepared for departure, and mount up for the quick journey. The Dominicans pause to watch as we leave. Their group is in disarray. Some have wandered off into the old ruins. I offer a friendly wave. But the monks glower with narrowed eyes. They know we're Sephardic exiles who've fled here to escape the Inquisition. If given the chance, they'd condemn *conversos* and accomplices like me, to be burned at the stake. Fortunately, they don't have that kind of power. But their malevolence is ever present, albeit veiled and indirect. As long as the Inquisition exists, we can never let down our guard.

CHAPTER 3

Ramla, Filastin District

Yonatan Déulocresca

We reach the caravanserai just before midday. The innkeeper gives each man a room, and supplies fresh linen and mattresses stuffed with fragrant newly cut rushes. Their servants bunk together. The pilgrims stow their belongings and secure them behind lock and key. Then we take them to the baths.

"Who would expect such fine marble floors and walls," says Lord Bacardi. "And for a desert, there's an abundance of steaming clean water."

After they wash, each one dons a freshly laundered *jalabah* made by locals. We escort them into the café where Shuli and Edna are expecting us. They've roped off a section of the café for the group. The midday meal includes a spicy dish of lentils and rice, freshly baked bread, olives, figs, and dates.

I sit across from my father, studying the way he converses with the visitors. As I nibble on a date, a hand brushes across my back. Turning, I see Shuli carrying a pitcher of wine, retouching patron's cups.

"I was worried about you today. I'm glad you got here safely."

"Why were you concerned? Everything has gone well, so far."

"That band of *Urbān* you displeased came here looking for you. It seems they saw the beacon in Jaffa too. They know you travel the Via Maris with donkeys."

My stomach sinks, and my heart starts to gallop. "What did you tell them?"

"Only that we didn't know where you went. It's the truth. But I think they sensed we were withholding information. You must be extra careful tomorrow. Have you told your father about the threat?"

"No, but I will."

She moves on to another patron. I again fix my eyes on my father, the man I love and admire above anyone. How can I tell him what I did? Even though I won the bet and tripled my wager; how do I admit I was gambling again? I can't bear the look of disappointment and pain in his eyes, losing faith in me. I've let him down. As unfair as al-Dabaa's demand was to return his lost wager; I've brought a menacing threat to my father, and to these travelers. Before we depart in the morning, I have to find a way to tell him.

When dawn arrives, father and I escort the travelers on foot to St. Nicodemus and St. Joseph of Arimathea church for morning prayers. Maybe I'll get a chance to tell father about the threat. Right now, Lord Bacardi has his attention, talking about the events in Milan. While the pilgrims attend worship services, we wait outside the tall metal gates. As we stare at the golden sunrise over the Judean Hills to the east, I try to raise the subject.

"I'm a little worried about our safety going through the hill country," I begin.

"I saw nothing out of the ordinary on my ride here. I think we'll be fine."

"But a band of *Urban* stirred up trouble here the day before yesterday."

"We'll just keep an eye out," father says.

I look skyward and sigh. My stomach knots. Why doesn't he hear me?

We return the travelers to the caravanserai and Edna's establishment, where we share a simple morning meal of warm bread, fresh butter, honey, and yogurt before saddling up the donkeys. With the servants' help, I load the pack animals with supplies and travelers' bags. When everyone has mounted, we head onto the Via Maris. Father and Lord Bacardi are at the front of our coffle, while I station myself at the rear to insure no one falls behind.

The undulating plain is sprouting fresh shoots of wild grass. Groves of almond trees on either side of the road are glorious with their white blossoms. The air is sweet with their fragrance. Flocks of sheep and goats graze on the new greenery and the morning fills with birdsong. But off in the distance, I notice a solitary rider on horseback perched at the top of a rise, watching us. My neck hair stands on end, and my gut turns watery. As soon as we come parallel to his position, he gallops off to the southeast. I have to warn my father. With my heart pounding, I swerve around the caravan of riders, speeding ahead to the front where my father rides.

"Father, I need to speak with you," I call over.

"We're almost to Kiryat-el-Inab. We can speak then," he says.

"Did you see that rider?"

He nods, but gestures to be silent, which I take to mean, don't alarm the pilgrims. I draw aside and slow my donkey to resume my place at the rear. But now I scan the horizon for likely danger.

Another hour passes and we reach the outskirts of Kiryat-el-Inab, the Village of Grapes. It is the center of a territory controlled by the Abu Ghosh clan. We will have to pay a toll to pass through the area with visitors. There is a spring beside the olive grove near the village. Father signals it is time to stop, and he guides his donkey off the road to where we can water the drove. He slides off his mount and gathers the travelers to his circle.

"There are many traditions about this place," he begins. "The

Crusaders believed this was Emmaus, the town where Jesus appeared to two disciples after his death, according to the Gospel of Luke."

The pilgrims draw closer with wide-eyes. But as he continues, I raise my gaze toward the shadowy grove beyond, and notice subtle movement between the trees. I cover my mouth to silence a gasp.

"They built a church here 400 years ago, but it stands in ruins today. This place is also associated with a Jewish legend. It's believed to be the town of Anatot, the birthplace of the prophet Jeremiah."

From behind the olive trees, half a dozen men on horseback come out of hiding and ride slowly toward us. I was afraid this might happen. My stomach sinks and I shake all over. They covered their faces with their *keffiyot*, all but their eyes. Some have drawn scimitars. Then, I see the alarm bloom on father's face. He looks back in the direction we just came. Over my shoulder, I see another half-dozen men on horses cutting off any chance of escape. Two men slide off their horses and gather up the tethers to the donkey coffle at the drinking trough. They bray in protest. Several men jump down, rush the pilgrims, and restrain them. Those who try to resist they knock to the ground, kicking and beating them. Some try to flee, but the horseback assailants easily intercept them. The marauders bind the pilgrims' hands with leather strapping. Someone shoves me hard from behind to usher me forward.

My father tries to reason with them in Arabic, but they tell him to shut up. In moments, everyone is bound and bunched together, surrounded by menacing thugs. Only I remain unbound, but I'm flanked by two men, one pointing a knife at my ribs.

Into the center struts al-Dabaa. He peruses the hostages one at a time with imperious pride. In front of my father, he stops and grins.

"Quite a prize we have here." He laughs. Then he turns toward me. The two men wrest my arms and shuffle me forward. Al-Dabaa looks down his nose at me.

He hisses. "Thirty hatikhot? A gold Sultani? That was your bet. You tripled your winnings. But now, for your insult, you will pay thirty gold Sultani. Or you will see none of these men alive again. Do you understand me, donkey-boy?"

I vigorously nod. "Yes, Sayid." The men release me with a shove, and I falter to one knee. When I stand and meet my father's gaze, his face crumbles in pain and disbelief and his eyes go glassy.

My voice catches when I try to speak. "I'm sorry."

"Not as sorry as you will be," says al-Dhbaa. "Now leave here, and bring me my money."

One guard brings a donkey for me. It's Giboor, my donkey's mate. I glance again at my father, but he lowers his head. He can't stand to look at me. After climbing on Giboor's back, I squeeze my thighs against his sides. He leaps into a gallop. My breath rasps and my hands tremble, holding the reins. I keep glancing back to see if any of them have followed me. When I reach the outskirts of the village, I slow and we catch our breath.

If I continue on the old Via Maris, I should be able to reach Jerusalem before nightfall. Dear God, protect my father, and all these poor travelers who trusted us to guard them from this very thing. This is entirely my fault. I should have kept my promise. This never would have happened. Shuli was right. My father will disown me if he survives. I couldn't live with myself if something happened to him.

What can I do now? I have to save them somehow. It's illegal for Jews to take-up swords or knives and go after them. I still have my remaining winnings, but it's only a fraction of what al-Dabaa demands. Father makes a good living, but I doubt I can readily put my hands on that amount of money. I have no grandparents, no rich uncles. Our primary method of earning a living is gone. They've taken most of our donkeys. My father's work for the last 20 years is up for ransom. If anything happens to him... I've got to stop thinking this way. It won't help. How do I even tell my mother? I'm stupid and I'm foolish. A stinking piece of camel shit.

I wind through the Judean Hills as quickly as Giboor will trot, passing through small villages and caravan stops. Finally, just before sunset, I reach the ridge across from Mount Zion and the tower of David. The tumbled down remains of ancient stone walls come into view. The warm blush of oil lamps glows from many windows. We usually enter the city from the northwest when we come from the sea. But that way skirts the Valley of Gehinnom, and after twilight it makes traversing that district chancy for a solitary rider, especially a Jewish one. They could tell immediately, by the piss color of my clothing. The last thing I want is another confrontation. I'll swing around to the southern entry point.

On the edge of the city near one of the last ancient portals, the Tanner's Gate, I leave my donkey at the stable. Now on foot, I hurry along the Cardo Maximus, built long ago by the Romans. My path crosses the Jewish quarter in the long colonnaded thoroughfare paved with cut stone, buffed smooth by time.

Our house stands just off the Cardo. Most buildings here are new by Jerusalem standards, only a century old. I veer down a narrow passageway flanked by pillars and rows of shops that are closing for the evening. When I arrive at the wrought-iron gate to our courtyard, mother has already barred it for the evening. She won't be expecting anyone to call. The sound of the bells may draw unwanted attention, but I yank on the small cord and wait. I ring a second time and there is movement across the courtyard.

"Who is there?" she calls.

"*Eema*, it's Yonatan."

She rushes across the courtyard. "Yonatan? What in heaven's name?"

She unlocks and slides away the stave. The weighty gate opens inward. I enter and my mother closes the gate behind me, bolting it.

She stares at me. "Is your father with you? What is happening?" she asks.

I pull back and answer with my head down. "Something bad, terrible. Let's go inside."

We walk across the tiled courtyard, around the small fountain to the entrance. The door is ajar. I push my way inside and unburden my shoulder bag onto the sturdy table where we share our meals. She pours me a cup of wine and sits down across from me. Her eyes are full with alarm and worry creases her brow.

I take a gulp of wine. "We set out from Ramla early this morning. Just as we reached Kiryat el Inab, a marauding band of *Urbān* attacked us. They'd been causing trouble in Ramla. The Halqa soldiers ran them off, but that only seemed to make them angrier."

"*Urbān*? What made them so angry?"

I lower my face and heave a great sigh. "Their chieftain lost a wager."

"A wager? Yonatan, you were gambling again. You promised."

"I know." I rub my forehead. "But I was certain to win, and I did win."

She throws herself back against the chair, covers her mouth and pinches her eyes tight. "What have you done?"

"I'm sorry. I didn't mean this to happen. I was stupid."

"Where is your father?"

"He's alive. All the pilgrims are alive."

"But where is he?"

"The *Urbān* are encamped near Abu Ghosh. They let me go. I must bring back the ransom money, or they might kill them. So, I came here to find help."

"Dear God. What are we going to do? How can we pay a ransom?"

"Don't we have money saved or assets we can sell?" I ask.

"Only money to bury us," she says. "How much are they demanding?"

"An exorbitant amount."

"Yonatan, how much?"

"Thirty gold Sultani."

"Unheard of. Impossible." Her eyes become glassy and she chokes back a sob. "We need to seek the counsel of Rabbi Bertinoro. They'll be finishing the Ma'ariv prayer service soon. We'll go to the synagogue."

She rises from the table, disappears into her bedchamber, and returns with her amber veil flowing beneath an embroidered tarbush. I follow her out the door, which she locks. Then we leave through the metal gate and hurry between the buildings back to the main road.

The entrance to our synagogue is at the bottom of the stairs. Members of the evening minyan file upward as we descend. The huge double doors with an arching lattice transom stand open. We linger while other worshipers clear out and the rabbi becomes available. He stands speaking to two other men in his dark blue robe and padded ring tarbush. He notices us standing here and tips his head.

"Señora Déulocresca? Is that you and Yonatan? We rarely see you at evening prayers. Come in and sit down. An urgent matter, I assume."

We hurry inside and take a seat on one of the many benches lining the walls beneath a coved ceiling and arches. Rabbi sits beside us. Mother removes the covering from her face.

"Joachim is in grave danger," she whispers.

Rabbi Bertinoro's chest heaves with a heavy sigh. "What has happened?"

"A cutthroat gang of *Urbān* took my father captive," I tell him. "He and 10 pilgrims are being held for ransom near Abu Ghosh."

He tents his hands against his snowy white beard. "This is dire news, indeed. I am so grieved to hear this. I assure you, Aularia, the members of the community will support your needs in whatever way we can."

"Can you bring influence with the authorities? Maybe they'll hunt for these men and bring them to justice," mother says.

"I will go straight away tomorrow to the Sheik and plead your case. Perhaps I can broker a deal. But you know the testimony of a Jew against a Muslim is inadmissible in court."

"Are you saying we should focus on raising the ransom, then?" I ask.

"That is a challenging dilemma. While the Ransom of Captives is one of the highest principles in our faith, as you know, our community survives on contributions from abroad. The addition of so many refugees from Spain and Portugal has stretched us thin. But this is an urgent situation. It's for the sake of a life, *Pikuach Nefesh*. I will put out a call to collect what I can."

"We're so grateful. Every bit will help," I say.

"Return home and wait. I will come to you when I have news."

On our walk back to our house, I turn toward my mother. "So, we're just going to return home and do nothing?"

"Yes. I trust Rabbi Bertinoro. He's going to help us."

I shake my head. "I'm sure he will try. But I don't want to waste time. I can't just sit on my hands."

"He has been our community leader for many years. His skill brought resolution to countless problems and conflicts."

"He may have helped with disputes over building a new plaza, or repair of waterways. But this is different. These lawless criminals won't negotiate. I don't think it will help."

We reach the gate to our home, now in full darkness. Mother pushes it open.

"That's just it, Yonatan. You don't think," she says. "You're impulsive, reckless, and your reasoning is flawed. Look where it's gotten you."

Her words fall like an enormous bag of feed on my chest. I step inside the courtyard, close and bolt the gate. "You don't understand," I say. "I have to fix this. I know it's my fault. You want to wait for an answer. So be it. But what if his efforts are fruitless? Meanwhile, time is running out and father could die."

Mother opens the door. Once inside, she removes her veil. I sit again at the dinner table and take another gulp of the wine she'd poured earlier. She is silent, but I sense her hostility and resentment beneath the surface of her sullen face. Her voice is like cold steel when she speaks.

"What is it you intend to do?"

"Raise more ransom money. It could take too long for the rabbi to gather funds. Tomorrow, I'll return to Ramla, and sell our remaining donkeys. Maybe these pilgrims brought money with them. Their captain might also contribute funds to ransom them. I don't know. But I have to do everything possible."

"So, you're going to run off again and leave me to deal with this by myself?"

"I'm impulsive, selfish, and my reasoning is flawed, remember? Whatever I do, it's the wrong thing. You don't seem to want me here very much."

She turns and leaves the room. Moments later, the door to her bedchamber slams.

CHAPTER 4

1515, Safed, Urdunn District

Aaron Déulocresca

Acrid fumes of mineral spirits accumulate thick against the coved ceiling. Paint brush in hand, I balance precariously high on the scaffolding. Rather than using tempera affresco, after the manner of the Italian muralists; I've resorted to mixing distilled resin from the terebinth tree with crushed minerals and beeswax to make the paint. This formula can be applied to dry plaster, and won't fade. An apothecary in Tiberius cautioned the compounds are highly poisonous, made with arsenic, cinnabar, and lead. But the lasting quality of the paint is what matters; because this is the first mural of its kind in all the Galilee or even Jerusalem. I'm blessed to be selected for this commission, and hope it is the start of many more to come. But the very act of crafting artwork itself brings me to a blissful state, like a mystical trance. This house of worship is unique. Devotees of Rabbi Isaac of Toledo, one of the Goanim of Castile, dedicated it to him. According to legend, the rabbi designed it using the symbols and numerology from the Kabbalah, the book of mystical wisdom.

The oil lamps illuminating my work burn low. I hurry to finish the foliage on a pomegranate tree before the light is spent and I have to stop for the night. Eventually, nine trees will decorate the arches that separate the ten pillars holding up the dome. Only four are complete. They represent the *Pardes*, the Orchard; an elevated realm of spiritual enlightenment that can only be attained through rigorous meditation on the Kabbalah. The Talmud recounts the legend of four sages who entered the *Pardes*. One went insane, one died, and a third became a heretic. Only the foremost among them, Rabbi Akiva, entered the Orchard and emerged whole again.

One lamp flickers and goes dark. I sigh. Reluctantly, I cover my palate with an oil-soaked cloth, and then maneuver on my belly to the ladder. It's best if I descend the scaffolding while I can still see. As I reach the floor, weariness overtakes me, but in a fulfilling rather than exhausted way.

Stepping outside the synagogue door, I begin my trek homeward beneath a star-filled sky. Unlike my once dread-filled walks homeward in Jerusalem, I look forward to what awaits me on arrival. There are things from the past that still haunt me, even after all this time. I keep those memories inside and have never spoken about them to anyone. When the opportunity to leave Jerusalem arrived, I jumped at the chance to study here. I count myself lucky to be admitted to one of the most revered houses of learning, Or Yakar. By the recommendation of my Jerusalem mentors, I had duly earned it. Rarely had they seen a man my age so dedicated, they said. The City of the Wise is my refuge from the world, my hermitage.

The moon is bright enough to navigate the winding roads through the hillside terraces. My pulse quickens from the steep climb. I clutch my *rida* tight against the brisk spring air. At the highest boundary of the village, a low rock wall surrounds a small plot of land. A humble stone dwelling stands firm, with its back against the hillside. The ground floor is an open bay shelter for sheep and goats. Suqi the watchdog barks as I approach, but recognizes me and goes silent.

I lean over the rock wall. "Just me, Suqi," I whisper, stretching my arm over the fence. I feel the dog's cold nose against the back of my hand and rub behind his pointy ears a few times. I trudge upward a short distance further to the entrance and rap on the door. The stave slides against the hasp and the door swings open. Moonlight casts a blue halo on Rehm's long dark hair. The hearth glows orange and warm behind her.

"*Salam Alekim*. You must be stiff and tired," she says.

Until she said that, I'd not even noticed the ache in my joints and the knot between my shoulder blades from holding the same position for so many hours. The aroma of her savory stew makes my stomach rumble.

"*Alekim salam*," I reply. "And yes, I'm ravenous."

I remove my *rida* and wash my hands and face at a simple basin and pitcher beside the door. I sink onto the bench at the table, whisper a blessing, break off a hunk of warm bread from the crusty round loaf, dip it in salt, and eat. Rehm ladles bean and spinach stew into an earthenware bowl and sets it before me. Then she returns to her loom, which supplies her livelihood. The rhythm of the warp beams shifting and the shuttle passing between them have become soothing and familiar. It is the sound of home, now.

The Or Yakar school had no open beds when I first arrived. I had to seek temporary room and board. It so happened, Rehm Kaled had a room to rent, and was willing to accept the meager stipend I receive from my parents, supplemented by my help with heavy labors. She is a childless widow, five years my senior, and a Maronite. The house and small flock were inherited from her late husband. Rehm sustains herself by weaving fine woolen cloth, making cheese, and selling the new lambs in spring. She makes her house comfortable with the rugs and pillows of her craft. There's a kitchen garden with a fig and a pomegranate tree. There is even a natural spring nearby. She has all the necessities.

I sleep in a loft high above the main living space. Residing here has been so agreeable, when a place opened at the school, I chose to remain here. That was two years ago. It does not matter that she adorns her walls with the icons of her Maronite faith. In fact, the first time I entered her home and set eyes on the artwork, I felt a twinge of excitement. Since then, I've studied them closely and even crafted a few replicas, selling them in the *shuk* and using the profit to buy her new dishes and crockery. In exchange, she serves only meat slaughtered by the Jewish shochet, soaked and salted to remove the blood, according to the dietary laws. It has become an ideal arrangement for us both.

But I know this idyllic life cannot last. "Study is all well and good," my father has said. "But to what end? At some point, you need a livelihood." Making money as an itinerant artist is seen as frivolous. I don't intend to enter the rabbinate. And I can't live off my parents' money forever. Is it foolish to think we could continue living together, making a humble living with our crafts? No one needs to know.

Before I even finish my meal, I begin to yawn. With a full belly, I stagger to the ladder and climb to the loft. I strip down to braes and pile into the short, but soft, bed. Closing my eyes, I yield to the trance of the loom. But after a short while, the rhythmic sound stops and the house grows still. Rehm opens the door to let the dog in, and then bolts it. I listen to the creak of the floorboards as she walks across them. It's my routine not to fully surrender to sleep until I hear her lay on her cot beneath the loft. But her footsteps continue to the foot of the ladder. I open my eyes, attuning one ear, waiting, listening. I turn over. In the soft glow of the embers, I see her silhouette as she rises to the top ladder rung. She stands at the foot of my bed.

"It's been eight years since I knew the touch of a man," she whispers. "My body aches just to be held."

I'm stunned. I know the ache she speaks of, but I never would have crossed that boundary. She's offering herself to me freely. A wave of gooseflesh sweeps over me. She saunters toward me, then pauses, lifts her robe and chemise, letting them slough to the floor. Rehm lifts the covers and slides under. The moment her skin makes contact with mine, every part of me comes alive. It's as if my body has been numb.

I've been asleep to all sensations for so long I cannot recall. She is like water on parched earth, seeping into the cracks, giving new life. These sensations awaken a hunger in me I've never known. She nestles against my chest. I enclose her with my arms, fumbling awkwardly to find a natural position.

"None of my husband's kinsmen have ever come forward to care for or claim me. I've had no suitor or even a friendship until you came."

"Eight years is a long time."

"Long enough to be convinced they never shall. I'm withering. In the last two years, you have filled that void, bringing your calming presence and steadfast protection. I am so grateful you are here."

"I never would have expected this. So many differences separate us, though we certainly aren't strangers. But let's be clear. You are a forbidden woman to me."

"I've been thinking about it for quite some time. I know what we are about to do is sinful. We'd be scorned by both our traditions."

"I'm certain it is punishable. If it came to light, we could be flogged or even stoned."

"You can still say no," she says, "and send me from your bed."

Should I become intimate with her? If I do, it could endanger our lives. And it betrays my own principles. But if I deny her, we will both continue to languish in the deep yearning for human warmth and affection. Why?

Her hand moves up my chest and shoulder and cradles my jaw. I want this, need this. I curl forward to meet her lips. Rehm slides one foot up the side of my leg, bringing her thigh over mine. Two lonely people. It seems inevitable. I roll her onto her back and glide into the warmth between her thighs. The bed frame creaks rhythmically like the loom, with the rocking of our bodies. I gaze into the face glowing with joy beneath me. Rehm's dark almond-shaped eyes gleam. This is one more secret I will bear, a hidden treasure no one needs to know about. Where this path leads is a mystery. But the ecstasy in my flesh whispers, *it does not matter*. I surrender.

CHAPTER 5

JUDEAN HILLS ROAD, BETH EL
Aularia Déulocresca

RIBBONS OF GREY and white clouds stretch across a misty blue expanse; a rather bleak and melancholy start to the day. My eyes ache from so many spilled tears. An undulating plateau with white limestone outcroppings stretches out before me; from hillcrests to lush dells, green with olive trees, cedar and juniper. This journey north from Jerusalem to Safed will last for two days. Every position on this stiff donkey saddle bites into my sit bones, tormenting me. But there's no other recourse. I must get to Safed to tell Aaron of his father's plight and beg for his help. The question is, will he even speak to me? My hand curls tight on the reins and I clasp my veil close at my throat with the other hand.

Beside me rides my travel companion, Rabbi Bertinoro. He is like the grandfather I never knew. He resembles a sage or biblical prophet in his indigo robe and tightly wrapped turban. "Please know how grateful I am that you accompanied me," I say. "Trying this journey by myself would be daunting."

His eyebrows draw together and he strokes his white beard. "For you to venture out alone is unconscionable," he says.

I lower my gaze. "Yonatan should have made the trip. But he rushed off so quickly, I doubt it even crossed his mind to ask his brother for help. He's like a wild ram sometimes."

"That, he is."

"Thankfully, Aaron has always been diligent."

I'm not sure the rabbi is aware, but since leaving home for his studies, I haven't seen or heard from Aaron in two years. Hopefully, a visit from Rabbi Bertinoro, who he's always revered, will ease the thorny silence between us. I'm certain it will devastate Aaron as much as it did me to learn his father is being held for ransom.

"You must be so proud. He's studying at one of the great houses of learning."

"We are, indeed."

"I'm happy to escort you," he says. "These are the most unusual circumstances. I've been meaning to visit Safed again and the Talmudic scholars I know there, while I'm still able-bodied. It's been years."

"Traveling to the Galilee brings back memories," I say. "The first time we visited was around Aaron's third birthday, for his first haircut. I still recall the *ḥalāqah* ceremony around the bonfires on Lag b'Omer. He had long hair to his shoulders, so wispy and fine."

"So, did you actually make the pilgrimage to the grave of Shimon bar Yochai?" he asks.

"Yes. After everything we went through in Spain, I wanted my son to have extra protection from malevolent spirits. Although Joachim said these were just old wives' superstitions."

He chuckles. "Ah, yes. The time-honored rituals of our womenfolk."

The midwives had told me to preserve Aaron's umbilical cord, his foreskin, and hair clippings for that night. I cast them into the bonfire, thrice whispering an incantation they taught me: *A token, a proxy, a substitute overrules evil.*

I stop short of telling the rabbi why I believed Aaron needed that extra protection. Except for my husband Joachim, I've told no one about the menacing evil that continues to haunt me, so long after fleeing the Inquisition. What good would it do to reveal it now? My posture slumps, and I bite my lower lip. Although, I still suffer. Could there be relief in sharing this burden? I gaze out from this ridge at the canyons below to the west. Everything here seems so remote.

"You two surely struggled to get a foothold in Jerusalem in those early years."

"Yes. Joachim was gone a great deal during the season of sail, bringing pilgrims and Inquisition refugees to our shores. With both my mother and grandmothers deceased, I had to rely on the midwives and healers to guide me in the early months. I drew strength and joy caring for Aaron, rocking him, suckling him, and watching him grow, day by day." I go quiet again, tucking my elbows in at my sides. That was only until he matured and his features changed. Before my eyes, the boy's appearance, and then the young man's, filled me with loathing.

Up ahead, I spy several crude stone dwellings and fences at the edge of a village.

"This place is called El Bireh by the locals," Rabbi says. "But according to tradition, it is Beth El, where Jacob dreamed of a ladder to heaven and the prophetess Deborah dwelled."

"Deborah? One of my favorite stories."

"Shall we stop here and water the donkeys?"

We reach the center of the village, where a spring fed fountain and watering trough serves the needs of travelers and residents. There's a small marketplace with covered stalls offering olives, bread, figs and dates. We slide down from the saddles and lead the donkeys to the trough. I want to be free of this emotional pain. My chin quivers. What should or shouldn't I tell him?

Rabbi Bertinoro buys a small portion of dates and we lead the donkeys over to a low stone wall. He invites me to sit and share the treats. I lower my eyes, staring at a troop of ants trudging in a line along the base of the wall, carrying burdens that seem far too large for their size.

"If I can be forthright, Rabbi Bertinoro, this crisis is just the capstone in a series of terrible things that have happened in my life. I have seldom shared them with others. The stories have remained buried secrets for decades. But I have felt such hopeless despair at times, I've lost my reason to exist. Now my husband's life is in danger and everything we've built together could crumble to dust."

When I glance over at him, Rabbi Bertinoro's hand covers his heart, and he is nodding and blinking. "It has never been my way to meddle in the affairs of my congregants. But when they come to me suffering, I am always ready to listen."

"Relations between Aaron and I have grown more and more strained the older he gets. I'm not sure he will even speak to me."

"This does not come as a complete surprise. When he was younger, I always wondered why Aaron would stay so late at the Bet Midrash. It was like he was avoiding going home."

"And it is entirely my fault."

"What is your fault?"

"After he passed the tender age, Aaron's hair grew-out the color of hazelnut, with a tinge of my copper; nothing like Joachim's raven hair and eyes. By the time he reached the age of six, the angle of his jaw and the sharpness of his nose left me no doubt who had sired him."

Rabbi's brows knot and he tugs on his beard.

"He became the living reminder, the haunting echo of the man who held me captive and repeatedly raped me, in Barcelona. The beautiful precious baby I had loved, nursed, and cradled was transforming into Friar Miguel Cirera. Each time I'd look at him, my insides would twist. Then the nightmares began."

He closes his eyes and shakes his head. "What a painful tragedy you endured. But what happened is not your fault. The blame lies with the offender."

"But he haunts me still. Aaron was a loving, dutiful boy. But every time I'd embrace him or show affection, the memories would flash in my mind of Cirera standing over me, whispering in my ear, groping me with his hands. I'd try to block out the recollection of those events. But the more I tried to forget, the more the memories intruded. Over time, I withdrew from my son more and more. I don't know how to stop the memories."

"I'm glad you revealed this to me, Aularia. For 20 years, I have held in confidence the disclosures of many. They too came to find healing and hope. Some had been tortured, others witnessed the brutal execution of loved ones, or suffered all manner of unspeakable acts at the hands of the Inquisition. Most blamed themselves, as you do."

"How could a good mother falter in her love for her first-born son? What a wretched mother that makes me. It has driven a wedge between us, and I desperately want to mend my relationship with my son."

"Have you ever considered explaining what happened to Aaron? It might help the healing and restoration."

"Never. When Aaron was born, we decided it would be best for him to know only Joachim as his father. Joachim thought it would harm their relationship and bring Aaron shame to know of my dishonor. So, we vowed never to tell him otherwise. And despite my dilemma, it was the right choice. Aaron has a strong relationship with his father."

"I understand and respect that."

"But you spoke of healing. Is that really possible?"

"Yes, it's possible. We have restored *refuah shlayma* to many."

"How? What must I do?"

"It begins by telling the story, the complete story. We can work on this together. But it will take time. First, we must address this present calamity."

"I agree. But why did this happen to me?"

"There are several reasons haunting memories can linger. The experiences are usually so horrific and soul-crushing it shatters our very sense of order in the world. Our beliefs, the very laws of nature, are obliterated."

"How very true."

"A common response is to think we must have caused it. Or we failed to prevent or stop it and are responsible. In our efforts to solve the puzzle, we relive those events over and over. Guilt and self-loathing follow, and then a yearning for punishment to free ourselves from it."

"Punishment?" I had been secretly inflicting pain on myself for years; pinching the undersides of my arms, plucking hair from the back of my neck and hairline, places no one could see. A sewing needle, a broken potsherd, could take away the guilt, dull the images that haunt me, and keep my rage at bay.

"Dear God in heaven. Rabbi, you describe my experiences perfectly. How do you know these things? Why haven't I figured this out, after all this time?"

"The Gemara says a prisoner cannot generally free himself from prison, but depends on others to release him from his shackles. I learned it is a predictable pattern, through the years counseling my congregants. It's the way we human souls deal with powerlessness and wanton cruelty. Just know there is hope."

"Well, you've restored my hope about seeing Aaron."

"I'm glad. Now, are you ready to move on?"

※

Safed, Urdunn District

Aaron Déulocresca

I brush off the surface of a flat rock and sit down near the opening to the cave. The water skin cork pulls out easily with a little thumb pressure, and I take several gulps. A group of us students climbed up here yesterday for an all-night study session. It's amazing to sit, pray, and just be in the company of the great rabbis buried here. More than anything, I came seeking peace in my life, an enlightened mind, and to resolve the enigmas that haunt me. As the sun comes up, I take a moment to admire the green shoots sprouting from the moist earth around me. Purple crocus perk their heads above the soil. A strong breeze sweeps up the hillside across the plateau.

The sky is a blend of pale blue, with clouds like heaps of lamb's wool drifting by.

Having finished morning prayers, the others file out of the cave. Here in these remote hills, Rabbi Shimon bar Yochai and his son Eleazar fled, hiding inside this cave. The Romans had executed the great Rabbi Akiva by flaying him. Legend says that they remained here for 12 years, sustained by the fruit of a carob tree, and the study of Torah. Followers entombed him and other influential teachers here. Though I'm light-headed without sleep, the hour has come for us to trek back down the mountain and return home.

The descent isn't nearly as strenuous and takes only half the time as the climb. It's made even more pleasant by our rousing songs. By the time I finally slog my way back to Rehm's welcoming cottage in Safed, it is past midday. I am hungry and just want to curl up on my bed and sleep. But as I approach the cottage, I stop in my tracks. Someone tethered two donkeys at the gate, which never happens. Who would have reason to call on Rehm, or me, for that matter? My heart races and my legs go spongy. But Suqi is just inside the fence, behaving as if there is nothing out of the ordinary. He greets me with a furious tail wag and a lick.

I enter the cottage, with Suqi by my side. I'm stunned by what greets me. Rehm is sitting at the table drinking mint tea. Seated across from her are my mother and Rabbi Bertinoro from Jerusalem. There is a grim expression on everyone's face.

"I was on Mt. Meron at a *Tikkun Hatzot*," I say. "I did not know you were coming."

Rehm stands. "Aaron, come join us. Your mother and the Rabbi have some grave news."

My stomach sinks as my mouth falls open. I have not seen my mother for two years and we did not part on the best of terms. I slide onto the bench beside Rehm and turn my face to meet the rabbi's gaze.

"We have traveled days to reach you, Aaron," says Rabbi Bertinoro. "This kind of news is best delivered face-to-face."

I shoot a glance at my mother. She says nothing, but tears well in her eyes.

"Several days ago, a band of marauding *Urbān* kidnapped your father with a group of pilgrims. They are demanding a ransom," he says.

I gasp and squeeze my eyes shut for a moment. "What? Slow down. Father's being held hostage?"

"Yes. And we need your help," says Rabbi Bertinoro.

I clasp my head with both hands. "*Ribono shel Olam*. This is terrible." I grow cold inside and my limbs go slack. "I can't believe this."

My mother speaks softly. "The Community of Jerusalem has raised a portion of the ransom, but it is not nearly enough. I've offered our funeral plots on the Mount of Olives for sale, but that still falls short. The only money we set aside is for your education, your stipend…"

I straighten. "Oh. I see. Whatever it takes, we must free him." This grips me at the core. I turn and look at Rehm, who shakes her head with downcast eyes. I stare at the tabletop, stroking my beard. "This is such a shock. Is there nothing more we can do?"

Rabbi Bertinoro clears his throat. "I approached the Sheik of Jerusalem with the matter. He was unwilling to broker a deal, as these men act outside the law and are unlikely to respect any influence or authority he might bring to bear."

"So negotiating is not possible."

"In addition, the Mamelukes have ordered him to send all available troops to defend the north from the threat of an Ottoman invasion. So, he could not spare the few remaining guards to mount a rescue."

I shake my head. "An Ottoman invasion? Does that mean it may not remain safe here in Safed for long?" I look beside me at Rehm.

"It may not be safe anywhere in the land. We don't know what war with the Ottomans will bring," Rabbi says.

"So, there is no one to enforce the law or protect us. Pardon me, Rabbi. But where is my brother, Yonatan? Was he taken as well?"

The rabbi exchanges glances with my mother.

"No," she says. "We don't really know where he is. We hoped you would find him. He had come to Jerusalem to tell us about this misfortune, but then left, saying he'd return to Ramla to sell off the remaining donkeys."

"Yonatan was also going to inform the captain of the pilgrim ship. Perhaps he could contribute to the ransom. That is all I know," the rabbi says.

My head is reeling. I take a slow, deep breath and try to put all this information in rational order. Rehm rises, brings another earthenware cup to the table, and pours me some tea. I send her a momentary smile and take a sip of the warm, soothing liquid. Suqi seems to sense my distress and comes over and lies down at my feet.

"So, what happens now?" I ask. "Do you want me to return to Jerusalem? Search for my brother? What can I do to help?"

Mother draws out a book with a worn leather cover from inside a bag at her hip. She slides it across the table to me. I pick up the volume and thumb through it.

"This looks like father's writing; some kind of navigation or travel journal."

"That's exactly what it is," she says. "Can you decipher it? Understand it?"

I study several pages more closely and recognize measurements, geometric and algebraic calculations, and star constellations. I study his illustrations and maps. "Yes, it's quite clear."

"This is not just any journal, from any ordinary voyage," mother says.

I lean in closer, studying her face.

"We have spoken little about the details surrounding our flight from Spain. We were younger than you are now. My father, Joan Bautista, was a wealthy spice merchant who the Inquisition murdered."

"That much I knew."

"What we never told you or Yonatan was that your father piloted a caravel owned by my father. He was smuggling much of father's estate in gold, silver, and gemstones out of Spain, hidden in wine barrels. My inheritance."

I gape with wonder. "What happened to it?"

"The plan was to transport it to Alexandria, where your father was to serve as agent and secure its safety. But the ship went aground on an island. Your father hid the wine barrels in a cave. But then corsairs arrived and commandeered the ship. He had to abandon the barrels to get off the island with fishermen. By the time the two of us finally escaped from Barcelona and arrived in Jerusalem, you were on the way. Your father continued piloting ships for a period. However, the opportunity never arrived to go in search of the island again."

I lean back, folding my arms. "So, they might still be hidden in that cave? Could that be, after 25 years?"

"There's no way to know. I had given up long ago ever recovering my inheritance."

"I mean, if father could find that cave, so could others. What are our chances of it being there? Or that we could actually find it?"

"Very true," says the rabbi. "The chance of it still being there is remote, with pirates combing the Mediterranean. But right now, the chance of saving your father's life is nil."

"Just to be sure I understand you. You want me to digest this journal, figure out where this place is, get on a ship, find this cache of riches, and bring it back to pay the ransom."

Rabbi Bertinoro and mother are silent, but stare at me with bent brows and glassy eyes. But what they're asking is impossible. Then, Rabbi leans forward.

"The mitzvah of *Pidyon Shevuiim*, ransoming the captives is of grave importance. You know this; not to mention the commandment of honoring your mother and father."

"I don't disagree. But I have no training, no familiarity with sea travel. What makes you believe I can accomplish such a thing?"

"Because, you're an excellent student," Rabbi Bertinoro says.

CHAPTER 6

Safed, Urdunn District

Aaron Déulocresca

I LAY ON my bed, curled up on my side, with Rehm nestled in my arms. Embracing her is comforting. I stare at the walls, aglow with the last flickers from the fireplace. Owing to my fatigue, I begged off giving the Rabbi and my mother an answer. We agreed to meet tomorrow morning, and then they went off to the *khan* to stay the night. I will make my decision by then. As bone-tired as I feel at this hour, my mind is a torrent of speculation and debate. This turned my whole life upside down.

"This entire situation is tearing me to ribbons," I say. "My father's life is at stake. And the smallest chance I have of saving him requires me to give up everything I hold dear. I wish I could tell them no. But there seems no alternative but to go on this voyage. I just doubt such an expedition will prove fruitful. And then what?"

She rolls over to face me and caresses my cheek. "And there's a possibility of you losing your own life on such an ill-fated voyage. It's unthinkable, especially when we just found each other, in such a rare coincidence of timing. Surely there must be another way."

"Well, I'll do everything in my power to find a solution." I roll onto my back and stare at the rafters. "I'm only leaving for my father's sake; not for my mother or her inheritance. He has been my main mast in the storm my whole life."

"But your mother came all this way to beg for your help. She needs you."

"You don't know her. I came here to get away from her ill-treatment and venomous temper, and now she follows me. She is cruel to the bone."

She sits up and stares into my face. "No one is cruel to the bone, Aaron. Something must have happened to her in the past that made her this way. I sense it beneath her passive manner and statue-like face."

"She doesn't treat my brother this way. She dotes on him. And he is a gambling, drinking reprobate. But me? She's always given me the impression that I don't deserve to be alive, or that I owe her something. What that may be, she never reveals. I am perpetually guessing."

Rehm shakes her head and lays back into my arms. "How strange that a mother would be this way toward her first-born son."

"It's as if I am bound by an unspoken contract to make up for some undefined debt. No matter what I do, how dutiful I might be, how strict in my observance, how studious; I fall short in her eyes. I cannot atone, and can never pay back the balance."

"But your father is not this way."

"Never. For years, father would keep me at his side." My voice catches and my eyes water. "Not only to guide me, he also protected me from her wrath."

Rehm rubs my arm. "Surely she must have loved you, and wanted to raise a good man."

I huff. "She's never told me she loves me, and has not held or kissed me since I was small. When I got older, she'd say she could not stand to look at me, hear my voice, or be in the same room with me. That's why

I would spend long hours in study. I'd complete my chores speedily, and then disappear to the roof where I could avoid her."

She sighs and cuddles against me. "What a hell that must have been for you."

"Until I arrived here and met you, I have not known a day's peace."

She turns to face me and wraps her arm around my torso. "It is the right thing to do, even though I don't want you to go. Your sense of duty to your family is something I understand and admire."

"But you are my family now, too," I say, squeezing her closer.

⚜

Seeing no other options, I'm traveling south by donkey coffle. The road skirts the coastal plain between rolling hills and swampy marshland. Large ibis and cranes pass in flight against the glowing twilight. The air is cool, but my skin is itchy and hot. Thirty gold Sultani is an astronomical sum. Rabbi Bertinoro and mother gathered five, and they hope more will yet come in. However, raising the rest is on my shoulders and those of my reckless brother, Yonatan. Hopefully, he has sold the donkeys. But knowing him, he's probably gambled away whatever profit he made on the sale.

There is so much uncertainty. My stomach churns, and I twirl the long strands of hair at my temple around my finger. Father and those in his charge may never see freedom again. How much time do we have? They could all die in captivity while we're sailing around, looking for lost treasure. It's so ludicrous. The thought of losing my father eviscerates me. And the enormity of this burden is like a pile of ashlar blocks on my chest. I'm weak and pathetic like a lost child; and I'm alone.

Torches of the caravanserai come into view on the southern horizon. Surely Shuli and her mother Edna must have heard what has happened, and they may know Yonatan's whereabouts. It's nearly dark when the tired donkeys crowd into the livestock pen. I dismount, gather my belongings, and go into the *khan*. A night's lodging only costs me a few *hatichot*. A good meal and a full night's sleep beckon me. But first, I head for the Turkish baths. After long journeys, cleansing oneself in the *hammam* is practically obligatory.

The attendants hand me a hammered metal bath bowl, mitt for lathering, and fresh towels. Once I've shed my clothing, I slide my feet into a pair of carved olive wood shoes and fasten a towel around my hips. I make my way to an open seat on the warm marble bench. A soothing calm settles over me as the steam fills my nostrils. Next, an attendant scrubs and rinses the dust and donkey sweat from my body. If only I could afford the time to linger and relax in the pool this evening. But the urgency of my mission prevails. I merely dip in the lukewarm water, dry off, and dress.

When I arrive, Edna's coffeehouse is bustling with patrons. The aroma of cardamom flavored café wafts in the air. Across the room, Shuli is pouring the hot brew from a cezve for a trio of Muslim traders. My eyes scan the room and locate an open table. Shuli's momentary glance catches on me and a wave of both welcome and concern spreads over her face as she hurries toward me.

"I'm so glad you're here, Aaron. Thank God," she says. "If only you'd come for a more joyful occasion."

"So, you know about my father," I say.

"Indeed. Mother and I have been distraught. We'll do whatever we can to help."

"I appreciate that. Have you seen my brother?"

"Yes." Shuli rolls her eyes with an exasperated sigh. "He's over there, playing Mancala out on the terrace." She gestures toward the arches leading to the courtyard. "I'm sure you're hungry and tired. Let me bring you something to eat. I'll let him know you've arrived."

Ramla, Filastin District

Yonatan Déulocresca

A hand brushes against my shoulder. Shuli lowers her lips to my ear.

"Your brother Aaron has just arrived from Safed," she says. I turn to look at her. She raises her brows with expectation.

"He has? Thank you," I reply. I give up my small wager to my opponent for his inconvenience. From the terrace, I stroll back through the arches into the café. My short-lived pleasure drains away as the shadow of old rivalries and unsettled resentments loom. Scanning the room filled with diners and café drinkers, my eyes finally land on Aaron. His long tawny hair and neatly trimmed amber beard stand out in a room filled with Bedouin traders. He sees me and rises from his stool. I weave between patrons and grudgingly accept his embrace.

"Shalom," he says, and gestures to the open stool. "Please, join me."

"I can't believe you came," I say, knowing it's only moments before his sarcasm and jibes begin. "How did you know I needed your help so desperately?"

He offers me some bread, but I've already eaten and turn it down.

"Mother and Rabbi Bertinoro came all the way to the Galilee to tell me," Aaron says.

"They did? Are they here, too?" I ask.

"No, they've returned to Jerusalem." He takes a sip of wine, but pushes his plate away. "However, they entrusted me with the paltry sum they've raised for the ransom. Rabbi believes more may yet come in. And mother is selling their burial plots. But in the meantime, we have to do everything possible to raise the rest."

"So, they explained the situation."

"Somewhat. All I know is that father and a group of pilgrims are hostages to some cutthroat tribesmen. Mother said you were here, trying to sell the remaining donkeys."

I nod. "Yes, I sold two of them, a gold Sultani each. It was a fair price."

"That makes seven out of 30. What other options do we have? We're a long way from 23. Have you contacted the ship's captain to inform him that they took his passengers captive?"

"Not yet," I say. "They're Genoese. I know a little Italian, but not enough. We need a translator."

"Then, first thing tomorrow, we can approach the local Catholic priests and ask if they have someone who'd be willing to accompany us to parley with the captain. Maybe they have means to ransom the pilgrims, and together with our funds, we can free them all."

I scowl. "Those monks are not likely to help us."

"Why is that?"

"First, we're Jews," I say. "And second, we're competitors. They make money off pilgrims, just like we do. They benefit if our business is brought down."

His brows knot and he groans. "Really? But we still have to try. Unless you know of someone else who speaks Italian, I see no alternative."

"Rabbi Bertinoro could have translated, but he's not here."

Shuli and Edna glide toward our table in their sheer veils and bangles. Shuli carries a tray with glasses and a bottle of spring water, which she sets on the table. Wearing rings on every finger, Edna holds a bottle of Arak. She pours a small amount of the anise flavored liquor into the glasses. She gives a glass to each of us, and then the two women draw stools to the table. I slide mine closer to Aaron to make room. We stare at the striking, mature woman with onyx eyes lined with kohl.

"Now that you're both here, I'd like to make a proposal," Edna says. Her voice is deep and smooth as velvet. She glances side-to-side, as if assessing eavesdroppers. She then reaches across the table and clasps my brother's wrist. He leans in.

"I'd like to offer you both a way to raise the ransom money. You could work for me here at the cafe, however long it may take. And it would be a help to us, as well. We could serve customers better and faster."

"That is very bighearted, Señora Yaakovi," Aaron says.

My stomach grows heavy. It seems a simple solution, both of us servants. But it could take years to earn enough. I don't know if al-Dabaa will wait that long.

Aaron turns to me. "What do you think, Yoni?"

I lower my gaze, rubbing my forehead. "Thank you for the offer," I say, staring up at Edna from beneath pinched brows. "But you both know all too well that my actions caused this misfortune. It's really my burden to bear."

Aaron jerks his head toward me and gapes, and then looks back at Edna. She clenches her jaw and bends one brow.

"I'm very grateful for your generosity," he says. "You have always looked out for us and our father. But we are working out a plan. If, in the end, our efforts come to naught, I hope your offer will still stand."

"Of course. Without hesitation." She pats the back of his hand and rises. "We have only love and admiration for your father, and want the best for you. Should you change your mind, let me know." She turns, crosses the restaurant, and disappears into the back room. Shuli lowers her face and clears away the dishes in silence. With a blank stare, she turns to the needs of other customers. I hope I didn't offend them.

Aaron stares wide-eyed at me. "What do you mean, you caused this?"

Here it comes. There is no easy way out of this. I lower my face. "I was about to tell you. We haven't talked about that yet."

He growls. "What happened?"

"Well, you know how I have always loved horses and *Furusiyya*?"

"Right. You got arrested for riding a horse."

"I've been studying master horsemen for years. Over time, I've discovered the secrets of their skill in sports and contests done on horseback."

"And so, what does that have to do with father's kidnapping?"

"I'm getting to that. There was a corps of free Mameluke cavalrymen from Egypt who came through Ramla and put on a Qabaq contest. Within moments of watching them warm-up, I knew I could pick the winner."

"The winner?" Aaron pinches his eyes shut, shaking his head. "Oh no, you didn't."

My gut becomes a twisted knot. "I know, I know. I promised to stop wagering. But in the end, I was right. I did win fair and square. How was I to know that the leader of the *Urbān* was a poor loser? He thought I cheated him out of his money and wanted it back. But I refused to give in. So, they encamped outside of Abu Ghosh and ambushed us."

Aaron covers his face with his hands and it takes a few moments to contain his anger. My heart is racing.

"Even if it was fair, you exposed the family financially by your risky behavior, Yonatan. That's nothing new, but this time you've provoked these cutthroats, and our father could die."

His words feel like a dagger jabbed into my chest. I hunch over, rocking to contain a flood of pain, and my eyes glaze. "You're right, I'm just an idiot. I'm sorry. I can't tell you how sorry I am."

He rolls his eyes and heaves a deep sigh. "Stop feeling sorry for yourself. How many people do you have to hurt before you'll take responsibility and rein in your urges? You're too damned impulsive."

"So I'm told. And told." My vision blurs and there's a catch in my throat. "You don't know how it is; feeling like you can never get a foothold, get a leg up. I'm trapped being a damned donkey herder. There's no path for me to build a future for myself, let alone marry and support a family." Hot blood rises through my chest. "The only advantage I have is my luck and my skill." I pound my fist on the table.

Aaron smirks. "Luck is an illusion. Wagering is foolish and wasteful. And besides, father will turn his lucrative business over to you one day; whether you deserve it or not. If he survives."

I look away. "I don't need a lecture," I say. "You're not the one who has to toil in donkey shit day in and day out. You've had it easy, Aaron. They did not give me the same opportunities as you have to be educated and sent away to a prestigious school. You're our father's spoiled favorite, *Yeled-tov Yerushalayim*."

"I'm not a *yeled-tov* or the spoiled favored one. You are. Mother never required you to do a thing, while she punished me for the smallest mistakes. The rules that apply to everyone else never applied to you, because you're the blessed child. I shouldn't have to come from my mountain retreat to fix what you've broken. You're right, you owe our family for the damage your obsession caused."

I'm about ready to punch that arrogant *zayin* in the mouth. "Mountain retreat, of course. You're used to hiding out, running off to the *bet midrash*, sneaking up to the roof, doing whatever you please. Where's your responsibility to the family? You just live off their stipend money."

"Oh, I take their money? How many times have they paid off your gambling debts?"

"Look. I said I would stop, and so I shall." My eyes burn, and I smear the residue of tears from my cheek with my fist. "Aaron, we'll never come up with a plan to save father if all we do is attack each other.

He grows silent for a few moments and then takes a deep breath. "You're right; so far we've accomplished nothing."

I look around to see if any other customers are watching our scrap, feeling raw and exposed. But the jumble of many voices and the clatter of plates and glasses seem to have blanketed our argument.

"I apologize," Aaron says, and pats me on the shoulder.

"To tell you the truth, I'm terrified, Aaron."

"We both are. That's the strange thing about the Déulocresca men. We get mad when we're scared. We get mad when we feel guilty. When we are embarrassed or hurt, we get mad. It seems to be the only note we can sing."

"Truth. My brother, the Sage."

CHAPTER 7

Ramla, Filastin District

Aaron Déulocresca

BIRDS CHATTER IN the trees as we walk to the nearby monastery of Arimathea. Nature usually brings good spirits on such a beautiful spring morning. But I'm filled with uncertainty and distrust. According to Yonatan, the friars from this monastery are not our allies. Will they have a hostile attitude and reject our plea for help? How then will we raise the ransom?

We're both clad in our usual coarse homespun tunics. The ochre vertical bands woven into the fabric and our amber tarbushes are dead giveaways that we're Jews. Nevertheless, I don't see how we can free the hostages without their cooperation.

In the company of my father as a boy, I relished the chance to see inside churches. But as we approach the pale stone edifice with a spearhead arch over the entrance, I'm fidgety and my stomach flutters. I open the door and the two of us enter the narthex. A huge icon hanging on the wall is stunning. The painting features the namesake of this church with a glittering gold halo. There is no worship service underway, for which I'm grateful. Interrupting prayers would get us off to a poor start. Two monks in faded brown robes busy themselves deeper inside near the altar. One looks up, pauses in his task, and hurries toward us. As he draws closer, his eyes narrow.

"Good morning, Friar," I say. "I'd like to speak to your Prior or Abbot."

"To what is this pertaining?" he asks with a fake smile.

"It's regarding a group of Catholic pilgrims in danger."

His eyes widen. He gestures for us to wait here, hurries back through the nave, and disappears into a side passageway.

Yonatan whispers. "At least he didn't make us leave."

"We'll see."

After a while, he returns with another older monk in a cassock, cowl, and hempen girdle. This man stops short, tilts his head, and looks us both up and down.

"Good morning. I am Father Ricardo Claver. It's seldom we have young visitors, especially Jews. You are seeking help from the Church?"

I speak up. "Yes, on behalf of Christian pilgrims. Our father transports pilgrims to Jerusalem. We just learned that a band of marauders has abducted him and a group of 10, who recently landed here."

The priest's brows pinch together.

"We need someone with knowledge of Italian who can go with us to parley with the ship's captain in hopes we can together raise the ransom to free them all."

"Ransom? Why haven't you reported this to the authorities?"

"We have, sir. But the governor just sent his troops to join the defense in the north against invasion of the Ottomans, and he could offer no armed intervention."

"I see. I remember a group of pilgrims out of Messina with a Jewish guide. They came here many days ago," he says. "Very well. I can send one of my friars to accompany you to report the hostage situation to the captain. I confess, this is not the first time such a thing has happened. Ransoming captives is an act of great compassion."

"As it is in our traditions, as well," I say and bow. "These times are becoming more lawless and hazardous."

"Yes, sadly. And a war is at our doorsteps. Perilous times."

For two hours, we travel by donkey in relative silence with one Friar Angelo. By midday, we reach the port of Jaffa where the group first landed. Yonatan approaches a familiar local fisherman with a small dinghy and pays him to ferry us out to the ship. When we reach the vessel, Friar Angelo requests in Italian to come aboard for parley, which they grant. The captain invites us into his quarters. We explain to the friar what has happened; al-Dabaa's demand, the sum we've raised, and the amount still needed to free the pilgrims. Friar Angelo translates the information to the captain. But this explanation progresses into a longer conversation between the two men. The captain glares at me and then Yonatan. My stomach flips and my pulse quickens.

When he finishes, Friar Angelo turns to us to translate. His face is grim.

"The captain declines your request." There is a snide tone in his voice and he looks down his nose. "He believes you may be the ones trying to extort money. He is only willing to have a priest seek to free the hostages. And if a ransom is needed, we will pay it through the Church as intermediaries, and not you."

I turn to Yonatan. His shoulders slump and he stares at his hands.

"Please, I came all the way from Safed to ask for help," I say to Friar Angelo. "We have already raised part of the ransom. Can we not work in consort?"

Angelo translates, but the captain purses his mouth, juts out his chin, and shakes his head.

"You can certainly donate your funds to the Church," Friar Angelo says. "One way or another, we will try to broker a deal. But there is no guarantee everyone will be freed."

I register his implied meaning. He'd be happy to free the pilgrims, but won't assure father's release. Rising bile burns in my throat. I again glance at my brother. With a subtle squint, I try to convey my rejection of any donation. He delicately nods, agreeing with me. They don't consider us trustworthy, but they'd love to have our ransom money.

"Thank you for your time," I say, and I rise. The friar gives a dismissive wave of the hand and remains with the captain, presumably to work out their own plan. Yonatan and I leave the ship, climb into the dinghy with the fisherman, and head toward the shore.

"I had a hunch it would not work," I say. "But we had to try."

"Aaron, they know who we are," Yonatan says. "As children of Inquisition fugitives, the animosity and mistrust between us and these Catholics is too great a rift to overcome."

"They can't hurt us here, but they sure don't have to help us."

"Exactly. So, now what?" Yonatan asks.

"Not to sound callous," I say, "but can't we pay the ransom for our father, and let the Italians liberate their pilgrims?"

Yonatan shakes his head. "Doubt it. Al-Dabaa demanded I return with 30 pieces of gold. I don't think it's negotiable. Looks like we'll have to accept Edna's offer," he says.

I shake my head. "It could take years to earn that much. We'd become indentured servants. But there is another possibility, albeit farfetched and a lot riskier. We've run out of options. This would be a last resort," I say.

Yonatan's eyes widen. "A last resort? What is it?"

"I have something to show you when we get back to the caravanserai."

"Tell me now."

I stare past him and briefly point toward the rowing fisherman. He gives me a quizzical look and then discernment awakens on my brother's face.

When Yonatan and I arrive back at the *khan*, I lead him to my sleeping quarters and take out the chronicle our mother gave me. I pull up the shade to let the late afternoon sunshine pour through the small window, illuminating the worn leather cover. Yonatan sits on the cot beside me, tips his head, and stares at it with creased brows.

"This was father's navigation journal." I say, surprised at the slight tremor in my hand. "It recounts his voyage on a caravel called the Jubilee, that belonged to our grandfather."

Yonatan leans back and folds his arms. "How did you get it?"

"From mother, when she came to Safed. She told me the vessel was smuggling much of grandfather's estate out of Spain hidden in wine barrels. They planned to resettle in Alexandria." I'm not sure why, but my heart is beating faster, as if I'm talking aloud about something forbidden.

Yonatan takes the journal from my hand and flips through it, and pauses to study the star charts and geometric figures. "How much was there?"

"There is no record of that, but our grandfather was the wealthiest spice merchant in Barcelona, so it must have been considerable."

"What happened to it?" Yonatan asks.

"According to father's account, the ship went aground in a storm somewhere in the middle of the Mediterranean. Father had to stash the wine barrels in a sea cave to protect them from corsairs, who later seized the vessel, stranding him," I say.

Yonatan stares hard at me. "This sounds like some kind of tale or legend from Orlando Furioso. Does that mean the wine barrels are still there?"

"Without venturing to this place, we have no way to determine that. But it's possible. Father wrote the cave is in an obscure place. The corsairs never found the barrels."

"Are you joking? It's like manna from heaven. What's stopping us?"

"Slow down. The journal also describes an old Crusader watchtower, where knights once kept surveillance. That means it would be a great hideout for pirates, too. To undertake such a voyage would be highly risky. It could take weeks or months to get there and back."

"It would take longer working for Edna to earn 23 gold Sultani, even with both of our efforts." Yonatan stands up and starts pacing. "Besides, you said yourself, it's about our duty to keep the commandment, honor your father and mother."

I take a deep breath. "You're right."

"When I think about everything our parents went through to get to this land, to give us life, the sacrifices they made. We've never taken those kinds of risks; escaping being burned at the stake, rescuing people," Yonatan says. "But everything they suffered was because of the Catholic sovereigns and the Inquisition." He brandishes the journal. "Imagine how different our lives could have been, had the Inquisition never existed. We've done nothing to redress the wrong our family suffered, and so many others like us."

"We could restore our family to its rightful place," I say. Something shifts inside me. What if this reparation is what I owe my mother?

Yonatan slowly shakes his head. "I wonder why they never told us about this until now. Did they ever try to recover it?"

"There's a lot about our parents' lives that remains a mystery. But if we did find it, perhaps I could mend the rift between mother and I."

Yonatan blusters. "So why did you wait until now to tell me? Why did you make us go through all that shit with the friars and captain, if you already knew about this?"

"It scares me to death. I felt I had to exhaust all other options before going down this path. This journey will be life threatening. We have to be wise about our actions. Neither of us has training as a mariner or navigator." I take the journal from him and fan through the pages. "I can comprehend it, but I wouldn't know how to use this information to direct a ship. And I'm reluctant to put this journal in just anyone's hands."

"Absolutely. But if we can find this cache and ransom father, I might actually be able to look him in the eye again."

"It appears the reasons in favor are stacking up," I say. "Besides honoring our parents, restoring our family's rightful place, we each have personal reasons to go forward."

"Indeed."

"But how are we going to get there?" I ask. "We need someone who won't rob us, or strand us? I had considered offering some captain a share of the fortune, assuming it's still there."

Yonatan huffs with a one-sided smile. "Could you see us walking up to strangers at a port and asking them to go on a treasure hunt? Someone would attack us and steal that book."

"There are a lot of unknowns." I gaze out the window, searching the sky, and then pin my eyes on father's journal again. "When we were rowing back from the Genoese ship today, a memory of someone leaped into my mind. You weren't born yet, but I still have vague memories of our father leaving for voyages with his apprentice. Do you remember Davî Salmonis?"

"That's a name I haven't heard in a long time," says Yonatan. "Of course. I used to think of him as our older brother."

"I did too. He is certainly someone who could help us. What has it been? A decade since we last saw him?" I ask.

"I think I was nine years old. But we'd have to find him first."

Yonatan Déulocresca

I find Shuli in the kitchen with cooks and helpers scurrying around, preparing food and drinks for their customers. However, since the Halqa troops left for the North Country, there are fewer patrons. But soon enough, arriving pilgrims and travelers will flood these shores and the coffeehouse will be busy until autumn. That is, unless the war spreads south. Shuli is loading a beverage tray with cups and plates. I take her by the hand and draw her into a storage room.

"Yoni, what is it? I have to deliver this before it gets cold."

"I know. This will only take a few moments."

"Alright, what, what is it?"

"I'm going to be leaving."

"Alright, I'll see you tomorrow." She turns to go.

"No, you don't understand. I came to say goodbye. Aaron and I are going on a voyage. I don't know how long I will be gone."

She whirls around. "What? A voyage? What are you talking about?"

"The captain of that pilgrim ship refused to help us. They believe we are the extortionists. So, we have to raise the ransom money ourselves or the thugs will kill our father. I have to do this to make up for what I did. It's my fault."

"How will going on a voyage raise money? You're becoming a sailor now? Are you *meshuga*? As usual, you're being impulsive and not thinking things through."

"You're usually right, Shuli, but not this time. Aaron came down from Safed because my mother and Rabbi Bertinoro asked him to. They gave him my father's navigator journal. It shows where he hid our family inheritance, so corsairs couldn't steal it. But he never went back for it. Mother and the rabbi believe we can find it to pay the ransom, and more. Don't you see? We could build a life together, a real life, Shuli."

She stares at me with mouth agape. Then she shakes her head. "Don't go anywhere. I'll be right back." She hoists the tray of hot beverages and scurries out of the kitchen. I want to tell her how mixed up I feel about all this, guilty, alongside hope and excitement. She returns a few minutes later with an empty tray. She sets it on the huge preparation table.

"Come outside with me," she says.

I follow her out the back entrance, past the bake ovens to the shade of several palms.

"If I understood you correctly, you and Aaron are leaving on a sea expedition, hoping to find some lost treasure. Do you know how ridiculous that sounds? How will you find this supposed treasure, if it in fact exists?"

I gently grasp her by the shoulders. "We have explicit directions. So, we're sailing to Famagusta to find father's former apprentice. We just need someone trustworthy who can guide us and not rob us."

"Rob you? You could get yourself killed in a whole host of ways."

"I've thought about that. But my father is going to be killed if we don't. I owe it to him. How else can we come up with the money?"

"Stay, work for it, save. My mother is sick with worry. She'll help you."

"You think al-Dabaa will take partial payments?" I huff. "I'm sorry. This is the only answer."

"Will you ever consider for once how the things you do affect other people?"

"Am I not? My father's life is at stake, and I'm risking mine to make up for my mistake."

She goes silent.

"Will you wait for me?" I ask.

She rolls her eyes. "What do you mean? I've been waiting for you to get your life in order for years."

"I'm trying."

She embraces me, then pulls back and looks up into my face. "God be with you."

※

Aaron Déulocresca

If the Christians won't help us, perhaps the Muslims will. The imam of Ramla has always been a kind man. He would give us sesame sweets when he'd walk by us at play. I stand outside the door to the White Mosque, a huge white marble structure with cedar and cypress doors and a stunning minaret. I hope to catch a worshiper when he comes to prayers.

On the cobbled road from the east, two gentlemen approach, each wearing a fine blue and red wool *durra'ah* over a long linen *kisa*. They drape their skullcaps with patterned *keffiyot*. They stare at me suspiciously, in my tunic, with urine-colored stripes.

"*Shalom Alekim.*" I bow. "It's imperative that I speak to the imam. If you please, would you pass him that message? I am Aaron, son of Joachim Déulocresca."

"The imam? Wait here."

A short time later, another man comes out and ushers me into the walled garden beside the mosque. It is a verdant paradise. The call of the muezzin carries from the minaret, and I realize I arrived just before the start of prayers. While waiting, I let myself take in the surrounding beauty, breathe in the fragrances. Water splashes from the central *shadirvan* and water channels used for the ritual cleansing. The hum of many voices rises from inside and is soothing and trance inducing, not unlike Jewish prayer.

After prayers finish, I watch as congregants depart. A bearded man in white and his escort approach me. When I recognize him as the imam, I stand and bow. He returns my greeting with a nod.

"Sayid Déulocresca. For many years, I've known your father. I respect him as a kind and honest man. A rumor has spread that trouble has visited your family."

"Thank you for seeing me, Imam. The rumor is true. A band of Urbān has kidnapped my father and a group of pilgrims. These visitors are so vital to the local merchants and services."

He closes his eyes and shakes his head. "Yes, I'm afraid enforcement of our laws and safety have crumbled under the threat of war. What are you hoping I can do for you?"

"We have raised a portion of the ransom. What I ask of you is that you receive and safeguard a sum of seven gold sultani as a good faith offer. My brother and I need time to raise the rest. I hope it can prevent this clan leader from starting to execute the hostages."

"I see. I suspect that a letter from me stating so may buy you some time. Do you wish me to release it if he grows impatient?"

"I trust your judgment." I hand him the small bag of coins.

"We will do what we can." He opens the bag, pours the coins into his palm, counting them. "Gamal, please make a note that we received seven gold Sultani from Sayid Déulocresca to safeguard on behalf of his father."

"Yes, Imam."

"*Salem Alekim*," the imam says.

"*Alekim Salem*," I reply.

CHAPTER 8

MARCH 1515, THE PARALOS

Aaron Déulocresca

THE SEA IS completely foreign to my nature. I've been green around the gills from the time we launched. Each rise and fall of the ship makes me want to hurl my guts out over the side. And worst of all, doubts again haunt me that this high-stakes odyssey will prove fruitful. A young page calls out the time, turns the sandglass at the binnacle, and another hour of sand begins its slide through the neck. Each turn is a reminder that we've yet to raise the ransom money. Jeopardy to our father's life and those of the pilgrims is increasing. Fortunately, this leg of our journey will only last a day. We will hopefully reach the port of Famagusta, a Venetian colony on the island of Cyprus, before evening.

Oddly, seasickness hasn't affected Yonatan in the least. He darts around the ship like a seasoned mariner, even though it's the first time at sea for us both. He's been studying the rigging and workings of the sailors with great interest. Our constitutions are as different as our stature and appearance. Few would guess we are brothers. He is like the oak; dark, robust and formidable; while I am more the willow; fair, slender, and nimble.

We learned from our mother that Davî Salmonis, father's former apprentice, is most likely in Famagusta. Our growing family forced our father to end his seafaring days. But Davî continued as a pilot in the silk trade, out of the port of Acre. He would visit us in Jerusalem during Passover season. Eventually, he met a woman from a Sephardic family on Cyprus, married, and moved there. Father only rarely receives letters anymore. So, I'm not sure if we can find him. He could be at sea. And even if we locate him; there is no guarantee he will help us. But it's our best hope.

Noise erupts from some kind of commotion below deck. A plaintive and urgent voice rises. Then, a woman emerges through the hatch, climbs onto the deck, and scrambles to the railing. She is veiled, wearing blouson trousers beneath a long tunic. Clutching the balustrade with a death grip, she vomits and retches over the side. I sympathize, wrestling with my own urge to disgorge, myself. Sailors nearby smirk and chuckle, exchanging mocking comments in their tongue, which I guess must be Greek. My brother Yonatan dashes toward her from across the deck. As I study her, my mouth falls open. It's Shulamit, Edna's daughter from the caravanserai in Ramla.

"What are you doing here, Shuli?" Yonatan asks. "How did you get aboard this ship?"

She groans, wipes her mouth, and takes a halting breath. "I'm wishing I hadn't." She stares at him and then lurches away, retching over the side.

I amble over to the pair. "Give her a moment, Yoni. She needs to recover."

"Well, there can't be much left in that tiny body," he says with a smirk.

Shuli turns around with a scowl and gives him a shove in the arm.

"Are you alright?" I ask.

She lowers her head. "Not entirely."

"I never expected to see you here," I say. "Do you also have business in Cyprus?"

"I'm not a stowaway, if that's what you're thinking. I paid for my passage, just like you did." She points at my brother. "I was afraid this one would get himself killed."

I lower my head to hide my smirk. "So, you thought you'd better monitor him."

"Don't laugh. My mother and I have stepped in countless times to keep your brother from acting on his reckless whims," she says.

Yonatan glowers in protest. "What do you mean?"

Shuli rolls her eyes and gives an indignant cluck. "What about that baby lynx you thought would make a nice pet?"

Yonatan bunches his brows and looks down. "Oh, that."

"Ah, I can well imagine," I say.

"Mother and I care deeply about your father," Shuli says. "I couldn't stand by and do nothing."

"You have good intentions, Shuli. Be assured, I'll keep my eyes on Yonatan, knowing his tendencies. But this expedition is likely far too dangerous for a woman. It's best if you turn around and go back to Ramla when we get to port."

She crosses her arms and frowns. "Well, I assumed I wouldn't be traveling alone."

"That's true," Yonatan says. "Why couldn't she go with us?"

I shake my head.

Shuli puts her hands on her hips. "I'm not without skills."

"She could be more help than a hindrance," Yonatan says.

I rub my aching forehead and gaze out at sea. "You cannot be serious. This will never work. We don't know where we're going or how to get there."

"We'll figure it out," says Yonatan. "We've got father's journal."

His mention of the diary strikes me like lightning. I glare in horror and bring my index finger to my lips, shaking my head.

"Let's tell the entire world. Shall we?" I mutter.

Yonatan's eyes widen and his mouth gapes. I survey the crewmen, assessing who may have overheard. But no one is near enough, and likely don't speak our language.

Shuli rolls her eyes again. "You see?"

I don't say it, but I'm wondering if Yonatan is the hazard. Maybe he should be the one to return to Ramla. Sometimes he's a ram in a potter's shed. But he caused this. He's obliged to at least try to make things whole. And if I'm honest, I feel woefully inadequate to the task. Yes, he is the oak and I am the willow.

"Let's first see if we can even find Davî. Then we'll decide. We may all be going back."

"Well, the offer to work for my mother still stands," says Shuli.

A stone lighthouse stands atop a massive Venetian-built bastion. Its silhouette contrasts against a golden horizon. As the ship enters the breakwater, a statue comes into view. It features a lion and cub on a pedestal. I make a sketch of them in my journal. Beyond the statue sits Famagusta's Harbor Citadel, the main entrance to the town, with a massive wrought-iron gate and portcullis. Shuli and Yonatan stand beside me with our bags, ready to disembark.

As soon as they lower the gangplank, we leave the ship, and trod up the wide cobbled thoroughfare to the main gate. How different the dock workers and citizenry all dress. Curious and suspicious eyes study us as we pass. We don't want to be so conspicuous. Shuli's and Yonatan's furtive glances tell me they feel as out of place as I do.

"We will need different clothes if we're going to fit in," I say.

"Do you suppose they place restrictions on Jews the way the Muslims do?" Yonatan asks.

"We're going to find out, soon enough," Shuli says.

Once we pass through the gate, we come to a huge central square. Great wealth built this place. The merchants and ship owners must lead lives of luxury. The builders of this city tried to replicate the ancient grandeur of Rome, with arches and columns. A huge, honey-colored cathedral stands directly ahead across the plaza. It has three large gables, canopied doorways, and a vast amount of carved stone work. In front of the church grows a very old fig tree of enormous size. It casts welcome shade over the courtyard. But it's the Jewish community that we seek, and its center is always the synagogue. If Davî Salmonis is still here, someone in the congregation will probably know him.

"Do you know enough Italian to ask where the Jewish quarter is, brother?" I ask.

"I'll try." Yonatan hails a passing well-dressed man. *"Per favore. Il quartiere ebraico?"*

The man scrutinizes us, and then politely gestures with his left hand back toward the gate. Yonatan thanks him and we retrace our steps. I spy an area in the surrounding colonnade where ornate wrought iron latticework fills the spaces between the pillars. And there is an arching gate, standing open.

"That might be it," I say, pointing.

The opening takes us through a narrow, dark passageway, and we emerge into a large open-air market selling many goods. Patrons hover around the stalls piled with vegetables and fruit, spices, bread, copper vessels, and cloth. The surrounding buildings are several stories high, built of the same beautiful stone, and with the same fine architectural details. That suggests that Jews here do not live an impoverished marginal existence as those in Jerusalem.

We approach the vendor at a stall displaying bolts of beautifully dyed silk. Yonatan asks him in Italian to direct us to the synagogue. He reveals that there are two houses of worship. One founded by Jews of the north, the Ashkenazim, and another started by refugees from Spain. Yonatan tries to interpret for us and asks directions to the Sephardic Synagogue. The vendor points the way through the northwest corner of the colonnade. I grow more hopeful that we might actually get some answers.

It's time for evening prayers as we arrive. Worshipers file through the arcade of white horseshoe arches into the Sephardic synagogue. We leave our baggage in the vestibule, and Shuli goes into the women's section. Yonatan and I greet our hosts, who offer welcoming but strained smiles. Something about us makes them uncomfortable. We take our turn at the wash basin along with the other men. All dress in the European manner; similar to the brightly colored garments worn by Christian pilgrims I've seen. But here, most wear black or indigo. They have strange form-fitting silk coverings on their legs, short belted tunics with their undergarments peeking from the neckline and seams; and the oddest coverings over their genitals; all of it laced together. It looks silly and uncomfortable to me, compared to the lose-fitting simple garments we wear at home.

"How long do you suppose they take to get dressed?" Yonatan whispers. I chuckle.

They also each wear a brass or gold symbol on their shoulders like the Latin letter O. It looks regal and elegant against the black, but I suspect it is not actually jewelry.

The *hazan* begins the service with a chant from Psalms. The familiar Sephardic melody makes me feel right at home. While Yonatan knows the melodies, he never excelled at reading Hebrew as I did. But he recites the parts he remembers. When at last our prayers finish, the rabbi approaches us straight away.

"Welcome, welcome," he says in Spanish. "You look like travelers from the Holy City."

"We are indeed," I reply. "I am Aaron Déulocresca, and this is my brother Yonatan."

"I am Rabbi Isaac Carrasco. What brings you to Famagusta?"

"We are trying to locate a family friend who lives here. We've known him since childhood, but lost touch with him over the years. He was a navigator apprentice to our father from Barcelona. We were hoping you might know of him. His name is Davî Salmonis."

The rabbi's brow wrinkles. "Salmonis? That name does not sound familiar. You say he was part of this community?"

"Yes, and married into a prominent Sephardic family."

"There are over 200 Jewish families here in Famagusta. The

majority are from Spain and Portugal. However, it is not uncommon among those fleeing the Inquisition to change their names, to decrease the chances that the Inquisition could ever identify them."

"The Inquisition? They're still hunting people after all this time and hauling them back to stand trial for heresy?" I ask.

"Yes, still to this day. But Cyprus is under the control of the Venetians. While it is a Catholic country, they're at odds with the Pope these days. In the 15 years I have been rabbi here, they have sent their spies only a few times. We made sure they did not find who they were looking for."

He says that in a manner that makes me wonder who I'm really dealing with. What lengths are they willing to go to in order to thwart the Inquisition? His revelation weighs heavily on my chest and a shudder passes over me. "So the man we know as Davî could be here, but he goes by an assumed name."

"Perhaps."

Suddenly, I realize the obvious. "I assure you, we're not Inquisition spies looking for him."

The rabbi stares intensely into my eyes, but is silent.

"We're Jews, born in Jerusalem," says Yonatan. "Our mother fled the Inquisition, and they murdered our grandparents."

The rabbi folds his arms across his chest. "There's a possible solution. I have in mind someone who regularly comes to morning minyan. Return tomorrow for morning prayers and wait. If he arrives, and if he recognizes you, he can reveal himself."

"Very well. We'll do that," I say. "Now, where might we find a place to get a meal and stay the night?"

"Just over here," he says, leading us outside. "They offer rooms and a kosher meal just down the way here at La Locanda. But before you go, there are a few vital things you must know. As Jews, I advise you not to leave the *giudecca* at this hour. They will soon lock the gates for the night. You will get stranded outside, which could bring the most undesirable consequences. Tomorrow, after prayers, you need to register as visitors, and you must purchase a badge designating our faith." He clutches the emblem at his shoulder.

We thank him and reunite with Shuli, who's been listening behind the *mehitzah*. Under a star filled sky, we leave the synagogue and make our way to the inn.

"This made me realize how much I have taken for granted," I say. "I'm astonished that the Inquisition still actively hunts mother and Davî after all these years."

"Living in a Muslim controlled land has its restrictions," says Shuli. "But at least we are not cowering under the shadow of the Inquisition."

"No, you're just taken for ransom by Arab tribesmen," Yonatan says.

"And here, you must wear a badge announcing you're a Jew," I say.

"It's a far cry better than the shit-colored clothing we're limited to," Yonatan replies.

"But being locked inside the gate makes me wonder," she says. "Is it to keep hostiles from getting in at night? Or is it a sign they fear Jews might get out?"

CHAPTER 9

March 1515, Famagusta, Cyprus

Yonatan Déulocresca

The morning is warm and bright. A gentle wind gusts through the window of our small room as we prepare to leave the inn. Aaron locks the door. But my insides are churning. I pick at my cuticles and fingernails. We walk the short distance to the synagogue. I hope we find Davî Salmonis at morning prayers. Shuli left earlier to comb the market for serviceable clothing and easy to carry provisions.

"I've been thinking," I say.

Aaron laughs. "Oh no, now we're in trouble."

"No, really. Watching those sailors on the ship, I know I could do what they do. If things don't work out with Davî…"

He interrupts. "You watched them for a day, Yoni. That doesn't make you an expert at seafaring."

"But I can do it. I could earn our way to the next port, and the next."

My brother looks toward heaven, shaking his head. "Slow down and focus on the matter at hand."

"What if Davî doesn't remember us?"

"He'll recognize us. You were young when he last visited, but I was 14."

"That doesn't mean he'll agree to help."

"You don't know that for certain. Don't predict the worst."

We enter the synagogue doors and the sanctuary. Benches surround a central *bimah* on three sides. A score of men are strapping on their *tefillin* and draping themselves in prayer shawls. We weave a path to a bench in the far corner. That gives us a view of the other worshipers and the entrance. Aaron opens his small embroidered pouch holding his prayer shawl and tefillin, and starts putting them on with the proper blessings.

"Where's your *tallit*?" he whispers.

"I forgot mine in Jerusalem," I say.

"Of course, you did." Aaron wanders over to a row of pegs near the entrance, borrows one of several spares hanging there, and then returns and hands it to me.

I wrap myself in the sacred garment and start humming along with the *hazan* as he chants the morning blessings. Worshipers continue to file into the sanctuary. I study them one by one. The dark silk and brocade clothes they wear suggest a proud and prosperous community. I catch glints of gold and gemstones on their hands, and modest gold and silver pendants at their chests. Jews are never allowed to show wealth like this in Jerusalem. It makes me wonder how they achieved it. Could someone like me, a simple donkey herder, learn to do the same? But these things could be mine if we found the hidden wine barrels.

We're in the middle of the *pesukei dezimra* hymns when a man joins the assembly, who grabs my attention. He takes his place amidst the benches on our right. His wavy hair and beard are acorn brown. He looks to be in his thirties, the right age for Davî. Then I notice a birthmark on his left cheek, almost hidden in his beard. This jogs my memory. Davî had such a birthmark. My stomach flips and my heart starts to sprint. I nudge Aaron with my elbow. He jerks his face toward me with a knotted brow. I casually gesture toward the man. Aaron stiffens and his eyes widen.

"It's him," he whispers.

As prayers continue, we both pin our gaze to him, hoping he will glance over. But it's not until the service is nearing the end that his eyes drift in our direction. He tips his head to one side and squints with a puzzled expression. Then he turns back to his prayer book. After we sing the final hymn, congregants remove their *tefillin* and prayer shawls, as do we. Rabbi Carasco is watching us from a distance as we sidle into the aisle and approach the man we believe is Davî Salmonis. He stands frozen, staring at us with curious alarm. Then his brows rise.

"I can't believe my eyes," he says. "Aaron? And is this Yonatan? It's been years."

"I wasn't sure you'd remember me," I say.

"Time passes, but I could never forget you or your family."

"We've traveled quite a distance to find you, Davî," says Aaron.

"Davî? It's also been years since I answered to that name," he says. "Call me Simon, Simon Mendes." He embraces each of us, but with restrained enthusiasm. Knowing he's hiding from the Inquisition, does our coming here threaten him in some way?

"And how is your father?" he asks.

I cringe. "Unfortunately, we…"

Aaron interrupts. "Is there a private place we may talk?"

"Certainly. Come home with me. We can speak candidly there," says Simon.

He leads us out of the synagogue and winds through the Jewish marketplace.

"The last letter I had from your father, he was planning to send you to one of the great houses of learning in Safed," he says to Aaron.

"Yes. I have been living there and studying for two years, and they've also commissioned me to paint a fresco," he says.

"A fresco? That's right. You're an artist. And Yonatan, what have you been pursuing?"

"I help run our family business guiding visitors on pilgrimage to the holy sites."

We arrive at a fine villa a short walk from the synagogue. I'm stunned by the beauty of the architecture and furnishings. Already I have a sense we can't persuade Davî, now Simon, to leave all this for our risky mission.

"This has been my home for the past eight years," he says. "The place belongs to my father-in-law, Signore Benjamin Franco, who is a financier."

The joyful sound of children's voices comes from a room off the central hallway. Two young boys come running toward us.

"*Abba*, you're home," says one little fellow with the same soft brown curls as his father.

"Good morning, Meir. How are you, Raffaele?" Simon kneels to give each child a hug.

"We have two special visitors, Signori Aaron and Yonatan Déulocresca, from Jerusalem."

"Pleased to meet you, Signori," the older boy says with a bow.

"Is Jerusalem far?" the younger boy asks.

"One day's sail," I reply.

"Can we go there, *Abba*?"

"Perhaps, one day. But now you must get ready for your studies. I will see you later." The boys scamper away.

"Their mother, God rest her soul, left us when Raffaele was born. He never knew her gentle ways. It took us many years to find joy and purpose again."

"Losing a wife and a mother can leave an indelible mark on one's soul," Aaron says.

"Didn't you lose both your parents to the Inquisition?" I ask.

"I did, 25 years ago. Your father and mother saved me, heart and soul. And I fear the reason you've come concerns them." He gestures to a doorway behind us. Simon leads us into a sitting room with damask drapes and fine upholstered chairs surrounded by tall cabinets and bookshelves. He invites us to sit. "Can I offer you café or tea?" he asks.

"Café," I reply, and Aaron nods in agreement. Within moments, a servant girl appears in the doorway and he instructs her to bring the beverages.

I'm saddened as the reality of his situation comes to light. After losing his wife, he'll never leave his children. The stakes are too high.

"Tell me what has happened," says Simon.

"Our parents are both yet alive," I say. "But some days ago, a cut-throat tribe of Urbān took our father and a group of pilgrims hostage on the road to Jerusalem."

"*Ribono shel Olam*," he whispers and covers his forehead with his palm, shaking his head. "He's like a father to me."

"We've raised some of the ransom, but unless we come up with an additional 23 gold Sultani, they may never see freedom and could die," Aaron says.

"Twenty-three?" He bunches his brows. "That's no trivial amount. Not an amount I can easily hand you. But I would without hesitation."

"What about your father-in-law?" Aaron asks.

"Signore Franco is a generous man. He might discuss a loan if he were here. However, this is sadly ill-timed. He sailed to Venice and isn't due to return for weeks."

"We hadn't really considered a loan," I say. "Our mother sent us on a different errand."

Aaron takes out father's journal and hands it to Simon. "She gave us this."

Simon opens the cover and studies the pages. Then he gasps, and his eyes widen. He searches my face and then Aaron's. "Do you realize what this is?"

"Yes," Aaron replies. "It's father's navigational journal. He details the location where he hid a cache of riches that belonged to our grandfather."

Simon straightens. "Your father used to talk about assets hidden inside wine barrels in a cave. He kept vowing the two of us would reclaim them one day. But then, you two were born. That day never came. I didn't know this journal existed."

"You're a navigator. Can you help us recover them?" I ask.

He looks skyward, sweeps his cap from his head and runs his hand through his hair. His eyes shift around the room and he wrestles with turmoil from this revelation. Finally, he blows out a long breath through pursed lips. "Forgive my hesitation, brothers. I would do anything to help your father. However, there are things I should tell you. I am a doubly wanted man; which is why I took a new name. The Inquisition still seeks me. They even came looking for me many years ago. But the men of this community protected me, shall I say?" He pauses and stares at each of us alternately.

Inside, I'm awe-struck by men willing to do whatever it takes to protect family and lives from unjust oppressors. "Justice," I whisper.

The corner of Simon's mouth draws up on one side. "But there's another obstacle. I can never set foot in a land under Spanish rule. The crown has placed a price on my head. There was a time that I piloted a ship that seized Spanish vessels. We plundered them to compensate for the fortunes lost by our people, who the Spanish forced into exile.

"Like you and our parents were."

He nods.

Something ignites inside my gut. "You robbed Spanish ships as retribution for the murderous Inquisition and the Alhambra Decree?"

"I did. We restored some semblance of life to refugees. You do not know the suffering our people have endured."

"Oh, but we do. Many of them have come to Jerusalem and Safed," Aaron says.

"That is a worthwhile cause," I say.

"But it comes at a heavy price," says Simon.

"We are looking for a trustworthy pilot who can guide us. If we recover this inheritance, you'd receive a share of it," says Aaron.

Simon crosses his arms. "A share of it? This is *Pidyon Shevuiim*. I couldn't take your inheritance." He studies the directions in the journal further. Then he rises, goes to a tall shelf, takes down a scroll case, and brings it to the table. He pulls out a map and unfurls it. We help hold down the corners.

"We are here. Based on what your father told me and what he wrote in the journal, the islands are somewhere around here between Tripolitanos and Sicily. That is the Spanish domain." He circles an area with his finger. But all I can see is ocean.

"There are several tiny islands here, too small to be noted on most maps. But those who frequently traverse these waters know them well. Pirates and corsairs comb this whole area. It's rather dangerous." He covers a yawn with his hand.

"In other words, there's a strong chance someone's already discovered it," says Aaron.

"And our whole endeavor could be pointless."

"That depends on how well your father hid it."

Aaron thumbs through the pages to a particular place. "Father wrote that the Janissaries were right there, carting off cargo from the Jubilee. But they never found the cave."

Simon studies father's notations and drawings. He strokes his beard and takes a deep breath. He looks at us. "Most interesting."

"We can understand why you could not leave your children and this haven to accompany us," says Aaron. "But is there someone else you could introduce us to, someone you trust?"

"Not here on Cyprus. Let me think about this. I didn't mention that I am the keeper of the Famagusta lighthouse. This is the end of my workday, and I'm desperately short of sleep. Later today, before sunset, I'll come and help you make a plan. In the meantime, head to the Port Authority. Find out which vessels are outbound in the next few days, and their destinations. And this…" He holds up father's journal. "Need I caution you? Sew it into the lining of your clothing, and never speak of it openly."

Aaron takes the journal and we both nod our acknowledgement.

"Until evening," I say. "Thank you."

Returning through the marketplace, we share a light meal of bourekas and oranges. Shuli is waiting for us at the entrance to the inn. She bought European garments and provisions, which we carry into the room.

"Well, I was half right," Aaron says, sitting on his cot. "He remembered us, but I doubt he will accompany us to find the hidden trove."

I gesture to Shuli to sit beside me. "But he said he knows someone who can," I reply.

"The bigger question is the wisdom of this expedition, altogether," Aaron says. "It's a high-risk venture with no guarantees. We could just stay here and wait for Signore Franco to return and request a loan."

"A loan?" says Shuli. "My mother will give you both a means to earn the ransom."

"I think we've already established that it could take years to earn enough," says Aaron.

"Why couldn't we try to find it while we're waiting for Signore Franco to return?" I ask.

"You underestimate the dangers of this journey. We could be killed if the ship sinks or pirates capture us and force us into slavery," Aaron says. "And if we find it; what's to say we couldn't then be robbed of it?"

"Oh, now who's predicting the worst?" I ask. "We have to take this chance. The wealth is rightly ours. If we don't go after it, we'll spend the rest of our lives wondering and regretting."

"Perhaps you would," says Aaron. "There are too many unknowns and risks."

"Father's life hangs by a thread. If Simon believes there is someone trustworthy who can help us, shouldn't we try? I owe it to father. And you said you hoped this journey might restore the rift you have with mother."

He huffs. "We'll see what Simon tells us. In the meantime, let's try out these European clothes, acquire the Jewish badges, and go to the Port Authority like he suggested."

CHAPTER 10

March 1515, Famagusta, Cyprus

Aaron Déulocresca

When you come to the crossroads, stand and look. Ask about the age-old paths. Which is the best road? Go that way and you will find rest for your soul. That is what the prophet Jeremiah wrote. Ambivalence and doubt cloud my path at this crossroad. Should we levy upon ourselves a debt? With accrued interest, we may never repay it in a lifetime. Or should we return home to months, or even years of servitude? If we embark on a perilous expedition to reclaim a trove of family assets; what if it is a mirage? No choice seems viable. But my father's life depends on making the right decision. So does my hope to see my mother smile at me again.

The three of us huddle around a stout table outside the inn's taverna, beneath a lattice pergola of climbing roses. Clouds stretch across the sky in variegated shades of orange and plum. While we wait for Simon, we share a bottle of wine served in Venetian stemmed glasses. I look at the people milling around the marketplace and the taverna.

At least we blend in with the locals now. Shuli found suitable second-hand European garments for each of us. But I feel a little ridiculous, like I'm wearing a costume or a disguise. Thankfully, the top is a modest length; a gown, they call it. It's worn over loose-fitting body linen with a cincture around the waist. But these tight leggings feel strange. With my beard trimmed and my tarbush replaced by an Italian toque, I look Venetian. So does Yonatan. He is in brown and I'm in faded blue. I've learned these are the colors of the servant class. Shuli wears a long dress with a short-waisted bodice that would immodestly expose her chest except for the gauzy chemise. The three of us also wear the circular brass emblem that signifies our faith.

From across the square, Simon approaches. He's dressed much the same as we are, but in vibrant green fabric, a color only Muslims may wear in our homeland. Hopefully, he'll bring the wisdom and experience we need to guide our decision and our path. He smiles and greets us, and I stand to embrace him.

"Good evening," says Yonatan and rises. "Let me introduce Shulamit Yaakovi. Shuli, this is Simon Mendes."

Simon studies her with a budding attraction in his eyes. "You didn't mention a woman accompanied you. You look familiar, Shuli. Are you also from Jerusalem?"

Her eyes widen. "No, from Ramla."

"We brought her along to look after the details, while we sort out the major matters," I say. "She's been a great help to us."

"I think we may have met before," Simon says. "Although I was 10 years younger, and you were probably eight or nine. If memory serves me, your mother had a restaurant in Ramla."

She tilts her head. "In fact, she still does." She keeps her eyes pinned to him with a hint of a coy smile.

"I've been there many times. You've matured into quite a lovely young woman."

She lowers her head and covers her mouth. Yonatan stiffens and his brows knot.

Simon reads his reaction. "The two of you are..." He slowly wags his finger.

"Family friends," she says. "Like you."

Color drains from Yonatan's face and his lips part. But no words come out.

"I see." says Simon and raises one brow as he sits next to me. "So, were you able to find out information about departing vessels?"

"Yes," I reply. "There are ships sailing to Rhodes, Alexandria, Messina by way of Crete, and Piraeus."

"Excellent. Here's what I think we should do," says Simon.

"We?" I lean in.

"Forgive me. It alarmed me when I learned two strange men had arrived looking for me. I hesitated, until I had time to reflect and remember many vital things. You see, your father saved me from the Inquisition, gave me a home, and a profession. I owe him my life. Although years have passed, I am still in his debt."

"Does that mean you'll go with us?" asks Yonatan.

"At least a portion of the journey. I want to ensure you're in good hands."

My heart thunders in my chest and my mouth goes dry. I take a sip of wine. "So, you believe there's a reasonable chance we can find this hidden inheritance?"

"If your father's journal is accurate, yes. And knowing him, it's precise."

"And it's a better choice than taking a loan from your father-in-law."

Simon leans back and folds his arms. "Can you guarantee a loan, have collateral, or employment to repay it?"

"Well, no," I say. My cheeks grow warm.

"My mother has offered them work," Shuli says.

"That's kind of her. I believe the cycle of time for a voyage would be more expedient. So, however far-flung it may seem; the journey appears to be your best course."

"I don't understand where your resistance is coming from, Aaron,"

Yonatan says. "You're the one who lectured us about redeeming the captives. It's a grave obligation, you said. And Maimonides wrote that delaying rescue is tantamount to murder."

"I know I did. It's just that I am not a sailor or a warrior. All the way here, I was seasick. No one ever taught me to swim or use weapons. I wouldn't know how to defend myself if I had to. Living under Mameluke rule does that to you. If things turn violent or dangerous…"

Simon leans forward. "Some of these things I can teach you, Aaron. But there are other ways to accomplish things than by violence. Sometimes it is better to avoid these in favor of intellect. That has always been your strength."

"I guess," I say. "Yonatan is certainly more cut out for a sailor's or warrior's life than I."

"That's why you make a good team. Your father never used a weapon nor resorted to violence, although he certainly knew how. Primarily, he used his mind to strategize how to conceal, masquerade, and misdirect, and he saved dozens of lives without a blow. He literally wrenched me from the clutches of a sentinel at the gate, disguised as a Catholic friar."

"I've heard similar stories, but not that one," says Yonatan.

"So, if we're all in agreement, Candia, on the isle of Crete, is our destination. It should be smooth sailing for 3-4 days with a fair wind to get there. It won't hurt to leave my boys for a week. I've explained the importance of this journey to my mother-in-law. Things will be fine until I return."

"Won't you lose your job at the lighthouse?" I ask.

"No. I share the duties with another keeper, who can cover my absence."

"What awaits us in Crete?" asks Shuli.

"Great question. Once we arrive there, I will make introductions. I've brought something to show you." He draws a folded piece of cloth from a small bag on his shoulder and spreads it over the tabletop. It is vibrant green and printed in gold, but well used and slightly tattered.

"Is this some kind of flag?" Yonatan asks.

"Exactly."

In the top portion is a framed passage in Arabic, I suspect from the Quran. A double-bladed sword and four crescents are emblazoned in the center with Arabic names. But in the lower portion is something I never expected to see, the Magen David.

"The Star of David! How strange," I say.

"We flew this on La Vengadora, where I served for three years. The crew included escapees from the Inquisition, both Jews and Moors, and Ottoman Turks. The Commander was a Turk, Hizir Pasha. He's known throughout the Mediterranean for his red beard as Barbarossa. But his second in command was an exiled Jew. I hope to introduce you to him. His real name is Gabriel Coron, but he earned a moniker, *Çiphut Sinai.*"

"Judgment of Sinai? That means what?" I ask.

"The righteous vengeance for the suffering inflicted on our peoples, Jews and Moors. You shall have no other gods before me. You shall not make for yourself an idol. You shall not murder. You shall not steal. You shall not bear false witness. You shall not covet. The Inquisition and Spanish did all of those things to us. And they are still doing them. We simply recovered what was ours."

"La Vengadora," says Yonatan. "The Avenger."

"You're a corsair," Shuli says in a whisper, her eyes gleaming.

"I was. In those three years, we successfully captured two papal galleys and a Sardinian warship. After that, we concentrated on commandeering Spanish trade vessels, and plundering Spanish controlled ports. We raided Cape Passero in Sicily and Reggio Calabria. We then distributed the spoils to help our people. Most of the ships we delivered to the Ottoman navy."

Yonatan shakes his head. "That's amazing."

"I'm both in awe and troubled," I say.

"How so?" Simon asks.

"Do you suppose that was the fate of the Jubilee, our grandfather's ship?"

He strokes his jaw and draws a deep breath. "Of course, they were flying the Catalan flag. Things were different 25 years ago. What I know is that since that time, the Ottoman Sultan has welcomed and aided Jewish refugees with open arms. He thinks Spain and Portugal are stupid to burn or expel prosperous, talented, and educated people."

"Amen," says Yonatan.

"If you have no objections, let's get on that ship to Crete. I must go to work now. Let's meet again in the morning and start preparations. I look forward to seeing you then." He reaches over and pats the back of Shuli's hand. She gazes into his face with an eager grin. Then he gathers up the flag, stands, and leaves us with a bow.

Yonatan is livid. He waits until Simon is out of earshot and then says through his teeth, "I can't believe you were flirting with him, Shuli. Right in front of me."

She stiffens. "I was not."

"You think I'm blind? Something was going on between you two."

"I was just being friendly."

"Don't tell me you're not keen on him. And he certainly noticed it."

I lean forward. "We have matters so much more important than this."

"Stay out of it, Aaron," Yonatan says. "I have a mind to send you home tomorrow, Shuli. You betrayed my trust. I give you my heart and this is what you do? I thought you loved me."

"I do love you." She lowers her head and mutters. "Just not in the way you imagine."

"What? What does that mean, not the way I imagine?"

"You want me to be your wife and lover. But that can never be."

He stares at her with his mouth agape. "Why?"

Shuli sits frozen except for the rise and fall of her chest with anxious breath. Finally, she breaks off the stare. "I may as well tell you." She glances at each of us in turn. "I'm your sister."

Yonatan's eyes widen. "Sister?" He bolts from the table, stalks away shaking his head, and disappears into the marketplace. I gape at Shuli, but have no words. Edna and Shuli have always seemed like family to me. Now I know it's because they are. I've sensed that father was miserable with my mother, although he never spoke of it to me. And I questioned my perceptions of their marriage, given my own feelings toward her. I guess I'm not surprised by this revelation. But the timing could have been better. Now, the wheels have come off the cart and turned everything upside-down.

"We need to go after him, find him," says Shuli.

"He just needs to cool off. Give him some time."

"No. You don't know what he's like, Aaron. I can tell you where he's gone. It's where he always goes when something upsets him."

"Gambling."

CHAPTER 11

Famagusta, Cyprus

Yonatan Déulocresca

It's better I walk away, rather than fly into a rage. How did I miss this? Can she really be my sister? But why would she lie about that? I'd dreamed of marrying her since we were children. Now that dream has been shattered. I just didn't want to see it and took her kindness the wrong way. Admittedly, she never seemed to feel the same way about me as I did about her. She'd offer treats, and hover around me. But that is what a sister does. There's a catch in my throat and my eyes blur. I always believed she was rejecting my affection because of some lack or defect. Now I know it was never meant to be, from the start.

The bazaar is a muddle of noises. Vendors hawk their wares, customers vie for the best price, horse's hooves clatter, and dogs bark. Lanterns are being lit. Shuli's revelation has scraped me raw inside, like the butchered lamb hanging beside clusters of sausages at the meat cutter's stall. I meander aimlessly, looking for anything to deaden the pain. Reminders are everywhere. Merchants stock their shelves with bolts of fine silk which a tailor could fashion into a bridal gown.

Those polished candlesticks could grace a family dinner table. My eyes glaze over.

I wander across the street to the potter's shop and admire the colorful patterns of his plates, bowls, and pitchers. They remind me of the pantry shelves at the caravanserai. Edna is my father's lover? I shake my head. I've watched them interact for as long as I can remember, thinking they were only friends. He'd always bring business her way, and she insured his guests were satisfied. But I never suspected this. They are probably still lovers. How blind could I be? That's why Edna offered to help. It all makes sense now. I wonder if my mother knows. What other family secrets might there be? But it all sickens me. I need to get out of here, away from all these reminders. If I leave the quarter, maybe something in the larger city can take my mind off this torment.

When I leave the *giudecca*, people are strolling around the central plaza and sitting beneath the gigantic fig tree. I recall there were drinking establishments along the waterfront when we arrived. As I thread between citizens heading toward the gate, I remove the badge from my shoulder. Maybe I can find a taverna where the Arak flows freely and there are games to be played.

Faint stars dot the sky beyond the watery horizon as I descend from the Harbor Citadel toward the quay. There's a cluster of seafront buildings. Sailors loiter near the taverna entrance, bantering. I peer through a bank of grimy windows. Men gather in small groups around table games. Some sit on cushioned benches against the wall, and others on squat stools. The smell of spirits draws me in the door and all tension leaves my body. Some patrons are playing backgammon and others play chess. I may not speak the language here. But it's no different from the variety of races and tongues at the caravanserai. Surely, there's a player willing to join me for a game. There's a table near a small group of players. I sit with my back to the wall and order a glass of Arak. Two men beside me are locked in a fast-paced round of backgammon.

After a while, another man enters the tavern carrying a backgammon board. He surveys the room and finally his gaze falls on me. He approaches, saying something to me in a language I don't understand, but his gestures imply an invitation to play. I nod and smile, welcoming him to my table. He opens the beautifully inlaid board of swirling olive wood and ivory. He does not dress as a sailor; rather in European clothes made of fine materials. He's perhaps a little older than I, a traveler or merchant.

My opponent hands me two stacks of ivory playing pieces, and he arranges his dark wood pieces on the board. I mirror the arrangement on my side. The server delivers my drink and a second for my new companion. He must be a regular patron with a known drink order. We each roll the pair of dice and I have the higher throw. We toast, I take several gulps of my drink, and we start the game.

A small crowd gathers around us. They jabber in his foreign tongue, advising him and even arguing. I'm used to playing in quiet, with deliberate moves, more like chess. Is this their custom, or are they trying to distract me? Having emptied my glass, I order another and let the noise fade into the background. Building a prime becomes my focus. The potent anise spirit makes me warm behind the ears, and calm spreads over me.

I easily win the first match. We shake hands, and he instantly starts setting up for a second round. I pat my chest.

"Yoni," I say, and then gesture toward him with an open hand.

"Luka," he replies.

I notice one of the other men is passing around a small hinged box, from which others are taking what looks like a waxy amber bean. I assume it must be *kaif*, the escape of the genie. He gives the box to Luka, who takes one and then offers it to me, smiling. It's been a long time since I tried any of that. I reach over and pinch the gummy oval and swallow it. I raise my glass again, take a swallow of Arak, and then we turn our attention back to the board.

In the corner, a man brings out a *bağlama*, begins strumming and sings. His voice and trance-like tune bring a hush over the room. Luka and I go three more rounds before the full effect of the *kaif* turns my head to pulp. A tingle spreads over my whole body and my vision alters. The pain lifts from my chest, and I no longer feel so broken. From the glassy eyes and giddy smiles on the glowing faces of the others, I know they feel the same. I thank Luka and explain my spinning head can no longer focus on playing. He seems to understand my meaning and invites someone else to take my place. I leave payment on the bar tray beside my empty glass.

I rise from the bench and weave between patrons toward the musician. Bobbing and swaying, the rhythmic spell of his song makes me lose myself. I don't understand a word of his lyrics, but it doesn't matter. Nothing matters. Two other men rise to their feet, lift their hands, and swivel their hips in a dance. I lean my head back against the wall, close my eyes, and let the music flow through me.

Time drifts away and before I fully realize it, the musician is putting his instrument away, the patrons have dwindled, and the place is closing down for the night. I trudge outside and look over the harbor. Most of the customers appear to be sailors, going back to their ships to sleep. Luka and his friends have disappeared. I'm still drunk and spinning, but I make my way up the hill and through the Harbor Citadel. But when I reach the entrance to the Jewish quarter, I find the gate sealed. The rabbi had told us this, but it seemed to slip through my mind. That was reckless of me. I can't get back to the inn. What now? Where can I go?

I'm a Jew who is outside the quarter after dark. Even though I'm not wearing the badge that identifies me as one, I think that alone could get me arrested. I saw city guardsmen patrolling in pairs with pikes earlier. Eventually I'm going to run into them. I could go outside the city walls. But like most ports, I put myself at risk of being attacked and abducted as a galley slave. But I can't stay here.

The only safe place to go is to the lighthouse. But I made such a fool of myself and treated Simon so badly. I wouldn't blame him if he turned me away. I need to apologize and make amends. Truly, I respect and admire the man. I skulk through the shadows of the arcade until I reach the Citadel. Two sentinels in chain-mail stand guard.

They survey me with narrowed eyes but let me pass through without a word. Torches along the ramparts and from the beacon itself cast long shadows under the star-filled sky. I hurry down the jetty toward the lighthouse, past the statue of a lion and cub.

At the threshold, I try the heavy door, but it is locked or braced on the inside. I pound several times, hoping he can hear me at the top. Then I wait, knowing it will take a while for him to descend. After a few minutes, I pound again. Within moments, the window opens and there's a pair of eyes.

"Who's there?" he says in Italian.

"It's me, Yonatan," I say.

"Yonatan? What are you doing here?" I hear the staves being drawn back, and the door swings open. "You shouldn't be wandering around the waterfront at this hour. It's not safe. Come inside."

I slip through the entrance and Simon seals us in.

He faces me, wide-eyed. "Why did you come here?"

"I was over here having a few drinks and lost track of time," I say. "I got myself locked out and had no place else to go."

He shakes his head. "I see. You can stay here and sleep it off." He turns and starts up the short flights of stairs leading to the beacon room and lookout. I trudge along behind him. Heat emanates from above as we draw nearer.

The lookout is a hexagonal room with windows on every side. A metal ladder at the center rises to the beacon. I stare up at the wondrous thing; a huge oil burning lantern surrounded by mirrors to focus the maximum light out to sea.

"Listen," he says. "I didn't realize that you and Shuli were courting. My interest in her was out of place. I apologize."

"Oh, no. I owe you an apology," I say. "We are not courting. Just my wishful thinking. In fact, I just learned something today that has turned my world upside-down."

"That bad? Is that why you were over here drinking instead of at the inn?"

"I guess."

"Sit down. Tell me about it."

I sit at a table spread with various items; a spyglass, log book, quill and ink, and a basket of bread, cheeses, and fruit. There's a hammered copper Moorish tea kettle and brazier on an adjacent bookshelf.

"Would you like some mint tea?"

"Please," I say, nodding. "I'm trying to make sense of it all. First, my father is abducted. If that weren't enough, Shuli revealed some family secrets I never knew my whole life."

He hands me a cup of tea. "Secrets?"

"After you left us, Shuli disclosed she is our half-sister. And all this time, I had harbored fantasies of marrying her, not knowing we were blood."

"I didn't know that either. But it does not really surprise me."

I squint. "Why is that?"

"I spent years with your father, and came to know him well; his struggles and his pain."

"I've always looked up to my father, admired his fine character. But he judges and criticizes me for my shortcomings. He wants an impossible standard of perfection, at which I was failing miserably. But now I see he has feet of clay. He's hidden a secret life and is really a fallen man. That has so shaken me, I feel like giving up on this venture altogether."

"Don't do that, Yonatan. There are no perfect men, no perfect lives. No one is without blemish."

"Blemish? He was unfaithful to my mother; fathered a child with another woman."

He blows out a long breath. "Your dear mother. And I emphasize, she is dear to me. She denied him all affection, refused to take him to her bed for years. That you are even here is a miracle."

"What?"

"He never told me why she stopped their intimacies. He once implied deep wounds haunted her from the past, the Inquisition, and such. I never learned the details. But he would never divorce her. He loved her and struggled to understand why she could not love him back."

I rub my forehead. "There's truth in what you say. She has grown colder over time, and withholds affection from everyone."

"A prisoner of her own history. But think about this. Little has really changed, except you know more than you did yesterday."

"They deceived us, Shuli, Edna, and my father."

"No, they simply kept their guilt private, to protect you."

"You have a curious perspective on things. But I don't know that I can easily get over this or forgive him."

"Not easily. These things take time. We are all bent and broken by life. We love in bent and broken ways. But to move forward, we all must make a choice. Either we embrace our pain, even though we may not know how to soothe ourselves. Or keep trying to escape it, which really just prolongs our pain and has dire consequences for us and those we care about."

I look down at the tabletop. "Your wisdom must be born of your own grief and losses."

"Indeed."

"How have you handled your pain?"

"Not well, at first. But I have children, and they have needs. Every night I listen to the soothing pulse of the waves. That is why I love the sea. The sea cleanses my soul. Of course, I pray and learn Torah. But I also take my eyes off myself and turn my actions toward helping others in need. These anchor me in the present, instead of drifting into maelstroms of the past."

"I don't know how to let go of the future I had dreamed of."

"You can still have all those dreams in the future. Only it will be with someone who can love you back. For now, take your eyes off yourself. It can transform you. You won't be the same man who left Jerusalem, any more than I am the same person who left Barcelona. Yes, you'll be taking a real gamble, risking your life."

The word gamble makes something awaken inside me. Tonight, as I played backgammon with Luka, I did not wager even once. That usual compelling urge never came. I just enjoyed myself. A weight, a burden lifts from my shoulders. It is not because of Arak and *kaif*, either. I realize my father is less than perfect, and that I am less flawed than I believed. Just human. I don't know how it works.

"I am on an uncertain path," I say, staring at Simon.

"Well, that's one way to describe it. Maybe a better way is to say you're completely free. There's nothing to hold you back."

I gaze off toward the starry night pondering what that could mean. Free.

CHAPTER 12

Famagusta, Cyprus

Aaron Déulocresca

The fog of insufficient sleep clouds my mind as I sit with Shuli over aromatic cups of café. She stares at her hands with a pained and watery gaze. We stayed up into the early hours, thinking Yonatan would return, but he never showed. Did he get himself arrested or meet some other sorry end? This turn of events could abort the mission. I would never go forward without him. I swallow dryly and take a deep breath.

Simon should arrive before too long. To distract myself while we wait things out, I sketch in my personal journal with charcoal, chalk and a metal point stylus. These I found while we were searching the marketplace for my brother. We also stumbled upon an apothecary, who sold us an herbal mixture of ginger, peppermint, and chamomile for seasickness.

Shuli studies my drawing of the arcades and buildings. "You've captured the images very well," she says and then she grows silent again.

"Thank you," I say. I sense she has more to say. I pause my drawing to look at her.

Shuli lowers her face. "Aaron, I feel I owe you an explanation."

"I figured when you were ready, you would offer one," I say. "May I ask you something?

"Of course."

"Have you always known we were family? Because I've always sensed there was more we shared than just a friendship."

"Sensed it how?"

"Just the abundance of love and laughter whenever we were all together."

"It's true. My mother only revealed who my father was when I reached the age of womanhood. She painted a picture of our family as a secret I could never talk about openly. I felt ashamed from that point forward. It made me believe that I was a mistake, an accident. You and Yonatan are father's rightful children and I am my parents' sin. I could never tell you, because it would spread that shame on your father and you."

I groan. "Oh, Shuli. I certainly don't see you that way."

"We all might have stayed in that blissful state. Mother could have kept it a secret. But Yonatan began to take a romantic interest in me. And innocently, I had started to reciprocate. Mother became alarmed about the risk of *gilui arayot*."

I stroke my beard. "Oh, absolutely. Incest would be a disaster. But why disclose it now?"

"Two reasons. This crisis with our father has devastated all of our lives, not just yours. I wanted you to understand my legitimate call to go on this journey, even though I have no claim to your mother's inheritance. Second, Yonatan misinterprets my actions, makes advances or expects affections I can't return. I had to stop him, but realize I didn't handle it gracefully."

"No, you didn't. But don't blame yourself for that. You did the right thing." I give her a gentle side-hug. "It might surprise you, but I am no stranger to shame, either."

"You? But why?"

"I grew up with a perpetual sense I did something wrong. But I don't know what. My mother was always irritated with me, but wouldn't reveal the reason."

"Is that why you work so hard to be some kind of *tzaddiq*?"

"A *tzaddiq*? No, I'm no holy man, although sometimes it seems others need me to be one. The simple way of life provides peace to me."

She sighs. "All of us have grown up carrying a mantle of shame. You know that's why Yonatan gambles, right? It's as if he keeps trying to redeem himself. Oh, the sins of the fathers," she says.

I close my eyes and shake my head. "Was it their sins? Or was it the sins of our grandparents, the choices that were forced upon them, and the brutality they endured that scarred their souls, and our parents' souls?"

"The Inquisition," Shuli says.

"That's our spiritual inheritance," I say. "But I've been trying to figure out how that operates. I like what the prophet Jeremiah wrote. We should look toward a better future. A day will come when we will no longer say: *the parents have eaten sour grapes, but the children's teeth are set on edge.*"

"What does that mean?"

"I believe it means we don't have to swallow their bitterness. It is up to us whether we eat our own sour grapes."

She gapes at me. "That sent a quiver down my spine, Aaron," Shuli says.

"It did? I understand it intellectually," I say, tapping my temple. "But I don't yet feel it. It takes one look from my mother, one sentence, and I'm reduced to five years old again, drinking her bile."

She gives a sad smile and rubs the back of my hand.

My thoughts drift to the source of my comfort, my own forbidden union with Rehm, her beautiful face and soothing embrace. I can't be angry at my father or blame him for turning to someone else. If only I was in my green hillside village painting frescos and playing with Suqi.

Merchants are opening for a new business day. Peering between shops and stalls, my eyes pause at the gate to the Jewish quarter. After a while, I glimpse a green toque and recognize Simon's curly hair. He comes through the entrance with Yonatan beside him. Tension releases from my shoulders and the vice around my chest loosens.

"Look," I say to Shuli and point. She shakes her head and releases a deep sigh. I'm both relieved and annoyed at my brother. But too fatigued to call him to account. He can be his own worst critic. Shuli is clenching her jaw.

"At least he's in one piece," Shuli murmurs.

"Good morning," says Simon. "We've just secured passage for four on the Euetêria, which leaves today for Candia."

"So, we need to get moving," says Yonatan.

I stand and give my brother a hug, then look into his face. "You had us so worried. I'm glad you're alright."

He turns to Simon. A private understanding passes between them in his glance, and then he again faces me. "I reasoned things out."

Reason is not an asset my brother often uses. Yonatan gives a one-sided smile and a new light has kindled in his eyes. A wry grin spreads across Simon's face. It seems his influence is having a favorable effect.

While Simon returns home to collect his things and bid farewell to his children, we gather our belongings, have the innkeeper brew the herbal remedy for nausea, and pour it into a flask. Then, we settle our account and depart. In the bazaar, we purchase some shelled almonds, toasted chickpeas, and flatbread for the journey. By mid-morning we await Simon near the lion monument. He joins us, carrying a heavy sea-bag slung over one shoulder and a cylindrical map case dangling from the other. He clasps the handle of a hinged wooden box. Then I notice the tooled leather scabbard at his hip with the hilts of two blades. When he sees us staring at them, he smiles.

"Just in case," he says, and pats me on the shoulder. That does not reassure me.

The Euetêria

Yonatan Déulocresca

Endless blue stretches above and below, blending together out near the edge of the horizon. This is the farthest I've ever strayed from home. Venturing out like this agrees with my nature. The salty breeze in my hair and nostrils fills me with life. I stand on the forward deck together with Aaron and Shuli listening to Simon's counsel.

"You will be less seasick if you face the direction of travel. Looking out sideways upsets one's balance and constitution. This is also a larger ship than the one that brought you to Cyprus, so you should feel the waves to a lesser degree."

I gaze upward, surveying the various parts of the ship, the masts, sails, and rigging, and the men tending to them. Like them, I don't seem to become seasick. I also watch the blue striped creatures coursing and leaping from the water out in front of the ship.

"What kind of fish are those?" I ask Simon.

"These are not fish at all," he says. "They're dolphins. Notice how they have no scales. They give live birth to their young, and seem to live in families." He unfastens the latch on his hinged wooden box, takes out a spyglass, extends it to full length, and adjusts it several times. He hands it to me. "Here, have a closer look."

I take the long metal shaft and peer through the lens. What enchantment unfolds before my eye as I study these curious creatures? "I've never seen anything like this before."

"You seem to have an interest in seafaring and ships," he says.

"Indeed. It must run through my blood."

Simon smirks, nods, and brings out another instrument of tarnished brass. The strange device has circular plates and levers that can spin around a central pin. He hands this enchanting tool to Aaron.

His eyes brighten. He's like a giddy child with a new plaything. He runs his fingertips over the plates, which are engraved with notches, numbers, and letters.

"This must be a navigation tool," Aaron says.

"Yes, it's called an astrolabe," says Simon.

"How is it used?"

"I'll show you. First, hold it out from your body by the ring and let it hang."

Aaron grasps the metal loop and extends his arm.

"Now, line up the plane of the astrolabe toward a point of interest, in this case, the sun."

Aaron alters his position and squints against the sunlight.

"You adjust this lever here, called the al-idad. Notice how the light casts a shadow from the forward vane onto the rear vane. You see."

He follows Simon's directions. "Yes, I can see it."

"Now, we read the angle measurement from the scale around the outside here." He points to the etched increments surrounding the edge of the tool. The Euetêria's actual pilot approaches us and asks to see the instrument. He and Simon converse about it briefly, and the man smiles and nods. He seems to admire the device and acknowledge Simon's knowledge of the skill. Then, he shakes Simon's hand and returns to his post.

Simon turns back to us. "The al-idad tells us the sun's altitude in degrees. This angle we can then compare to charts and tables to determine our latitude."

"What is latitude?" I ask.

"How far north or south we are. In the middle of the sea, there are no landmarks or signposts to tell the right path. We have to use the sun and stars."

"That seems like wizardry," I say.

"No," says Aaron. "Just mathematics."

There he goes again, always with his jibes. He can't resist an opportunity to make me look stupid. But I'll just let it go. We've already had enough trouble, and it will only set us back. I stare at the spyglass. "May I use this a little longer?" I ask Simon.

"Certainly. Just mind the glass. It's precious to me and not easily replaced."

I nod and smile, but inside I feel like they both regard me as a careless child.

"Now, if you'll come with me," he says to Aaron, "I'll show you how to chart our course. We'll take this reading multiple times during the voyage so you can practice."

I watch them go back below deck, leaving Shuli by herself. Our eyes meet for a moment. There's a lot I need to say to her. But I'm not ready to face it right now. I turn away and wander to the other end of the ship. Lifting the spyglass, I survey what else must fill these waters.

CHAPTER 13

The Euetêria

Aaron Déulocresca

THE WATER ROLLS aside in white-capped curls as the prow cuts a path through the sea. I stand peering over the gunwale near the bowsprit. Sails above and behind me bulge with the wind. I've grown more accustomed to the undulations of the vessel in the water. But despite the relatively calm conditions, my legs are spongy and restless. Do I have what it takes to face this gauntlet? I don't know a thing about launching an expedition. And the only time I've ever led anyone was for a Talmud discussion. I'm a defenseless fool.

"How are you this morning?"

I turn toward the voice and see Simon in his green toque, with his head tilted to one side and a kindly half-smile.

"My seasickness has mostly subsided," I say. "But I've a knot in my chest."

"That crease in your brow says you're wary about something. We're only two more days out from Crete; closer than ever to reaching our goal."

"Yes, and closer to untold dangers." I gesture toward the two men clad in thick leather jerkins standing guard beside a heavy crossbow on the forecastle. "Everyone is armed with a weapon; swords and daggers of all sorts. I know you said intellect is an essential defense. But I'd be an easy kill."

"The blades are also tools to cut thick lines, as much as they are weapons."

"I want to meet the challenge ahead. My father's life is at stake. I'm unprepared. You well know, they never allow Jews to carry weapons in our homeland. I don't have the slightest idea how to use one."

Simon folds his arms and nods. "I understand."

"Yonatan, at least, brought his donkey whip and is quite skilled at using it."

Simon's eyes aimlessly search the deck for a few moments. "Neither of you should have to resort to a donkey whip." He raises his gaze to meet my stare. "Come on. Let's gather the others and remedy the situation."

We locate Shuli and my brother and assemble in the cramped but open deck area in between the cargo bays. When Simon brings out his rapier and a short sword, my pulse thumps hard in my throat.

"If someone pulls out a blade," he says, "you must assume he intends to use it. So, you must be ready to defend yourselves. Once you've learned the skills to protect, we can take the next step and introduce some basic attacks." Simon points to the pouch at my waist. "May I borrow one of your pieces of chalk, Aaron?"

"Certainly," I say. I fish a small white chunk from my bag of drawing materials. My hand trembles when I hand it to him. He notices, but only smiles. We watch him trace out a large circle on the deck and make angled lines through it. Then he returns the chalk and pats me on the shoulder.

"Who would like to go first?"

A trapdoor opens in the pit of my stomach. I turn to my brother. "If you don't object, I'd like to observe first. Why don't you go."

"Gladly," Yonatan says. Simon stares at me with one raised brow.

"Yonatan, I want you to stand here," says Simon, pointing to the edge of the circle. Yoni positions himself and studies Simon with great interest.

Simon hands the rapier to Yonatan and steps to the outside of the circle opposite him. He points the short sword toward him. "Now, extend your arm forward from the shoulder. If you'll notice, this circle is roughly your striking range." He sidles around the edge of the circle and Yonatan follows his movement, pointing the sword.

"Always try to maintain this distance, adjusting your position to match your opponent." Yonatan swipes and jabs with the blade. Then Simon signals him with one hand to stop. Then he pinches the tip of the blade.

"Your opponent could strike you here." He brings the tip to his throat, and then he moves the tip to his left chest. "Or the heart, of course. This would instantly be fatal." Then he positions the tip at his navel. "If he damages any vital organs in the belly, you'd die a slow and painful death. So that is what we want to avoid."

I cringe and glance over at Shuli, who pins her eyes on Simon.

"Your assailant knows these vulnerable spots. So, he will try to stab you there. With your life in danger, your position and posture are vital."

"How do you know all this?" Yonatan asks. "I've never even held a sword."

"On one of my voyages, we transported a master of swordsmanship, another *converso* escaping the Inquisition. He practiced the True Skill, *Destreza*, which is based on principles of reason and geometry, a whole discipline. He taught me to fight."

His manner of teaching and the simple principles have captured my interest. This is just what I was asking for. My fear and misgivings gradually drain away.

"As you can see right now, facing forward, Yonatan is fully exposed.

I could easily kill him. You never want to expose your front to your opponent. Rather, turn profile, and bend your knees."

Yonatan follows his instructions.

"Now, you've made it harder for me to get directly at your vital points. And you've increased your reach. You want to come toward your rival just off center." He motions to the angular lines across the circle. "You do that by slowly circling and studying your opponent for the best angle. Every time he tries to jab at you, you block him. Try it."

Yonatan moves around the chalk circle and Simon mirrors him. Yonatan makes several swipes, awkwardly at first, but he gradually becomes more adept.

"You're getting the idea." After more practice, Simon turns to me. "Aaron, your turn."

My heart leaps into my throat. "I've never done anything like this."

Yonatan jeers. "Not one of your many talents?"

"No." I blow out a puff of air. If it weren't for Yonatan's many talents, I wouldn't be having to learn to sword-fight. But I decide to dismiss his heckling.

"Just because it is something new, don't underestimate yourself," says Simon. He takes the rapier from Yonatan and holds it out to me.

The sword feels lighter in my grasp than I expect. Yonatan steps aside and I replace him in the circle. Standing profile, I position my feet. The rise and fall of the ship make balancing tricky. As I extend my arm with the rapier, a surge of power wells up inside me. Lunging seems to come naturally, and I extend my other arm behind me for steadiness. I shadow Simon's transit around the circle, swiping and jabbing to block him. The movements become easier than I expected, which surprises and emboldens me. Simon's eyes widen and a smile spreads across his face.

"You see? It's not that hard," he says, and then glances at Yonatan. "Both of you. It is essential that you practice these skills daily until the movements become second nature. But there is much more to learn."

I glance at Shuli, who has a pleading look in her eyes. "Would you like to try?" I ask.

Yonatan huffs and crosses his arms. She nods enthusiastically and comes to the circle. I hand her the sword and get out of the way. She steps to the edge of the chalk line, positions her feet, showing confidence, balance, and agility. Simon cocks his head with a smile. Her lunges and stabs spur a playful response. With his next lunge toward her, she deflects his knife and quickly jabs at his middle. Simon laughs and steps backward. "I can tell someone's already trained you," he says.

"My mother," she says. "She's very skilled with a blade."

"That's true, she is," says Yonatan.

Simon counters with his own riposte, striking the rapier blade out of his way. "I'd never have guessed." Then he stops and turns to me and Yonatan. "Just now, Shuli was executing a move called *atajos*, a strategy not only to protect your life but also to disarm your opponent. There are different variations and hand positions which I will teach you later. But you have a capable sparring partner and didn't even know it."

"You're just full of surprises," says Yonatan with a sneer.

I scowl at him for his sarcasm. Then I turn to my sister. "Shuli. I had no idea you were so skilled. All this time, I worried about how to protect you. But you could very well protect us."

She lifts her chin with a smile. "With practice, we'll all be better prepared for what lies ahead."

❧

Yonatan Déulocresca

Calls of the boatswain send the crewmen scrambling to prepare for docking. I lean against the portside gunwale beside Simon, taking in the scenery, as the Euetêria enters the gleaming aqua waters of the harbor. Shuli and Aaron stand a short distance away on the starboard side. The palms and cedars waving in the breeze invite me to stroll a sandy pebbled shore. But everything that happens in the next few days could determine father's fate. Nothing else matters. My stomach flutters and I grip the railing.

"I look forward to meeting this Gabriel Coron you spoke of," I say. "I hope he's willing to help us. So much depends on it."

"Our first task is to find him. But I'm sure you won't be disappointed."

The same sort of quay as Famagusta's juts out into the bay from the main gate. There is even a similar lighthouse.

"Candia looks a lot like where you live," I say. "The Venetians must have used the same building plan."

"But Candia is much larger and even more grand than Famagusta," Simon replies.

I study the crenulated walls and corner towers that encircle the massive ramparts. Beyond the city to the south, a spectacular range of blue mountains still crested with traces of snow spans the horizon.

"Jews have lived here since the time of the Maccabees," says Simon. "The Greeks strongly influenced them and some still speak Yevanic, a kind of Greek written in Hebrew characters."

"Not unlike us," I say, "only we speak Spanish written in Hebrew script, even though we never lived in Spain."

"Similar."

"You must have spent a lot of time here to know all that," I say.

"It was a place we harbored many times. I came to know the area and community. But it's been years since I last visited."

Aaron comes over. "Either we'll end our search here, or go forward to hunt for the family assets. There are really no other options left for us."

"There's always work at the caravanserai," Shuli offers.

"Let's hope it doesn't come to that," says Simon. "You have so much at stake. So, once we get situated, we'll make some preliminary inquiries, do some reconnaissance."

"Reconnaissance?" asks Aaron. "Does Senor Coron live in hiding?"

"In a manner of speaking, for the same reasons I do. But I have an idea how to find him."

"Somehow, I had this silly picture in my mind. I thought he'd be at the harbor on a ship ready to sail," says Shuli.

Simon shakes his head with a chuckle. "Not quite. There's likely a ship, but it's probably not anchored here in so obvious a place."

"Why not start at the synagogue?" Aaron asks.

"Jews also live outside the city. There are numerous rural settlements that surround Candia which produce cheeses, wine, grain, and fruit. Naturally, refugees from Spain and Portugal settled there, which is where we'll find him."

"Jews can own land?" I ask.

"We can. While not extended to full citizenship, and we pay heavy taxes, in most Venetian colonies, Jews can own property, homes, and businesses. We also have protection under the law."

This new possibility jars loose a hope buried deep inside me; a yearning for something I was always denied.

"Even though you sailed with him years ago," says Aaron. "Would he consider such a venture now? If he has settled down, like you, what motive does he have to take to sea again?"

"There's a chance. I doubt his rancor for the Inquisition and the Spanish monarch has waned with time. The man I know would jump at an opportunity to redress wrongs done to our people."

I don't understand Aaron's constant doubts and second guessing. He seems overly cautious to me. Although, I admit I've always been the kind of man who runs headlong into what looks great at first, only to discover later all the reasons such a move was a mistake. My actions are the reason we're here. So, perhaps I should take a lesson from his caution. A myriad of things could go wrong. But we don't know how long al-Dabaa will wait before he kills our father. Time is running out. This next journey will likely change our lives in ways none of us could imagine.

CHAPTER 14

Candia, Crete

Yonatan Déulocresca

THE NORTHERN GATE at Candia's harbor stands beside the Jewish quarter, another city within a city. We wander down the main artery through the walled maze of passageways. One could easily get lost here.

"The Zudecca differs from the Jewish quarter in Famagusta," says Simon. "Christians actually choose to own homes and businesses here, too. It's considered the most desirable and beautiful part of the city."

The streets are spotless. I catch sight of sparkling Dermatu Bay. Mansions overlook the waterfront along the north and western walls. Simon points east to a giant church and monastery built next to the wall, but on the other side of it.

"At liturgical times, the bells toll loudly just to remind us the Christians are still here, looking over our shoulder. Fortunately, the Venetians have no fondness for the recent popes or the Inquisition. So, it's officially banned from holding trials here. But Inquisition spies from Spain and Portugal still present a threat. They've been known to abduct people."

We enter the reception area of a large inn. Across a terrazzo floor, a bank of open doors leads out onto a terrace with a fountain. Benches, shrubs, and flowers surround the edges. Once we arrange our lodgings, we agree to meet up for supper. Shuli and Aaron explain that they still have a touch of nausea and headache from the voyage and wish to stay behind. Simon and I stow our belongings in a shared room and embark on a mission, hoping to locate Gabriel Coron.

I thought we'd return to the embarcadero to survey ships docked there. But Simon leads us the opposite way down a stone-paved passageway lined with shops. Entrances are decorated with carved archways. The doors have wrought iron grillwork. Balconies or shuttered windows cast cooling shadows from the stories above. Crates jut into the walkway, bulging with early spring vegetables and fruit. The aroma of fresh baked bread, roasted garlic, and herbs come from the entrances.

Simon gestures to the sign of a wine merchant. "Let's stop in here." We go inside, and he greets the man in Italian, starting a friendly conversation. I don't understand everything they say, but I catch the words rosso and bianco, and guess they refer to kinds of wine.

Simon turns to me. "Would you like to taste some wine?"

"Yes, but I thought we were trying to find your friend," I say.

"We are." He turns to the merchant. "*Sì, grazie, il vino bianco.*"

The merchant pours two glasses with a little white wine and sets them on the counter. We each take a sip.

"I know nothing about gauging the quality of wine," I say.

"You put your nose to the cup and smell." He shows me. "Often there are hints of various flavors and aromas you don't expect. Then you taste for how sweet or tart it is." He turns back to the merchant and asks if they make the wine here in Crete.

"No, *da Trieste. Ti piace?*"

"He asks if we like it," says Simon.

I nod and smile at the merchant. "I like it well enough."

"I'll buy some to take back to the inn," says Simon. He again asks the merchant a question. The name Coron and the word *vino bianco* catch my attention. But the merchant speaks too quickly for me to understand. He shakes his head. Next, he disappears into an adjoining room for a few moments. I hear an exchange of words, and then he brings a small pottery ewer back to the counter. He fills it with wine from the cask and presses a cork stopper into the mouth. We finish what is in our glasses. Simon pays the merchant, hands the vessel to me, and we depart.

"I don't understand what we're doing," I say.

"I was trying to find out if he'd heard of and sells a variety of white wine produced in the Malevisi valley. He told me he's familiar with it, but has none to sell."

"But why are you so interested in wine? Don't we have other priorities?"

"Coron brought me to a place in the Malevisi valley south of Candia several times. We looked over some property he'd purchased with Spanish plunder. He hoped to establish a winery there. His parents and grandparents had been prosperous winemakers and owned a vineyard for generations in Spain. But they lost it and their lives at the hands of the Inquisition. If he indeed planted a vineyard, it's been long enough for the vines to have matured and he could produce wine now. The valley is about half a day's ride."

"Ah, I understand now," I say. "When we find the wine, we find him."

When we exit the wine shop, I notice a dark-haired man and another balding one loitering beside a shop selling olive wood bowls. Each wears a leather jerkin not unlike those guards aboard the Euetêria. They study us a moment through narrowed eyes, but then hurry away. I'm unsure whether it's because we're speaking Spanish or they overheard what we were saying about Gabriel Coron. The hair on the back of my neck stands on end. Simon's brows pinch together, but he says nothing.

We wander farther along the market passageway, and visit three more wine merchants. Meanwhile, I'm growing warm behind my ears from all the wine tasting. Finally, we enter the shop of our fifth *vinaio*. This time I ask the question.

"Good afternoon! Do you have wine from the Malevisi valley?" I ask.

The merchant replies too quickly for me to comprehend, but Simon translates. "He says we've come at the right time. The Malevisi sells out rapidly in spring."

My vision is blurring when I ask if we may try it. He nods and brings out the tasting glasses. The wine is fragrant, with hints of apricot and quince, and not too cloyingly sweet. Simon offers to buy several casks to ship back to Famagusta on his return voyage. The merchant writes the order. Simon pays him, takes the receipt, and we leave the shop.

"We now know for certain that Coron's winery is producing," he says. "Next, we'll dispatch a courier to take a message announcing our arrival. Then tomorrow, we'll rent horses and travel out there."

"Horses? We're allowed to ride horses?" I ask.

Simon chuckles. "Yes, Yonatan, we can ride horses without getting arrested or fined."

"A miracle!" I want to dance for joy. But as we begin our return trek to the inn, I notice the same men at the end of the passageway to our right. When we turn onto the Stenón, I glance behind us.

"I think we are being followed," I say.

"I noticed them, too. They're likely just thugs who prey on customers with full purses. But they could also be mercenaries hired by the Inquisition. They may have overheard us speaking Spanish. Come with me."

He dodges between two stalls dangling net bags of figs and clusters of dates. We dash down a side passage. The course winds back and forth but finally ends at an intersecting corridor. Simon darts left, and I follow him. But this way turns out to be a cul-de-sac surrounded by a stone wall.

Simon ducks behind a buttress. I'm just about to stoop behind a hedge when someone shoves me from behind. A boot thumps the back of my knee, and I fall to the ground. The pottery ewer flies from my hands and shatters on the paving stones. The dark-haired man holding a knife hauls Simon out of the recess.

"Who are you and what is your business here?" the knife-wielding man says in Spanish.

"My name is Mendes. I'm a lighthouse keeper from Famagusta. My business is my own."

"I am from Jerusalem." I say. "So, this is how you welcome guests to your city?"

"You claim to be from Jerusalem. Yet you speak Spanish. Get up," the balding man orders, yanking me by the arm. He pulls a lathe-turned club from his waistband and raises it, ready to strike me. Then he shoves me backward against the wall. Over my captor's shoulder, I see the other man holding the knife at Simon's throat. Simon's eyes blaze with rage, but he doesn't budge.

"You have been going from shop to shop asking about a particular vintner. Why? And don't tell me you're just interested in buying wine."

"He's a friend," says Simon.

"We're not mercenaries or spies, if that's what you think," I say. "But perhaps *you* are."

He huffs. "Is that so? Prove you're not emissaries of the Pope or the Spanish Monarch."

I take out the registration card I saved from Famagusta, which shows I am a Jew.

"That means nothing. You could forge or steal that."

My anger and the wine are getting the better of me. I glance at Simon again. He blinks at me with tight lips, which I take to mean, don't do anything stupid. I try the one thing I know will make the fact indisputable. I raise the front of my brown tunic, pull down my braes, and wave my circumcised phallus at them. "Argue that away, you assholes!" I shout. But they just roll their eyes and laugh.

Simon hisses with clenched teeth. The thugs both glare at him.

"If the man we seek is who I believe him to be, he would not take kindly to this treatment. I sailed with him as navigator for three years."

"Delightful story," says the dark-haired man with a knife.

"Turnaround," my balding attacker orders. As I start to turn, he shoves my shoulder hard, slamming my face against the stone wall. Pinning me with one hand, and then his whole body, he wrenches my arm backward. Pain shoots down from my shoulder. I balk and flail to free myself. But he smashes his baton into my ribs. The stabbing pain paralyzes me for a moment. I don't know what to do. My heart is pounding against my collarbone. He quickly wraps a cord around my wrist. Then grabs the other one, snugly securing my hands behind me.

A surge of energy pumps through my body. I want to run. But I wouldn't get far before he caught me again. Then the risk of being beaten or killed would be even greater. My captor forces me down several passageways, jabbing my back with his baton. There are so many turns, I quickly lose my bearings. I hear Simon and his captor shuffling behind us.

"What gives you the authority to do this?" I shout.

"Shut your mouth!" A jab in the back of my head silences me.

We stop in front of a huge oak door with wrought iron strapping. The balding man opens it, revealing a shadowy brick cellar. He pushes me inside. Simon stumbles and almost falls after the knife-wielding man shoves him hard. The door slams shut, sealing us in darkness. The sound of metal scraping against metal tells me they've bolted the door.

CHAPTER 15

CANDIA, CRETE

Yonatan Déulocresca

FROM HIGH ON one wall, a dim shaft of light filters down through dust motes into the darkness. A small window fitted with decorative iron grillwork lets light and air into this dank enclosed space. My shoulders go limp and I drop my chin to my chest. I still reel with drunk unsteadiness. Lord God, what are we going to do now?

"Are you alright?" asks Simon.

"Yes, only bruised a little. How about you?"

"I'm unharmed. Let's see if we can untie our bonds," he says. "Stand over here in the light. Turn so I can see the knot."

I back into the shaft of sunlight. Over my shoulder, I watch Simon stoop as he studies my wrist bonds. He rears back.

"Hmm. Now, that's interesting."

"What is it?" I ask.

"A Spanish bowline."

"What does that mean?"

"It's a common knot used by sailors. That and the belaying pin your captor held suggest they're probably seamen," says Simon.

"You mean Spanish navy?"

"No. More likely pirates or mercenaries."

"Well, can you untie me?" I tug on one side, only to find it tightens the other.

"Hold still. You can't loosen it, but let me try." He turns his back to me and I feel his fingers plucking at the cords. In a matter of moments, he frees one hand. I untangle the other myself. Then I turn around and untie Simon's bonds. Walking to the door, I try to open it. But as I guessed, it's bolted shut. I take a deep breath, and the tension in my neck and shoulders loosens.

"Maybe we can call for help," I say, and point to the window. I slowly feel my way around the shadowy room. "There might be something we can push to the window and climb out."

Simon shakes his head. "Looks too small to squeeze through that opening. The best way out is through that door. Let's prepare for when they open it."

We find an old wooden crate and several empty wine casks.

"We can turn this into weapons if we smash it," says Simon.

We each grasp a cask and take turns pounding on the crate. After many blows, it splinters and breaks apart. We pull the crate into pieces and each of us chooses a slat.

"What's the plan?" I ask.

"To get away. You stand right there beside the door, ready with that board. I'll stand here, hiding my plank behind my back. The light from the open door will fall on me. I'll shade my eyes. When I drop my hand, that's the signal. I'm hoping by rushing the door, we'll catch them off guard. But we can use these planks as clubs, if we need to."

"So do they plan to force us to be galley slaves, or turn us over to the Inquisition?"

"From their questions, I doubt either of those motives."

"What do you think they want, if not to rob us or enslave us?"

"I'm not sure, but I'm beginning to wonder if they might be Coron's men, and believe we are spies," says Simon.

"What? His henchmen?"

"Could be."

"But why attack and entrap us?"

"We're strangers. They don't trust us. We'll know soon enough."

My mind swirls and my guts become watery. All this trickery and spying confuses me. Waiting is torment, as we squat on the casks for stools. We keep silent to hear any foot traffic or conversation outside. But I hear nothing for a long time. The rectangle of scant sunlight on the floor gradually drifts and narrows with the sun's movement. Finally, someone pulls the rasping metal stave aside, making us jump to our places. I raise my board, ready to bash the first person through the door in the face.

The door swings inward with a whine of the hinges, but no one enters. I peer at Simon. His brow knots and his mouth falls open.

"Hold on," he says, and he holds out his palm.

A man steps into the doorframe. A hooded cloak obscures his face. He pulls his hood back, letting it fall to his shoulders and reveals long dark hair.

"Umberto?" Simon asks.

"Dâvi?" he replies.

Both men are smiling at each other, and they embrace.

"It's been too long, brother." Umberto says.

I lower my board and step out of the shadows.

"Yonatan, this is Umberto Alvo, boatswain who served with me on La Vengadora."

Standing outside the door are the two other men staring wide-eyed with mouths agape.

"I figured Coron might have scouts lying in wait," Simon says. "Your men wasted no time intercepting us. They're first-rate."

"We take no chances and give no quarter to Inquisition spies," says the balding man.

"It might have gone far worse for you," says the other captor.

"But you raised a doubt when you claimed to be a navigator. I knew Umberto would recognize such a man."

Umberto gestures to the balding man. "This is Mossé Satellis, from Barcelona and our chief gunner." He points to the other man. "And this is Isaac Abramo, a mariner from Palma and our guardian."

"You're all Sephardim?" I ask.

"Yes. The Alhambra Decree made exiles of our families, one and all," says Umberto.

"Please accept our apologies for rousting you," says Mossé. "But we can't be too vigilant. I hope I didn't injure you."

"Not badly," I say. "Apology accepted."

Now the pieces of the mosaic are falling into place. All these wine merchants, perhaps all shopkeepers in the Giudecca, are part of an invisible web. They must alert Coron's men when suspicious visitors arrive. These crewmen are like secret guardians, preventing the Spanish or the Inquisition from getting their claws on any fugitive. They operate right under the noses of the Venetian authorities. I've never met tough, powerful Jews like these. At home, most Jewish men are passive, weak, and submissive to our Muslim overlords. But the brawn and cunning of these Sephardim are like the warriors and heroes described in the Prophets and Writings.

Umberto gestures for us to come out of the cellar into the alleyway. It's twilight. He dispatches Isaac to Malevisi to inform Caron.

"Again, our apologies," Umberto says. "Perhaps I'll see you tomorrow, and you can tell me what you've been doing all this time. I hope the rest of your evening is more pleasant." Umberto and Mossé turn and walk away.

Simon and I stare at each other a moment, shaking our heads. Then we begin our return to the inn. I look forward to seeing these men again, too. A tingling sensation sweeps over me, making me smile. How odd, after being beaten and locked up by them. What valuable lessons might I learn if I sail with men like these? I look over at Simon.

"Tell me. What exactly is a chief gunner?"

❧

Sunrise. I'm awake and full of vigor. But when I mounted this haggard mare, my mouth went dry and I couldn't catch my breath. It's the first time I've ridden a horse since I was punished for it four years ago. We ride in pairs, headed southward, away from the city. A well-trodden dirt road passes through rolling hills, densely overgrown with evergreen shrubs, laurel, and myrtle. Simon leads the way, side-by-side with Shuli. She turns to him and says something. They exchange smiles and even laughter, which tugs at my gut, even now. I divert my attention to birds wheeling overhead in a brilliant sky, where luminous clouds drift by. Sheep with long shaggy coats graze in grassy dells. The fragrances of cedar, rosemary, and orange blossom waft on the warm air.

"These hills remind me of Safed and the Galilee," Aaron says. "I'd much rather be there, but this place is beautiful."

"I never thought the day would come that I'd finally be riding a horse again. Even though it's a well-used stable nag, it fulfils a long-held dream."

"It doesn't feel much different from a donkey," Aaron says, "just higher off the ground."

"No. There's a vast difference. Did you know, if I lived here, I could own and even raise horses and ride whenever I pleased?"

"Are you considering doing that when all this is through?"

"Possibly. Once we've freed father."

"If we free father," Aaron says, with an emphasis on the if. "Today we'll find out whether we should even trust this man, Coron, or will go back empty-handed."

"Must you always think in black and white, Aaron? Simon trusts him," I say.

"Yes, but I will decide for myself if I'm willing to place my life in his hands."

"I've never met such highly skilled guardians and sailors among

Jews. They've championed justice for our people in the past and continue even now intercepting spies of the Inquisition. I want to learn everything I can from them. No more hesitation, Aaron. Time is slipping away."

"Listen, we don't want to fall prey to double-dealing thieves and cutthroats. They're pirates, Yonatan. Remember?"

There may be an element of truth to what he is saying, but I will not admit it to his face just because he's condescending again. Or maybe he's just frightened. Should I be?

We come through a craggy pass that opens into a long valley stretching to the interior as far as I can see. They parceled the landscape like a chessboard of orchards, crops, and pasture, separated by crude rock fences and slender cypress. It takes the better part of the day to cross the curving road, the air ever warming with the sunshine. We finally reach a sprawling vineyard after midday. Row after row of trellises lush with green leaves and budding fruit crisscross the rolling hills and scale upward on terraces across a stony ridge.

We pause where the road branches off. A double wrought-iron gate stands open on this side road. Above it hangs a painted sign over a metal archway displaying the rising sun and the words Los Viñedas de Sol.

"This is the place," says Simon as he steers his mount through the portal. My belly flutters and I peer upward at the distant buildings on the crest of the promontory. We ascend the ridge, switching back and forth across a rocky bluff. Massive stone ramparts come into view, encircling the base of a huge stronghold. It looks like it was once a fortress or a monastery.

At last, we reach the plateau and a broad path leading to the estate. A hexagonal structure dominates one end of the building, and a turret overlooks the valley on the other. Thick stone walls surround the property with a massive wooden gate. Above it, framed in wrought iron scrollwork, is a sign bearing the same insignia of the rising sun.

A guard with a pike stands just outside the gate. Upon seeing us, he hurries inside the enclosed courtyard.

They draw the gate back and several grooms rush out to meet us. Simon dismounts and one of them takes the reins. The rest of us slide from the saddle and the grooms lead our horses across the square to what I presume is a stable or corral. To our left, a man dressed in burgundy velvet stands atop a veranda with a colonnade of arches that spans the face of the entrance. He descends the short flight of stairs and strides across the courtyard toward Simon. Silver stubble flecks his sun-bronzed jaw. The wind rifles through his pewter-colored hair, hanging long to his collar. His withering, dark eyes and flared nostrils carry the vigor of a charging bull. He smirks and places his hands on his hips. "For a supposed navigator, it certainly took you long enough to find this place."

Simon laughs and the two men embrace. "Only five years."

"Closer to ten, my friend."

I'm struck by the instant familiarity between them, as if no time has passed at all. Coron pulls back and glances our way. Simon extends his hand. "These are the sons and daughter of Maestro Joachim Déulocresca, the navigator from Barcelona I told you about, who saved my life and taught me his trade."

"Welcome to my home," he says. "I am Gabriel Coron. The name Déulocresca is still whispered with reverence among our people for the lives he saved. I'm honored to meet you."

This is the first time outside the small circle of elders in Jerusalem that I've heard my father so described. Warmth kindles behind my eyes and my chest swells. I glance at Aaron, who stares with parted lips. Coron offers his hand to me with a grin.

"I'm Yonatan," I say, "And this is Aaron, and my sister, Shulamit."

"Shulamit?" says Coron, as he admires her. "The beauty that inspired King Solomon. *Shuvi, shuvi, Ha Shulamit, shuvi, shuvi, ve nekhezeh bakh.* Welcome."

Aaron covers his smile as Coron quotes the Hebrew verse from Song of Songs. Light sparks in Shuli's eyes.

"Please come in and meet my family and take refreshment. You've gone to considerable trouble to travel such a great distance. I look forward to learning your reasons. But first, let us celebrate your return." He turns and leads us across the cobblestone square, past a central fountain. We ascend the flight of stairs to the veranda graced with chairs, benches, and tables. Wide double doors stand open, welcoming us inside a huge salon with a massive central fireplace, now dark in this warm season. A young man stands beside two women, one older, the other my age. They wear velvet and silk with gold embroidery. My eyes affix to the young woman, her brown hair gathered at the nape of her neck beneath a pearl-studded hairnet.

"This is my wife Doña Soledad Bienveniste Coron; my son Olivar, and my daughter Aldonza," he says.

Aldonza's dark eyes meet mine and her cheeks grow rosy. There's a tingle behind my ears that trails down my neck. Doña Coron invites us to sit at the long table set for a meal. We each take a seat. She rings a bell that signals to her servants. They enter carrying trays and bowls and serving our plates with mounds of field greens, rice, roast fowl, and fresh baked bread. Coron pours white wine from a blown glass vessel into stemmed drinking glasses.

"This is my vintage, Malevisi del Sol," he tells us. "The landscape and climate here have proved perfect for growing grapes."

When everyone has been served, Coron makes a blessing over the wine and bread and we begin the meal.

"I don't know what your brother has told you," Coron says, "but my family once owned an immense vineyard in Alto Turia northeast of Valencia. We produced white wine for generations until the Inquisition robbed us of it."

"Yes, I told them," says Simon. "And I purchased several casques of this delicious Malevisi to take back to Famagusta. It's in part how we found you, that, and Umberto."

Coron chuckles. "He found *you*."

Aaron leans forward. "Your family shares much in common with ours," he says. "Our grandfather was a wealthy spice merchant, with his own caravel. He and our grandmother lost their estate and lands and died at the hands of the Barcelona Tribunal. Praise God, our parents were fortunate enough to escape."

"I knew they rescued Simon as a boy, but did not know of your family's losses. It is an all too familiar tale brought to my door many times. Is it restitution you seek?"

"In a manner of speaking," I say.

"I assumed as much. But we will discuss it after our meal. First, let's toast to enduring friendship." He raises his glass and we join him. Then he recites the Hebrew blessing for milestone occasions, "Blessed are You, Sovereign over all, who has kept us alive, sustained us, and brought us to this time."

We all respond with "Amen".

The meal is delicious and Coron keeps the wine flowing. When we finish and chant the final grace, Olivar takes Shuli's and Simon's belongings and shows them to their rooms. Aldonza leads Aaron and me down another hallway to a different wing of the hacienda.

"How was your ride to our estate?" she asks.

"Magnificent," I say.

She raises her brows, and her dark eyes widen. "This valley is truly a beautiful place, with pasture land, ponds and streams."

"It seems the perfect place not only for a vineyard, but for raising horses," I say.

"Oh? Have you raised or cared for horses?"

"Yes, that's what I do. Horses, donkeys, mules. I care for the transport and pack animals, taking pilgrims to and from Jerusalem. That's my father's business."

"But life under the Mamelukes can be very restrictive," says Aaron.

"I know nothing about that," Aldonza replies.

"Unless you are a Muslim, you cannot ride a horse."

"How dreadful. We have no such restrictions here."

"It must be like a Garden of Eden," I say.

"I hope to one day raise horses," Aldonza says. "We have a special breed, native to the island."

"Is that so," I say. "I'd love to see it."

"Wonderful. Perhaps tomorrow I can show you, and we can take a ride together."

CHAPTER 16

MALEVISI VALLEY, CRETE

Yonatan Déulocresca

CORON TAKES US on a tour of his winemaking operation. We stroll from the grape press to the huge vats being cleaned and readied for the fall harvest. Descending into the vast cellar in the caves beneath the compound, we survey the barrels and casques lying in rows, aging. An overpowering fragrance of wood and wine permeates the air. Afterward he leads us out to a pergola overgrown with grape vines where chairs and benches afford a vista over the upper terraces and the valley below. He invites us to sit and offers yet another glass of wine. This might give us a chance to ask for his help.

"All that you see here I've restored to my family," Coron says. "But to whom much is given, much is required, as the prophet Amos wrote. Restitution does not come free, it is hard earned," he says. "Consider this endeavor well. I must tell you, more was lost to me than just my estate and lands. The suffering that comes with the murder of your parents, and being a hunted fugitive, injures your soul."

His words make me think of my mother. What was she subjected to at the hands of the Inquisition that made her so bitter?

"The line that divides restorative justice and revenge becomes faint. Transgress that boundary and you are no different from your persecutor. That mistake is easy to make when your eyes blur with tears of rage. For many years, I've had to confront the sins and ghosts of my own actions."

Simon leans forward. "You speak truth. Since the days of La Vengadora, my perspective has changed, too," says Simon. "Tell me what you came to understand in these many years?"

"For over 20 years, we have worked to reclaim the value of assets lost and confiscated from our people. And this summer is no different. But I've learned to ask myself again and again, whose life will be blessed by my choices? What wound will be healed; what damage will be made whole again? Does not the prophet Micah tell us: Act justly and love mercy, and walk humbly before your God?"

"The way you quote the prophets, Señor Coron, tells me you are dedicated to *Halachah*," says Aaron.

"As a young man, I was going to enter the rabbinate. I couldn't attend any of the great houses of learning. My parent's murder steered my life in another direction."

"Aaron is studying at Or Yakar in Safed," says Simon.

"Is that so?"

"Yes, with Rabbi Saragossi."

"So, tell me, what is it you are seeking?"

"We have a dire need, Señor Coron," I say. "Our father is being held for ransom, along with a group of pilgrims, by a clan of ruthless tribesmen. We can't pay the ransom."

His brows pinch into a knot and he frowns. "I see. *Pidyon Ha-Shevuiim*, Ransoming the Captives. That is no small priority."

"But there is more," I say. I glance at Aaron and Simon, knowing I'm about to jump off a cliff. "Our grandfather tried to smuggle his assets out of Spain, to re-establish the family in Alexandria. Our father piloted the ship bearing them. They went aground in a storm near some islands. He hid the cache in a sea cave. But he could never return for it. It's our hope you can help us reclaim it."

Coron relaxes and the tension leaves his face. "Most interesting. So, it's not revenge you seek, only your family inheritance. What makes you believe it's still there?"

"According to our father, a ship of Janissaries arrived and commandeered the vessel and cargo, but never discovered the cave," Aaron says.

"How will you find this island and cave?"

Simon leans forward. "Based on Maestro Déulocresca's description, I believe it's Isula Pelagie."

"Isula Pelagie? Well, well. As we speak, we are preparing for a voyage to Djerba. It would be a minor detour. We could transport you there to search; although there are no guarantees we can find this cave. However, there are certain conditions you must understand and agree to. We can discuss this in greater detail later."

"What sort of conditions?" asks Aaron.

"We will probably encounter Spanish ships. In fact, that is our mission. You must be willing to fight and kill enemy attackers. I have seen men lose an arm or an eye, or have their belly sliced open and their guts spilled out. We could be captured and imprisoned ourselves."

My legs grow restless and my insides quiver.

Coron smirks. "The Spanish won't hesitate to kill you. And our crewmen will see your presence as a hinderance and a burden that could endanger their lives." He studies our faces as the gravity of his words registers. "Do either of you have experience with weaponry, combat, or sailoring?"

I lower my face but glance edge-wise at Aaron. He shakes his head with pursed lips.

"I have introduced them to swordsmanship," says Simon. "And Aaron knows how to take bearings."

I roll my shoulders to loosen the tightness gripping me and shift in my seat.

"I suggest you sleep on it tonight. Get some rest. We can speak further and come to an agreement. I wish you a pleasant evening." Coron rises to depart and then turns to Shuli. "And one more thing. I'm afraid we never allow women onboard the ship. I'm sorry, my dear, you will have to remain here or return home."

Our eyes drift to Shuli, who drops her head. Her eyes become glassy and she frowns.

At first no one speaks. There is only the sound of the breeze through the trees and birdsong. Coron returns to the villa, leaving us in the pergola gazing at the sunset over the western hills in a blaze of reds and oranges. The breath of the ocean meanders through the valleys, cooling the sweat on my brow.

"I'll accompany you back to Candia," says Simon. "And I'm happy to escort you back to Jaffa, too, and make sure you arrive home safely."

She meets his gaze and nods. "Thank you."

"Who's going to spar with us after you leave?" asks Aaron.

Shuli's mouth draws up on one side. "You can spar with each other. You're always squabbling, anyway."

Aaron peers at me from the corner of his eyes. He snickers with a shake of the head.

"Walk me back," she says to Simon and rises. They saunter side-by-side along the flagstone path to the villa.

I turn toward Aaron. "What's your measure of Coron, now?"

"I didn't see the slightest hint of deception," Aaron says. "Coron is rather forthright, in fact. He's a man with similar leanings to mine, a man of Torah."

"I can usually tell if someone is lying by the way they shift their eyes as they speak. He was telling the truth."

"He clings to the scriptures for guidance. That assures me the man has a conscience. I realize scripture can be used to justify all sorts of wrongs. But I trust he will really help us."

I fold my arms. "Some things he said stopped me cold. I hadn't fully realized the possibility of losing an eye or an arm."

"Or being killed."

"Yes, and to take another man's life. I don't want to become as depraved as our persecutors," I say.

"I fear more the prospect of collecting my own ghosts and sins," says Aaron. "I've been saying this from the beginning, Yonatan. You just ignored me. Or perhaps the gleam of gold you hoped to find blinded you. Now you see what I've feared all along."

"You were right, Aaron. We're risking our lives, and our souls."

"Even so, I'm willing to sail with Coron. But if you're overcome with doubt, you can still return with Shuli and Simon tomorrow."

Aaron Déulocresca

My brother has lost his spine. The risks of this undertaking have finally sunk into his thick skull and his usual foolhardy impulses have cooled. On the other hand, I seem to have found my backbone. I trust that if we go with Coron, we can do our part and he will help us find the island. Hopefully, we can recover the family's assets. But there will be an uncertain cost. We could find ourselves in jeopardy at many points on this voyage before we return home. Our skills are still too new to be any assurance. But the more we practice, the better prepared we'll be. Perhaps I can buoy my brother's courage if I engage him in more mock battles.

I look over at Yonatan. He stares off toward the sunset, his jaw set and eyes grave. "The night is young. There's still time to strengthen our swordsmanship skills."

"I'm rather drunk," he says.

"Come on," I say.

He nods in agreement but seems uncommonly somber. We find Simon seated on the portico with Shuli when we reach the main house. He happily gives up the rapier and short sword for us to practice. In the courtyard between the stairs and the fountain, we take positions.

We thrust, jab, and deflect. Our efforts seem to grow more earnest than ever before. Simon and Shuli watch in silence with solemn faces.

After a period of dodging and clashing swords, a sweat soaks my collar. My shoulder is growing fatigued from holding out my arm so long. Behind me, I hear a male voice laughing. I turn to glance over my shoulder and see Mossé Satellis watching us. At the same moment, Yonatan thrusts forward. He nicks me on the corner of my jaw, just missing the vein in my throat. I recoil and clasp my face with a yelp.

Yonatan gasps. "Oh my God, Aaron. I'm so sorry. I didn't mean to get you. You usually dodge out of the way."

I touch my beard, feeling wetness. When I withdraw my hand, I see blood on my fingers and stinging blooms as salt from my sweat meets the open wound. Shuli and Simon stand up.

"Are you alright?" Shuli asks.

Simon bounds over. "Let me look at it," he says. I hold my face where he can inspect it. "It's small, but might be deep," he says.

Mossé Satellis comes over and clasps me on the shoulder. "Put pressure on it," he says. "It will slow the bleeding."

"I'm alright, really," I say, but heed his instructions. "We were practicing to better prepare for this voyage."

"Better prepare?" Mossé says with a smirk.

"My God, I could have killed him," mutters Yonatan.

"But you didn't," says Simon. "You've gotten used to his moving in a certain way."

"Unfortunately, real attackers are never so predictable," adds Mossé. "Imagine someone more skilled who is very intent on killing you. Come with me."

Yonatan returns the blades to Simon, and we follow Mossé back inside the residence. He leads us down a side hallway, opens a heavy door, and ushers us into a large room with weaponry. From a cabinet, Mossé brings out a small coffer and opens it, revealing small bottles and jars, instruments and linen wrappings.

"This is achillea, made from yarrow powder. It will staunch the blood." He sprinkles some powder onto a square of linen and hands it to me. "Hold it to the wound."

I press the cloth to my jaw and look around the room.

"This is unbelievable," says Yonatan.

Swords of all sizes, battle axes and pikes line one wall. Padded gambesons and hauberks lie out on a central table. To our left, they've mounted shields of various shapes. On the right, racks bear strange devices made of wood and tubular metal. I have never seen anything like them before. Below them in a glass-lidded cabinet nestled in velvet are smaller versions of these weapons. My belly flutters and my knees go soft.

"I've only heard stories about these," says Yonatan.

"What are they?" I ask.

Yonatan huffs. "That is an arcubus," he says, pointing. "And those are matchlock pistols."

"You are correct," says Mossé.

"How wondrous," he says. "I would love to learn how to use them." Then he turns to me. "These propel metal balls or pellets at high velocity using explosive powder. I heard they can kill a man far off in an instant."

"Explosive powder?" I ask.

"That's right," says Mossé. "They are very affective. But it takes time to reload them once fired. You'll still require good swordsmanship skills if you face hand-to-hand combat. But these weapons, when used well, can prevent your having to. You can drop a man before he even gets in range," says Mossé.

"How do you know about these, Yonatan?"

"Well, when you spend as much time at a military crossroads as I do, where sailors and soldiers encamp, you hear their stories. But the Mamelukes reject their use."

"To their own peril, if the Ottomans invade," says Mossé.

"Will you teach us how to use them?" I ask.

"Captain Coron asked me to help you be better prepared. We don't sail for a few more days. We've got time."

"I can hardly wait," says Yonatan.

CHAPTER 17

Malevisi Valley, Crete

Yonatan Déulocresca

The odor of fresh hay mixed with horse dung meets my nostrils when I enter the stable. Morning light falls through the open doors onto the beaten sod floor. A groom is already hauling buckets of water and food to the stalls, five on each side. I wander down the central corridor looking for the horse I rode here. I'd love to ride while I still have the chance. In the corner stall, I see the legs of someone standing on the other side of a dark, majestic horse. A soft voice speaks to it while brushing the animal. A head pops up above the horse's withers and I recognize her. Aldonza.

"Good morning," I say.

"Yonatan. I was hoping to see you this morning." She comes out from around the horse holding a brush. Her eager eyes study me with a smile.

"And I was hoping to ride with you. Looks like a glorious day." My gut flutters as I walk toward her. "Simon will return to Candia today and take the horses with him."

"It's a good thing we have an early start. I was just saddling my horse," she says as she draws her horse out of the stall by the reins.

Aldonza tosses her head and a single long braid swings around her shoulder. Her loose-fitting blouson trousers peek through the open sides of her emerald embroidered tunic.

"Tell me about this beautiful animal. She looks to be about fourteen hands."

"Yes. It's called the Messara breed, native to this island. Her bloodlines go back centuries to ancient Crete."

"I've never seen a horse quite like this. The blueish-black coat and silver speckles are like a starry night."

"That is why I named her Estrella."

"May I?" I gesture toward the brush and she hands it to me. I give the horse a few strokes with the firm bristles.

"The breed has a unique inborn gait, known as *aravani*," she says. "They say it is like a camel's gait. It doesn't make the rider rise and fall, even at a gallop."

"That's amazing. I'd like to experience that for myself."

From the entrance to the barn, we hear voices in conversation. Both our heads turn. Simon walks beside Coron. They stare at us, wide-eyed. Then Coron frowns and his brows pinch together. Are we doing something wrong?

"Good morning," I say with an awkward smile. The hair on the back of my neck rises.

Aldonza frowns and bows her head. She draws her horse by the reins, passes me, and walks toward the entrance. In a momentary glance, a silent message passes between father and daughter. Coron's eyes follow her until she's exited. Then he turns to face me.

"Aldonza was just telling me about the Messara breed," I say. My mouth goes dry. "I'd hoped to go for a ride this morning."

"I'm sorry," says Simon. "There won't be time. We're about to leave. But I could use your help to get the animals ready for the return journey."

Coron narrows his eyes as he looks me up and down but says nothing.

"Certainly," I say. I turn toward the tack room. A groomsman exits carrying a fine leather saddle. He takes it to the courtyard where Aldonza has tethered Estrella. I find the bridles for our rented horses. With the help of the stable hands, we make the horses ready for travel. But when I lead two mounts out of the barn, Aldonza has gone. Perhaps there will be another chance to ride with her before we sail. But I get the impression her father would disapprove. The last thing I want is to offend him.

Aaron comes out of the residence with Shuli. Everyone is now assembling in the courtyard. Coron embraces Simon and then kisses Shuli on the hand.

"I'm very grateful for your help, Simon," says Aaron and they embrace. I look at my older adopted brother with admiration and gratitude.

"I am in your debt for all the things you've taught me, all the ways you've helped," I say.

"It's the least I could do to repay your father. When you do finally see him again, express my love. You're always welcome in Famagusta."

"I'll tell him," I say. Then I turn to face Shuli. We stare at each other for a few awkward moments. Then I smile at her. "Thank you for always looking out for me, sister. Sorry you can't go with us. I hope you have a safe journey home."

She throws her arms around me, squeezes me tight, and then steps back. "May God bless you and keep you, always."

They mount their horses and exit the gate, with the other two horses in tow. Aaron and I follow them out to the road and watch until they've descended the esplanade and are no longer in view. I'm now adrift in strange waters without Simon. My heart is leaden. I will miss them both.

∽

Aaron Déulocresca

Mossé has shepherded us into a box canyon back in the hills this morning. High cliffs rise in the distance beneath a brilliant cloudless sky. Someone affixed burlap bags of straw stacked to chest height with targets in black and red paint. A row of bottles and clay jugs balance on large rocks and boulders with shards scattered at their base. It's clear this spot isn't set up just for us. They've used it for shooting practice for some time, away from curious eyes.

Removing his cap, Mossé runs his hand over his balding head, and then replaces it. "Captain Coron has given orders to train you to defend yourselves and the ship, even though you are more like passengers," Mossé explains. "So, today I'm teaching you how to use firearms."

I notice my brother's wide grin as he bounces on his toes. My pulse quickens and a rush of energy awakens in me, but not without forethought. "We do need to protect ourselves. But that means we must make orphans of some other man's children," I say.

"Must you fuss and waver over everything, Aaron?" asks Yonatan.

Mossé rumples his brow. "First, the Torah requires you to protect your life and that of others," he says. "Just remember Aaron, these people would kill you without a second thought; and see your mother burned alive, if they got a chance. And they executed your grandfather. Feel no guilt, my young friend."

My gut twists as I absorb his logical argument. But I still reflect on Coron's warning about reckoning with ghosts and sins. Will I do the right thing with this new power?

There's a wooden shelter and a table to the side. Mossé has laid out several long and short weapons. There is also a wooden chest with compartments holding balls, pellets, and flasks of black powder. I run my fingertips over the satiny hard wood and polished brass fittings.

"Here is how a matchlock works. This flash pan holds the gunpowder, right here," he says, showing us the slide-away cover on the pistol. "It's ignited with a candle wick we call a serpentine. See here, it is in a movable clamp. By pulling this lever, it curls around to meet the powder." He shows the movement with the wick cold. "Now you try it." He hands the pistol to me and gives another to Yonatan. "Squeeze the finger grip gently and feel how the lever moves."

"Next, we load it with ammunition." He pulls out a metal rod from the bulbous end of the pistol and shows us how to load it with powder, a small ball, and wadding, tamping it into the barrel with the rod. We copy his movements and prepare the pistols in a similar manner. He pours the black powder into the small chamber. "Now we're ready to light the match," he says. He holds one end of the wick to a burning candle inside a lantern, positions it in the clamp, and then blows on it to keep the tip smoldering. He then guides us to prepare our weapons.

"We're now ready to fire. But before we do, I want you to be aware. This will make a startling noise, and it has a fair kick. Hold your weapon out like this and look down the barrel to aim it and then fire." We watch as he points to the target and squeezes the finger grip. In a flash of light and a deafening boom, the ammunition explodes out of the barrel. The air fills with smoke. It jars me out of my skin. But despite a thundering heart, I stick to the spot.

"Alright, Aaron. Step up here and take a shot," Mossé says.

My hand trembles as I hold out the pistol. Mossé comes over. "Steady your hand by using your other one underneath." He shows how to cup one hand with the other for support. I aim the pistol and squeeze the lever. The match arches to the pan of explosive powder and I feel the pistol jerk as it detonates. The smoke stings my eyes.

"Good job. The blast takes a little getting used to. But you even hit the target.," says Mossé. "Be aware. The ball will lose altitude as it travels. Depending on how far away you are, you need to aim slightly higher than your intended target. Yonatan, your turn."

My brother does not hesitate. He walks up to the firing line, takes a wide stance, closes one eye, aims at the clay pots, and fires. He misses the mark and huffs.

"Try again. More practice will help your accuracy, but these pistols are not too precise. With the arcubus, though, we often use pellets, because they cover a wider range and do more damage. Let's reload."

Shooting practice continues while the sun makes its transit across the sky toward midday. We each try various weapons and ammunition until the supply Mossé brought runs out. We pack up the weaponry and start the trek back to the family compound.

"Alright. It's a start," Mossé says. "Until we sail, I want you both to do little else but practice shooting and swordsmanship. You know enough now you won't likely need further guidance. But Coron will be here, if you do. I've got to make the ship ready with arms and ammunition."

"We're most grateful for your instruction and patience," I say.

"You'll both do fine."

When we arrive back at the armory inside the former fortress, Mossé instructs us on how to clean the weapons and put them away when we've finished. He then leaves us to the task.

"I don't know about you," says Yonatan. "But I feel better prepared for this journey."

"I'm getting there," I reply. "But I've been thinking about something you said earlier. I know that unless you are a qualified *Shochet*, the law of our land restricts Jews from owning any blade longer than the width of a hand."

"And so?"

"You mentioned the Mamelukes have rejected the use of firearms."

"They're trained in the old code of hand-to-hand combat. Use of firearms is considered dishonorable. Nobody has them."

"So, they're completely baffled by them."

"You could say that."

"And, there are no laws forbidding us from having or using them?"

Yonatan rears back. His eyes wander as he sorts through the implications of this. "None that I know of." He folds his arms and tips his head. "Why?"

I let that realization sink in a moment, and then smile at him. "Just curious."

CHAPTER 18

La Represalia

Yonatan Déulocresca

At the Candia harbor, I stand dockside with Mossé Satellis and my brother Aaron. I shade my eyes from the morning sun as I survey the corsair ship for the first time. Flutters fill my chest and belly. We're about to embark on this vessel into the unknown. The craft sits high in the water as tall as a three-story building at the after-castle. Made of polished tawny oak, she displays brightly painted pavises on the sides, including Coron's blue and gold sunrise emblem. I study the activity on the deck and above it. A loading ramp extends from the wharf to the opening in the gunwale. Men wheel containers onboard with a hand truck. A group of sailors maneuvers the yard arm and pulleys to lower heavy crates into the hold.

"This is La Represalia," says Mossé.

"It's the most magical craft I've ever seen," I say.

"I assure you," he continues. "This vessel is modest compared to a warship. But she's a rare beauty. They built her caravel style, with planks set edge-to-edge rather than overlapping."

"How is that better?" Aaron asks.

"It makes the ship lighter and faster. And it also allows for gunports, which you couldn't have on the old clinker-built cogs. See, she has two cannons fore and aft." He points, wagging his finger.

I widen my eyes. "Our grandfather's ship was a caravel," I say.

"Is that so? This one is larger and finer than those built decades ago," Mossé says. "Notice her high rounded stern with the ornate trim on the after castle. She has one square-rigged sail on the foremast. The other three are lateen-rigged."

"What does that do for the ship?" I ask.

"That makes it very nimble and easy to maneuver. Here, you're going to need these," he says. He hands us each a large folded gauzy piece of cloth. I take the cloth and wrap it around my neck. Mossé's eyes fix on something behind us. I turn to see Captain Coron arriving by horse at the wharf with his son Olivar. Olivar leads Coron's mount away, and the captain goes into a dockside tavern.

"Looks like we're about to assemble," Mossé says. "Come with me."

He leads us through the tavern's arched portico. We follow him to an alcove with open shutters overlooking the water. The man who took Simon and me captive, Isaac Abramo, stands guard at the entrance to the alcove. He keeps surveillance on the other patrons of the tavern. Daylight illuminates a heavy table flanked by sturdy benches. A familiar face greets us: Umberto Alvo. Two others sit there who I don't recognize. One man wears a dark robe and sits before a parchment document with a quill and ink. The other wears a tall white Turkish headdress. Coron gestures to the bench and Aaron and I join the others seated. Coron stands at the head of the table.

"Gentlemen, if no one has yet introduced you, these young men are Aaron and Yonatan Déulocresca from Jerusalem." Then he turns to us. "Let me present our navigator, Khizr Balcan. And this is Señor Sevillano, who is the scrivener. I believe you're already acquainted with Mossé, Umberto, and Isaac. I've invited Señor Sevillano here today to assist us with an amendment to our *Hezchem*.

"*Hezchem?*" asks Aaron.

"Correct. An official contract. Every sea voyage we lay out an agreement in writing, detailing the expectations between us and the members of the crew. We do this to spell out the compensation and avoid misunderstandings. This is, after all, a business enterprise."

I nod my head and glance at Aaron.

"Understandable," he says.

"You've asked for our help and we can offer that aid. But just so the senior officers understand what you are proposing, let me clarify. Yonatan and Aaron are seeking to recover a cache of family assets, which they believe are hidden in a sea cave. According to our former navigator, Davî Salmonis, it is on an island in the Pelagie chain. They want us to transport them there so they can search for it."

I glance around the table at the solemn faces and discerning eyes. Umberto strokes his beard and Khizr tugs at his long moustache. My pulse surges.

Coron continues. "They face a dire situation. Their father is being held for ransom. So, it is a mission of mercy for *Pidyon Shevuiim*. We can make some allowances. But it cannot come without expectations."

He stares at us with a stern face. "I want to ensure you understand our side of the matter. We typically plan journeys between 20 to 30 days long. There are enormous costs involved, everything from fitting out the ship to our supplies of gunpowder, shot, tar, rope. Then there are the provisions for the crew and sundry items; everything from candles to crockery. We like to offer our sailors an advance on whatever spoils we may take to insure their loyalty. Then, the governor of the Isle of Djerba is entitled to one eighth of our gleanings, captives, merchandise, bullion. And we deliver any ship we seize. Then there are port taxes and fees. But understand, it is a costly undertaking."

All the officers are nodding their heads and mumbling their agreement.

"If I may say so, Captain," says Umberto. "We would have these costs regardless of whether we take on their errand, or do not."

"Of course. I'm not expecting them to defray any of those costs. But it may impact our opportunities for profit. The trip there and back cannot be gratis. So, what I propose is a contract partly paid for by their labors on the voyage to Djerba, and also a share of the assets. That ensures we unite everyone behind the effort and they all have a stake in its success."

"When you say a share of the assets, what does that amount to?" Aaron asks.

I lean forward. "We don't even know how much is there, if anything remains at all."

"Half for you and the other half divided equally among the crew and officers."

"Half?" Aaron and I say it at the same time. My stomach sinks.

"We have five officers, four gunners, and sixteen crewmen at your disposal for a rather speculative venture," Coron says. "So divided 25 ways, a share is probably not very much."

"That's true," I say.

"I see your point," says Aaron. "We can't expect you to do it just for the sake of *rachmanut*."

"What if we never find the cache, or it has already been discovered?" I ask.

"That is the risk, isn't it?" says Coron.

"One we're all taking," says Umberto.

"The officers and crew have already signed our *Hezchem*," says Señor Sevillano. "It's completely voluntary, but you must agree to the terms in order to move forward. So, if there's no further discussion, we need you to sign the *Hezchem*."

Aaron and I look at each other for a few moments. My mouth goes dry.

"I'd like to have a word with my brother, if I may," Aaron says and rises.

"Certainly," says Coron.

I follow Aaron out of the alcove into the tavern. There are other patrons drinking and it's hard to hear over the drone of voices. Aaron waves me closer so he can speak into my ear. I bend toward him.

"Do you think we should go through with this? Half our assets. It seems too much."

"He didn't sound like it was negotiable. What other choices do we have? We've come too far to turn back now, empty-handed."

He rubs his forehead and huffs. "Alright. I hope we don't regret this."

We walk back into the alcove. Aaron's hand trembles as he reaches toward the document. Señor Sevillano slides the parchment toward him. Aaron reads through the text and slowly takes a deep breath. Dipping the quill in the ink, Señor Sevillano offers it to Aaron. My brother takes the quill and signs his name. Then Aaron turns to me. I swallow dryly, pinch the quill between my thumb and fingers, and scrawl my mark beside Aaron's.

"Very well," says Coron. "Welcome to the crew. Mossé, I want you to take Yonatan under wing to teach him to be a gunner, as well as sailoring skills. And Khizr, I'm assigning Aaron to assist you with navigation duties. I will expect you both to serve watch, help with routine tasks, defend the ship, and attack our enemies if called to do so; which is likely. That is our mission."

Inside, my gut swirls with a mix of jittery excitement and dread. This voyage is no longer just about finding the money to ransom father. Now, Coron and his men have a stake in finding our family inheritance, too. I don't know if this is a good thing, or if it will be a fatal mistake.

⚜

After sharing a meal with Aaron and toasting to our voyage, it's time to go aboard. Aaron heads up the gangplank and takes the stairs toward the observation deck where Khizr stands. When I arrive on deck, I see the boatswain, Umberto, standing there. He's yelling directives to the crew. If I'm going to live amicably alongside these crewmen, I must earn their respect. To make myself useful, I offer to take a turn at the capstan. Umberto gestures to it without hesitation. With pulleys and ropes attached to the yards, we grunt and groan to lower a large crate into the hold. Once we finish the load, a new crewmate turns to me.

"If you don't cover up, you'll boil your brain, *Nuevo*. Then your face will blister and your lips split open. It will spoil all the fun."

Earning a nickname already makes me smile. My partner wears a gauzy cloth like the one Mossé gave me earlier. His is wrapped in an unfamiliar style. But it protects him from the sun. Most of the sailors seem to wear them.

"How do you wrap it so it won't fall in your way?" I ask.

"I'll show you, *Nuevo*," he says.

I pull the square of cloth from around my neck and hand it to him. He first makes a slipknot toward one end. Then he throws it over my head. The knot rests at the nape of my neck. He pulls the other half forward over my face. Next, he gathers it into a twist at my forehead, and then wraps it twice around my head. Finally, he tucks in the ends, and loosens the slipknot, allowing the fabric to fall down my back. It feels snug and secure, but out of my way.

"It keeps sweat out of your eyes, too. Cover your face like this." He pulls one side of his *keffiyah* across his face and pokes it into the other to shield his face from sunburn.

"Thank you, brother. Tell me your name?" I ask.

"Call me Saadia, Saadia Benatar," he says.

"I'm Yonatan Déulocresca."

"Nice to meet you, *Nuevo*. Now we have work to do."

Once we've loaded all the cargo, the next task is to maneuver the ship into the open sea. Being *nuevo*, I'm little use here. But I pay attention to Umberto's commands and study the crewmen's actions. They loosen and fasten lines and sails and adjust the rigging. They haul up the anchor and we slowly glide out of the harbor.

When I see Mossé again, I approach him. "I would like to learn how to tie the common knots. Especially the Spanish bowline."

"Spanish bowline?" Mossé asks.

"Isn't that knot used to tie two things together?"

"Indeed. But how do you know that name?" Mossé asks.

"Wasn't I wearing one?"

His belly shakes with a hardy guffaw and he grins, nodding. "Yes, you did."

He takes me aside and teaches me half a dozen common knots. "The crew don't take kindly to clumsy novices on the shrouds. Best to stay clear unless Umberto orders you. But I'll show you the guns later."

For the rest of the afternoon, I sit atop the after-castle stairs. Over and over, I practice the knots. Maybe tomorrow Saadia will show me where and how to use them. By the end of the day, my hands are blistered and raw. I'm covered with sweat and salt, and every muscle and joint aches from turning the capstan. But I don't care. Now evening, it's a pleasure to share a bowl of beans and *galleta* with these robust men below deck.

Some crewmen are Turks and Venetians. They have families waiting for them to return to Crete. But most are Sephardic Jews like me and my new acquaintances, Saadia and Manoa. They have sun-burnished faces, crisscrossed with scars. My thoughts turn to my father and the scar on his temple. I can well imagine how a loose line in a storm can be deadly. I'm sure it's only a matter of time until I bear my own scars. What would he think of me being here?

Below deck, it reeks of unwashed bodies, piss, and tar. After a while, I cease to notice. It's easy to distract oneself by a game of cards and a cup of ale. Along with other crewmen, Saadia pulls off his *keffiyah*, revealing his long, dark mane, like mine. With his onyx eyes, he looks more like a brother than Aaron.

"Real gambling gets you whipped, *Nuevo*," says Saadia, as he deals the cards for a game of Parar. "But you're free to wager all the almonds and chickpeas you wish."

I laugh. With those stakes, no one is apt to cheat or brawl. Before long, I find my eyes drooping against all efforts to stay awake. I finish the hand and bid my crewmates a *buenos noches*. Locating my blanket, I curl up in a corner and fall deeply into oblivion.

∽

We wake to calm waters and a fair wind. Our heading is due west toward Malta. It will take us three days to reach the island. There is nothing but open sea in between. According to the steward, the closer we get to The Straits, as they call them, the more likely we'll meet whirlpools and storms. These can be so fierce it can send ships to the bottom. Now that we're set on our course, today our efforts turn to cleaning and repairs. Umberto sets me to scrubbing and polishing, which I eagerly carry out. I still catch glimpses of the work in the harpings above.

Several other ships cross paths throughout the forenoon watch. Turkish or Venetian vessels sail past in the opposite direction. But shortly after two bells in the afternoon watch, a voice from the crow's-nest again calls out. "Vessel on the starboard bow." Our pilot and Umberto climb to the forecastle deck and examine the horizon with the spyglass. But unlike previous sightings, Umberto now returns to the officers' quarters, presumably to inform the captain. There is something different about this vessel. It's heading the same direction we are, but is to the north of us. After a short time, Umberto comes out on the main deck.

"Alright men, let's have a closer look." He then directs the helmsman to turn the rudder and orders men to shift the sails. After a few moments, the Represalia gently veers toward the other ship.

Manoa stands beside me, coiling rope. "I heard the boatswain say it's flying a Spanish flag and could be a cargo ship."

"From the width and depth of the vessel it looks like a näo," says Saadia, as he secures a line with belaying pins. "It's rather far out to be alone. They usually travel in convoys."

"Maybe they're sailing from Sicily."

"Well, we're going to scout them out. Get ready, *Nuevo*," says Saadia.

A flutter erupts beneath my ribs, and my pulse quickens. We're about to chase down a Spanish ship. I swallow hard. Our ship has been sailing windward on the westerly Levant, with help from the Gregale, a crosswind from Greece. That gives us a tactical advantage. The other ship would have to turn into the wind to attack us. But they can evade capture downwind if they're a faster vessel.

We track the ship flying a red and yellow flag for several hours, just watching. Finally, Captain Coron comes out onto the deck. "Let's show them who we really are, and see how they like it," says Coron. He orders the winged lion flag of our home port to be brought down. I study the corsair flag as they haul it up. There's a death's head in the center between a crescent moon and the Magen David flanking it, against a half-black and half-green field. It's not long before the Spanish vessel shifts their sails and turns southwest to put distance between us.

Gradually, we leave the Gregale's range, slowing our course. The Levant also weakens, and it takes until early evening before we pass the horn of Benghazi. Then, the hot gale off the desert, the Ghibli, blows strong crosswinds northward. The Spanish ship, now a dot on the horizon, takes advantage and multiplies the distance between us. She finally disappears from the western skyline.

"She's still out there," says Coron. "We'll find her."

At sunset, I go below deck to join my crewmates. It's Tuesday, so tonight there will be meat and wine.

CHAPTER 19

La Represalia

Aaron Déulocresca

The sky is black and filled with a myriad of glittering stars. A waxing crescent moon is rising behind us. With a few more turns of the sandglass, I'll finally be able to go back to sleep. They divide the night watch into three parts; first watch, sleep watch, and dawn watch. Sleep watch is the worst, because it breaks the night in the middle, destroying any chance of adequate rest. Since duties are rotated, everyone must take a turn, and tonight is mine.

Finding a decent place to sleep on the main deck is a blessing. Earlier, I staked my claim just outside the forecastle where the junior officers all lodge. Beds or berths are reserved only for them. Like the other sailors, they gave me a blanket and sack filled with straw for my pillow. While the lower decks have more room; they reek from the stench of rot, piss, and the sticky mixture of tar and pitch used to seal the ship called *alquitrán*. They're also plagued by insects and vermin. Here at least the air is cool and fresh. I can stave off another bout of seasickness.

Why anyone would choose the life of a sailor is beyond my understanding. It is difficult to tolerate being trapped in close quarters for days at a time. But to imagine living here for months is no better than being in prison. At least in jail, one has the advantage of a cell. There is little chance of drowning or being eaten alive by monsters of the deep.

There is no privacy, either. But regardless, I must do the most loathsome thing of all. I can't rest until I visit the gardens. They're paradoxically called that, because they reek. I carefully creep around sleeping bodies scattered across the deck. This is the way to the latrines, located all the way at the beak of the ship. Hiding behind the majestic, sword-bearing angel figurehead is a filthy secret. On both sides, a foul and slippery lattice floor and open railing juts out over the sea. It's a dangerous prospect in the surging waves to balance, just to relieve oneself. You risk your life just to piss. As waves splash onto the prow and soak my lower legs, I clasp tight to the railing with one hand and pull the front of my braes down with the other, letting my relief flow into the sea spray.

Over my left shoulder, there's a faint light. I turn my head, peering around the decorative carving. A man stands on the fretwork on the other side of the figurehead. How can he hold a lantern and the railing while taking a pee? The lantern is moving back and forth. Is he signaling to someone? My heart starts to thunder as I peer into the darkness ahead. Against the slight contrast where the sky meets the sea, I can make out shapes, outlined in moonlight. Lord! Those look like longboats. A quiver runs down my spine and my limbs grow loose.

I scramble back to the deck and shout. "Longboats approaching, dead ahead!"

Immediately, Umberto runs out of the forecastle toward me. One of the lombarderos clambers his way from the mainmast. Other sailors nearby are on their feet.

Umberto calls. "What's happening?"

"Two longboats are headed our way from the west. I think we're about to be attacked," I say and point.

He runs to the port-side gunwale and peers across the dark waters. "Devils. They've launched a cutting out against us," he says.

"I saw someone in the gardens signaling with a lantern to them," I tell him.

His eyes widen. "A lantern? Find him," he says to two men standing nearby, and they dash toward the latrine. He throws open the hatch and blows on his whistle. "All hands on deck," he shouts. "Aaron, run and alert Captain Coron," he instructs me. Then he hurries to the arms chest and begins handing out weapons and ammunition.

I try not to trip over anyone on the deck as I go toward the after castle. "We're about to be boarded, get your weapons!" I repeat as I pass. I see my brother's head emerge from the lower deck. "Get a pistol and an arcubus, right now!"

He rears back. "What's going on?"

"That downwind ship is attempting a sneak attack," I say, and continue across the deck toward the stern. Scaling the stairs, I open the door to the officer's quarters and call out. "Captain Coron. The boatswain has called all hands. We're under attack."

I hear him mutter as he comes flying out of his quarters with only one boot. He pulls on a second and puts on a thick leather jerkin. Khizr is right behind him. They rush past me, down the stairs to the binnacle. Captain starts shouting orders.

Sailors position themselves along the gunwale with crossbows or pikes in hand. Others bring buckets of water and wet blankets. They spread them out to extinguish any flaming arrows. Men get on the lines, furling the sails to protect them.

Mossé comes running over. "Come to the observation deck," he says, and I ascend the stairs with him. He rushes to a chest of weapons and grabs two firearms. Many more lie inside the trunk. "Start loading scatter shot in these," says Mossé. We quickly begin making the weapons ready to fire and hand them out to crewmen.

"To the gunwales," shouts Coron, "and may God be with you."

I grab an arcubus and tuck a pistol into my waistband. Hurrying down to the weather deck, I join the other sailors. The moonlight outlines the men hunched two-men-deep along the port side. I glance over my shoulder and see the sliver of moon high on the eastern horizon. The ship and crew are ready to launch our full barrage against the invaders.

A few steps away, Mossé is facing two sailors restraining the struggling man they've apprehended. Mossé turns to me. "Aaron, is this the man?" he asks.

"I never saw his face," I say. "But by the looks of his wet zaragüelles, he was standing out in the gardens."

"I'd cut his throat and throw him overboard, but the captain may want to question him first," says Mossé. "Put him in the brig."

The man glares with defiance as they tie his hands. "You'll pay for this, heretic worms."

"Oh, will we?" Mossé huffs, and slugs the man in the jaw. "We'll see who pays. Take him away." The two sailors force him toward the opening to the lower decks.

Moonlight now glints on the water, leaving an outline around the dark, approaching long boats crammed with attackers.

"They're nearly in range, boys," says Mossé. "Be sure your wicks are lit. Wait for my command."

I grip my arcubus, finger on the trigger, and blow on the fuse so it glows red. Then I aim toward the longboats. I can see the oars rowing.

"First row, raise your weapons," orders Mossé. "Fire!"

All along the gunwale, flames flash in the darkness and smoke fills the air. Then a volley of arrows follows. Next, the first row ducks down to reload, and the second row fires our weapons. The distinct sound of bullets or arrows from the enemy whistle overhead and makes a thunk as they shatter and embed into wood. Men gasp and cry out beside me. My heart is at my throat and I hunker down and peer between the balusters. Cries of agony rise from the boats, too.

"Fire at will," shouts Mossé.

As the boats close the distance, I fit my pistol between the balusters, aim, and fire. Others to the right and left of me loose arrows or send another volley of scatter shot toward the invaders. A grappling hook launched by a crossbow, flies over the gunwale and catches there. They're trying to board us. Two sailors dodge and duck as they try to dislodge the thing. I turn with my back to the gunwale and reload the powder and shot for my arcubus. Then I reload my pistol. I turn back to face the enemy.

One of our gunners lobs hand-sized bottles that explode when they break on the wooden boats. The *alquitrán* inside ignites into flames on their clothing and skin. The attackers scream and writhe in pain. Some stand up and jump into the water to douse themselves. A man is swimming toward the knotted rope of the grappling hook. I have to stop him. I fumble with my pistol. My hand is shaking when I try to aim it, but I squeeze the trigger. The shot must have hit him. He stops swimming and sinks into the deep. Wincing, the urge to vomit grips my gut. I take my arcubus, point it at our attackers and let go a scatter of bloody damage, with a growl.

I keep reloading and firing until I finally run out of ammunition. The Spanish ship's profile is now visible. Firing from the long boats has stopped. Umberto and a handful of others free the grappling hook and use it to capture the nearest long boat; dispatching any surviving enemies and dumping their bodies into the sea.

Doctor Alamosa is slowly making his way among the wounded, assessing their injuries. They help those who are severe to the infirmary. I get to my feet and survey my shipmates, looking for my brother. Finally, I spy him crouched next to another man, who is lying on his back. Yonatan presses his hands against the man's shoulder to stop the bleeding. I hurry over and he looks up at me. Blood is oozing from a gash on his cheekbone. I take a knee beside him.

"You're bleeding. Are you alright?" I ask.

"I dodged a bullet, but not quite enough."

"It almost got your eye," I say.

"Stings a bit. Glad to see you're in one piece."

"Men fell on both sides of me," I say. "I was lucky, but I ran out of ammunition."

Doctor Alamosa arrives and takes charge of the wounded crewman. Yonatan goes to a bucket. He spills a little water to wash the blood from his hands, and then bends over, splashing the side of his face. As he straightens and combs his hair with his fingers, Captain Coron approaches us.

"You're wounded," he says to Yonatan, clasping him by the shoulder.

"Not too bad," he replies.

"Be sure our physician looks you over." For all his previous resistance to bringing us aboard, the man actually seems to care. Then he turns to me. "Mossé tells me you're the one who discovered the spy. Had it not been for you, we might have suffered much heavier losses."

I stare at Coron's approving smile and then at my brother, who stares wide-eyed, shaking his head. My face grows warm.

"It was just by coincidence," I say.

"A coincidence?" says Coron.

"I was in the gardens, sir."

Coron erupts with laughter. "Well, good timing, then."

The three of us laugh a moment. Then we survey the crew, putting things in order and caring for the wounded.

"What were the Spanish trying to do?" asks Yonatan.

"They wanted to eliminate us as a threat. Probably, the intention was to set fire to the ship, blow the powder kegs, and kill as many of us as they could without sustaining damage to their own vessel," the captain replies.

"But why not just blow holes in our hull with their cannons and sink us?" I ask.

"That would require them to let us get close enough to retaliate and take damage. They may be carrying something or someone valuable or important."

"Well, they're 14 men down, now," says Yonatan. "They didn't count on us being ready for them."

"That's for certain. But when they don't see our sails on fire and there are no explosions, they'll realize their attack failed and will probably flee. There's no time to wait," says Coron. As the Talmud puts it, "If someone is coming to kill you, rise up early and kill them first."

I don't know if I accept Coron's interpretation of tractate Berakhot 62b in the Talmud. What determines an obligatory war was a matter of dispute among the Rabbis. But there's no time to debate that now. Someone is trying to kill us.

CHAPTER 20

LA REPRESALIA

Yonatan Déulocresca

UMBERTO GATHERS TOGETHER those who are still able-bodied onto the weather deck. A good wind out of the south flutters through his dark hair, gleaming blue in the moonlight.

"They wounded seven men, one severely. But we can be thankful no one died," he says.

I touch the tender wound on my upper cheek and count myself lucky compared to others.

"La Represalia took no damage, so now we're going after those bastards. I need you boys to climb the shrouds, unfurl and adjust the sheets. If we sail full and bye, we can pick up speed."

Hot blood pulsates in my throat and I flex my fingers in readiness. Saadia jabs me with his elbow. "Let's go, *Nuevo*."

We race to the foremast rigging, ready to grab the lines and make the sheets taut, while other crewmen climb the shrouds to unfurl them. From the stern castle, Captain Coron studies our progress as we catch the wind. Once we've shortened the distance between us and the Spanish vessel, Captain yells to Mossé Satellis.

"Looks like we've got ourselves a lovely little Spanish carrack. Let's give the vixen a pinch on her haunches."

"Sí, Capitán. We'll let her know we're on her tail," he shouts back.

Mossé waves to me and several other men and we follow him below.

"I want you to watch how we do this, Yonatan. It's not all that different from loading your arcubus, but much larger," he tells me. I observe as four men pack the two forward cannons with powder and balls. "Our aim isn't to damage or sink the ship," he says. "We want to seize it. If our goal is to take booty to sell at a profit, there's little point in destroying it. We're just trying to intimidate."

"Won't they fire back?"

"Oh, they'll surely try. But because we've killed a quarter of their crew, when their men get on the guns, there'll be fewer on deck, making it easier to board."

The Spanish vessel flees downwind, and we pursue for a length of time. When we are in closer range, Mossé orders the gunners to prepare to fire. The right gunner loads the canon with powder, while the left gunner stuffs in wadding. Next, a ball the size of a grapefruit is thrown in and everything rammed tight. Then Mossé turns to me.

"Stay well clear," he says. "It's very dangerous and very loud. Cover your ears."

I step back out of range of the cannon's rearward thrust. Mossé then peers out to judge the distance as we close in, and then he moves aside.

"Ready? Fire!"

The volley cracks the sea's silence with deafening booms and flashes, filling the space with smoke. The force of the explosion makes the deck quake beneath my feet. The thunder resounds in my chest and I steady my stance. Above deck, cheers of crewmates celebrate our retaliation for the attack. The cannonball strikes the water a short distance from the Spanish ship, as intended.

Climbing back up to the main deck, I rush over to the gunwale to see the reaction. The Spanish waste no time before returning fire from their rear cannons, showing their intention to fight. With the moon now overhead, sailors appear in their shrouds, scrambling to change its sails and rudder. They're trying to bring their full bank of cannons to face us. I hold my breath and my mouth goes dry.

"Trim the sails," shouts Umberto. Everyone rushes to get on the lines again. We shift our heading to lie as near the wind as possible and our helmsman steers a diagonal course toward the prow of the other ship. This puts them at the wrong angle for their cannons to hit us.

"Ready arms and prepare to board," shouts Mossé.

All the crewmen, including my brother and I, reload our pistols and arcubuses, refill our supply of black powder and shot. I also strap a cutlass onto my hip. When we're ready, Aaron and I cross the deck and approach Umberto, who is now standing at the binnacle with Khizr.

"Where would you like us, sir?" I ask.

He looks us over for a moment. "Aaron, you'll go in the second wave. Cut down anyone still putting up a fight. Those who surrender, you line them up along the gunwale with their hands tied behind their backs. Gather all weapons."

Then, he turns to me and takes my arcubus, and hands me a pouch. I glance inside and find two grenados, one glass, the other of perforated metal, a smoke bomb.

"Yonatan, take two pistols. Find Saadia and Manoa. As soon as the second wave boards, you come in behind and scout out the lower decks. Find whoever might be holed-up there and kill them. Or if they surrender, bring them above board."

Kill them, at close range. A shudder sweeps through my whole body and my chest pounds hard. The crew of the Spanish ship launches a barrage of gunfire toward us. They've lit several lanterns and the enemy crewmen are lining up on their deck, just as we are. My eyes search the cluster of men crouched beside our gunwale. I stoop down and scramble over to my friends.

"Come with me. We've got a special task," I say.

Mossé orders the men to the forecastle, dividing them into two boarding parties. We scale the stairs and huddle behind them. It strikes me that my brother is among this group and about to go into hand-to-hand combat. Even though he has on a leather jerkin and carries a buckler and cutlass, this could be the last moments we will see each other alive. I weave a path to him and clasp him on the shoulder. He turns to meet my stare with wide-eyed surprise.

"Yonatan!" he says.

"God protect you."

We grasp each other tight by the forearm. My gut clenches and throat swells.

"Fight well," he says.

I turn back to the assigned task with my comrades. Blood throbs in my ears and every muscle and tendon tightens. I become keenly aware of my surroundings, as arrows and shot fly overhead. I raise my gaze to the enemy's shrouds and crow's nest, against a background of dim lantern glow. High above the fray is an archer with a crossbow aimed down at our ship. He intends to pick us off. Then he turns his aim toward our observation deck, where the captain stands. In an instant, I know his intent. This weapon may not have great range or accuracy, but I have to do something. My hand shakes. I steady my grasp, aim, and fire my pistol. He hunches forward, drops the bow, and then he falls, rebounding off the shrouds to the deck. My peers watch the man fall, too, and both look at me with gaping mouths. Several men in the boarding party turn around, annoyed.

"Hold your fire."

"What are you doing?"

"Sniper in the crow's nest." I say and quickly reload to be ready for our task.

"Good shot, *Nuevo*," says Saadia.

I take a deep breath and prepare to move.

Mossé calls out. "We're here to deliver the Judgement of Sinai. Don't hesitate."

We have the higher ground, and use several grappling hooks to pull the ships together. The enemy crew continues shooting arrows and scattershot toward us. We hunker down behind our shields.

"Boarding parties forward," shouts Mossé. Men pile over the gunwale holding pikes and shields. The enemy meets these with swords and spears. But a few blasts with scatter shot from the arcubuses at close range drops them bloody on the deck. Men are groaning and flailing in pain. The first rays of sunlight glow from the east as the second wave prepares to board.

"Surrender, and we won't slaughter you all," shouts Mossé. "Second wave, take position!" The cluster of crewmen including Aaron squats beside the gunwale. After the enemy volley, there's a pause as they reload. Mossé orders the men to cross over, amidst smoke and thunder. In the dim light, the fumes, and battle cries of wrestling bodies and clashing blades, I lose sight of my brother.

⁓

Aaron Déulocresca

Pools of black blood spread out over the forecastle of the Spanish ship. Long, eerie shadows splay across the deck with the first rays of sun. Three men lie dead at my feet and two others writhe and groan in the death throes. None of them are from our crew. I take in the entire array of carnage as I descend the stairs into a grim haze. Some Spaniards see our advent and flee toward the stern castle.

"Lay down your arms and we won't kill you!" I shout. Cutlass and buckler in hand, pistol in my waistband, I plunge into the melee alongside five others. Metal against metal rings in my ears. The screams of agony, grunts and groans mix with battle cries. I know what I must do. We are the finishers. I jab my cutlass into the back of a man locked in struggle with a young sailor with whom I prayed last evening. His blood splatters all over my hand and wrist as I withdraw the blade. The assailant falls to the deck. I use the point of my sword to knock the knife from his hand and then slash his throat.

I spin around to assess what comes next. A Spanish sailor is choking one of ours, pinning him down with the handle of a pike. I swing my blade against the side of his neck and he slumps over, gushing blood everywhere. So much blood. I retch. Now freed, the blood drenched target of his menace grabs the pike and we pivot to the next skirmish. We move to fend off an axe wielding attacker, using a pike jab to the belly and a blast from my pistol.

The choleric humor rushing through my veins is keeping me alert and vigilant. My breath comes fast and heavy. Atop the stern castle, two of our crewmen are squaring off with a third man. It's the Spanish captain. One pins the captain's arms back. The other aims a pistol point blank at his head and fires. Then they lever his body overboard.

The remaining Spanish crewmen witnessing this, throw down their weapons, hold up their hands, and back away from further fighting. Some fall to their knees, pleading for their lives and pissing themselves. The battle seems to have ended quicker than I imagined. No one wants to die. How quickly life can be cut short.

My face goes slack and I rub my chest. The smoke burns my watering eyes. Our men on the bridge lower the Spanish standard. As the sun breeches the horizon, the black and green corsair flag rises on the flagpole. A wave of giddiness spreads over me, but I also want to cry. Along with my sailing brothers, a cheer bursts from my lips. In the pink glow of the dawn, I realize the entire night has passed and I have not slept.

≼

Yonatan Déulocresca

I stare down through the lattice grill covering the hatch. My heart booms at my throat. This could be the most treacherous of situations. They could cut us down with ready pistols before our feet hit the lower deck. Perhaps I could get them to fire their weapons and then descend before they can reload. I grab a belaying pin and drop it down the ladder with a clatter. There seems to be movement stirring below, but the roar on deck makes it difficult to make-out. They could have axes or pikes.

Saadia hollers down into the hold. "We have killed your captain. Lay down your arms and come out if you want to live."

"Come take us, if you think you can," someone shouts back.

I look at my two companions. "Alright, amigos, I say we smoke them out." I ignite the fuse on the smoke bomb and when the thing begins to fume like hell, I pitch it down the hatch. After a few moments, smoke spreads and pours back up through the opening.

Several men fumble their way to the bottom of the ladder. With red eyes, they gasp for air and climb out. When they reach the deck, we bind their hands behind their backs. Manoa marches them to the gunwale. Five in all turn themselves over. Then I see something I didn't expect; the partly shorn head and black robe of a Catholic monk. Two of them grapple their way upward, coughing and squinting against the sting of fiery pitch. My heart turns to stone. I've interacted plenty with scornful monks in Ramla, but a sinister menace emanates from these two.

I point my cutlass at the throat of one monk. "How many others remain below?"

"No others on the gun deck, but there are some on the orlop."

Once we have this handful secured, Manoa stands guard with pistols aimed at them. Saadia and I go down the ladder, covering our faces. Saadia rushes over to the gun ports, opening them to get a crosswind and clear the smoke. I locate the fuming thing and fling it out into the sea. We make a quick search of the gun deck but find the clerics were telling the truth. No one else is on this level. We climb down to the orlop deck where we find the surgeon in the infirmary, attending to two wounded men.

"Your ship is now under the command of Captain Gabriel Coron. As long as you make no move against us, you'll come to no harm," I say.

The physician nods with little enthusiasm. We make a quick weapons search and gather a few knives. Saadia stands guard over the disabled captives while I search the rest of the deck. I take a lantern and make my way to the cargo hold and brig. There is plenty of water, food stores and a galley, but the cook must have gone topside to fight. Shadowy forms totter back and forth in a dark corner of the brig. My gut clenches when I reach it. Staring out from the crisscrossing bars are two young faces, tear-stained with terror in their eyes, a boy about ten, and a younger girl. Behind them in the cell is a man about father's age and a younger woman. This can only mean one thing.

"Please don't hurt them," the woman pleads when I approach the bars.

"Don't be afraid," I say. "Let me get you out of there." I look around until I locate the keys and unlock the cell and open the door. The man steps forward and scrutinizes me up and down. Images of my father's captivity invade my mind.

"How did you come to be imprisoned on this vessel?" I ask. I already know the answer.

"The Inquisition was transporting us to Spain for trial," he says.

I smile. "Not anymore, they're not."

His face brightens. "God be praised."

"This ship is now under the command of Captain Gabriel Coron, *Çiphut Sinai*," I say.

"Judgment of Sinai, what does that mean? Who are you?"

"My name is Yonatan Déulocresca. We carry a letter of marque from the Ottoman Sultan, giving us license to intercept and confiscate Spanish vessels and goods in these waters. Our crew is made-up mostly of Jewish exiles from Spain, from around the Mediterranean. We see it as justice and restitution for losses caused by the Inquisition and the Alhambra Decree."

His mouth drops open. "It's a miracle." He shakes his head and his eyes turn glassy. "You do justice for our people and honor your family name."

I swallow hard as my own eyes grow teary, knowing where my father is at this moment and how he came to be there. My gut twists.

The man drops his gaze and pulls himself together.

"What is your name, sir?" I ask.

"Medina, Avram Medina."

"Honored to meet you, Señor Medina. If only it were under better circumstances. We are liberating this ship. There is still fighting on deck. You can best protect your family if you wait over here in the galley." I hand him one of the knives I collected. "I'll return to let you know when it is safe."

☙

Aaron Déulocresca

I search for the nearest bucket, toss it over the side to draw water, and pull it back on deck. Bending over, I rinse my face and hands. The carnage surrounding me makes my insides heave again, and I cover my mouth with my palm. But only bile burns my throat. I close my eyes and splash water on my face a second time. Then I lean with my back against the gunwale, gasping. It's over. God protected me. But I had to take men's lives to save my own and those of my fellow crewmen. After a few moments, I catch my breath and stand upright. Gazing out at the rosy sunrise, I rock back and forth and whisper the first prayer upon waking. *I'm grateful before you living and eternal King, who returned into me my soul with compassion. Abundant is your faithfulness.*

On the other side of the deck, wisps of smoke rise from the hatch. My pulse surges, knowing that a ship catching fire is life-threatening. They assigned my brother the task of clearing the lower decks. But men clamber out, one after another, coughing and gasping. My pike-wielding crewman hurries over to assist Manoa to bind their wrists and ankles.

Mossé and Umberto come toward us to assess the situation. Mossé looks me up and down, appraising my blood-splattered jerkin, and offers a grim smile. He pats me on the shoulder.

"Well done, Aaron," he says.

My eyes fix on Manoa, who is securing the wrists of a Catholic cleric, now standing on deck. My mouth drops open. Mossé turns to see the source of my surprise. A second cleric stands near the opening to the lower decks. Umberto and I rush over to assist taking them into custody. We've nearly finished securing them when Yonatan emerges from below, reeking of burning pitch.

"There are two wounded and a physician in the infirmary. Saadia is guarding them." Then he leans toward Umberto and whispers something.

"Go inform the captain," he says.

Yonatan nods and rushes toward the prow, crossing back over to La Represalia.

Umberto moves to the binnacle and calls out, "Brave friends, fall in!"

Except for those guarding prisoners, the bruised and bloody crewmen gather around.

"You've fought hard and well. I know you're all exhausted. But we must put this ship in order and prepare to sail for Djerba. You two, get our wounded to our infirmary." He points at two well-muscled crewmen capable of hefting a wounded man over two gunwales and down ladders. "Manoa, Aaron, and Nico, help me move our casualties over here. We'll cover them with a tarpaulin. And then escort the prisoners to the brig. Half in this brig, the other half in La Represalia. The rest of you, clear and swab this deck, put everything in order."

The sailors shake their heads and mutter with bitter smirks, but move back into action. Umberto, Manoa, and I carry two of our dead crewmates under the shelter of the after castle and cover them.

"Nico, I'm assigning you to stay with the bodies for now," Umberto says.

We are about to usher our captives down to the brig when Yonatan returns.

"Hold off, just a few moments. I have Captain's orders." He then climbs back down the ladder and within minutes, the face of a little girl emerges from the hatch, followed by a young boy and then a woman. Finally, a man climbs out, followed by my brother. Everything stops. One and all watch with furrowed brows and pained grimaces.

"These innocent people are the Medina family, who had fled Spain to Ragusa," Yonatan says. "But these murderers pursued them." He points to the clerics, "and kidnapped them from their home to stand trial for heresy in Spain. We saved them from certain death."

My tired eyes glaze and a knot grows in my throat.

Yonatan continues. "Captain Coron asked me to escort them to his quarters." He leads them toward the forecastle. Everyone now shifts their stare to the Catholic clerics. Threats and profane names multiply.

Umberto raises his hand. "We have spilled enough blood today. Despite our sentiments, these men are civilians. Captain Coron will determine their fate."

"We all feel the fire of wrath," says Mossé. "But it is not for us to seek revenge. That would make us no different than they are. Let's get back to work. Rest assured; they will see justice."

CHAPTER 21

La Represalia

Yonatan Déulocresca

THE DOOR TO his cabin stands open when we reach the captain's quarters. He's arranged five place settings around the central table with the morning meal.

"Welcome," says Captain Coron, and ushers the family inside. "Come in. Take a chair."

There's the usual barley porridge, but also hard-cooked eggs, Cretan figs, and dates. The children squeal with gleeful looks at all the delights and then at their mother, who nods her permission. Coron turns to me, handing me a fig.

"Thank you for escorting them, Yonatan. I must speak to the family in private. But if you would, please stand by." He gestures to the exit.

I take my post at the balustrade beside the stairs leading down to the main deck. Most of the crew is still aboard the Spanish vessel. They are busy as an anthill, climbing over every part of the captured ship. Only a handful remain on La Represalia. Our navigator, Khizr, and his page stand above me on the observation deck. And the dawn watch and a gunner are at the prow. There may be others below.

My eyes grow soft and all the tension leaves my body. Since boarding this ship, I've seldom had a moment's solitude with time to even think or reflect. My stomach is growling. It's the first moment in many days I've even considered my own needs. This entire time, my effort has been to do my part as a member of this crew. I didn't stop to think or hesitate. I just did what needed to be done, even when a fiery ball grazed the side of my face. Protecting the ship and crew from invading assassins was the priority; and then stopping a crewmate from bleeding to death. And just now, liberating a family from the Inquisition. I've just been through the most violent bloody whirlwind and survived. My skin tingles with this sense of being so alive and my heart is full. The salty smell of the sea, the smoke, the sweat, the gunpowder, and the sweetness of a ripe fig on my tongue. What a contrast to my life in Ramla.

In Ramla, I was always concerned with how I was being cheated, or what was being denied to me. I was watchful for any remark I could take as an insult, and would hold on to it with angry bitterness. Shuli once said I was impulsive and reckless; that I never consider the consequences of my actions on others. And that recklessness resulted in my father being taken hostage.

But during this voyage, I've been too busy to think about what I want or need, or even my wellbeing. What others call impulsiveness saved the captain from a sniper's arrow. Was it reckless to climb down the ladder of an enemy's hold? Or was it readiness to face danger? It once seemed that I could never do anything right. I was always in trouble. But maybe these faults and shortcomings can be used for good in this world. Caring more for the lives of others, without benefit to myself, has given me an unexpected gift. A sense of honor.

The door to the captain's cabin opens, and he steps outside. "Would you look after these two while I speak to their parents alone?"

"Certainly."

The children stare at me and then their parents. The girl's lower lip trembles.

"Don't worry," I say. "We're just going to sit here on the steps for a short while."

"It will be alright," says their mother. "We'll be just inside."

They return to the cabin and close the door.

"Tell me your names," I say.

The boy puts his arm around his sister. "I am Sami, short for Samuel. And this is my sister Rina. What is your name, Señor?"

"You can call me Yonatan."

"Are you a sailor?" Rina asks.

"I guess you could say so. I'm the captain's helper on the ship. But where I come from, I care for horses and donkeys, and take visitors on journeys to the holy city of Jerusalem."

Their eyes widen and a curious smile brightens the boy's face.

"Jerusalem? Are you taking us there now?" he asks.

"No. We're taking you to safety, a city where you won't have to be afraid anymore."

The door opens again and the parents step outside with the captain. The children stand-up and race to embrace their mother.

"They're going to stay here in Umberto's cabin. He will take charge of the Spanish ship until we reach our destination," says Coron.

"Very well, sir," I say with a nod.

"Report back to our chief gunner for your next assignment."

"Yes, Captain."

"Oh, and let me just say, you've rather impressed me, Yonatan. The way you're carrying out your duties with diligence and compassion. Well done."

"Thank you, sir."

As I start back toward the Spanish ship, the captain's choice of words echoes in my mind. Diligence and compassion. That is the first time anyone has described me that way.

Aaron Déulocresca

By the time we separate the captives and secure them all in the brig, the sun is well above the horizon. Our cook reignites the galley fires. While he prepares a hot meal, Umberto gives us leave for morning prayers. We are just about to start when the page from La Represalia comes over, summoning me to the captain's cabin.

I glance down and realize I'm still dressed in my blood-stained jerkin. When I arrive at Coron's quarters, I quickly remove it, leaving it beside the door. But the sleeves and hem of my tunic still bear the dark red signs of battle. I knock and Coron bids me to enter. To my surprise, the captain is not alone. Also seated here is Dr. Alamosa, who is not only a physician, but a man educated in *Halachah*.

"Please have a seat, Aaron," says Coron. "I asked you here because of your knowledge of the Torah and Talmud. Along with Dr. Alamosa, I'd like to deliberate over several points of the law and come to a decision."

"A decision?"

"Yes, as you know, we're holding two inquisitors in the brig."

I take a deep breath. "The entire crew is riled up against them, and they seek their blood."

"Not surprising, since most of us have lost loved ones, homes, land or businesses because of the Inquisition. Who of us doesn't want to just cut their throats and throw the bodies overboard? But they are civilians."

"Well, that's debatable," I reply. "They're by no means innocent. As Mossé told me; these men would see your mother burned alive, if they could."

"So, we may feel they deserve it," says Coron. "But we must ensure we do the right thing in the service of justice. Should we execute them, or turn them over to be sold as slaves, or held for ransom? There is certainly a financial aspect to our decision. I want to hear arguments for and against. You see, in 20 years, this has never happened, that we actually captured the henchmen of the Inquisition at sea during a battle. Furthermore, the victims of their murderous intent are with us, too."

Dr. Alamosa leans forward. "In the Mishna, in order for an execution to be carried out, it required a Sanhedrin of 23 judges to approve the death sentence."

"But those standards apply to Jews within the community, not enemies," I say.

"Correct," says Coron. "It would be one thing if this were amid battle. But the immediate battle is over, even though a greater war continues. So then, how are we to regard our non-combatant captives?"

"The only direction we have in the Bible," says Dr. Alamosa, "relates to the conquest of the land of Israel and specific peoples like the Moabites or Canaanites."

"Which says, *leave no soul alive*. But that does not apply here, either," I say.

"Why not?" asks Coron. "Aren't they an idolatrous nation that forced their religion on our people?"

"I could see how one might argue that way," I say. "But the rabbis were more concerned with OUR moral character as a people, and our conduct; that we not become cruel and wrathful."

"I agree," says Doctor Alamosa. "We're commanded to have compassion and mercy toward our enemies."

"However, there is one category that I think may still apply," I say. "That of the *din rodef*, one who pursues another intending to murder. Failing to stop the *rodef* violates the commandment, *do not stand by as your brother's blood is spilled*."

"So, you're saying if you catch someone who is pursuing another with the clear intent to murder them, you're obligated to pre-emptively kill him?"

I nod my head. "Exactly. But there are conditions."

"Such as?" Coron asks.

"One must be certain the person actually intends to murder," I say. "Also, that killing the *rodef* is the only way to save the innocent."

"We know these men have killed before. If we don't stop them, they'll continue their crusade to hunt down forced converts and burn them alive as heretics. If we were to let the friars go, they would not stop. They would kill again."

I throw myself back against the chair. "That they were transporting a family for trial proves their intent."

"Every man on this ship has a story, testimony to their murderous actions and intentions."

I meet Coron's gaze and nod my head. He strokes his beard. We both look at Doctor Alamosa, who is nodding with his eyes closed.

"Thank you, gentlemen. I have my answer," says Coron. "Justice is served."

"One other thing," I say. "According to our law, any punishment must preserve human dignity, and be swift to cause the least amount of suffering."

With his elbow on the table, Coron presses his jaw against his fist. His eyes aimlessly search the middle distance. Finally, he blows out a resigned breath.

"Regardless of the malice we feel, or how much we might wish them to suffer, we are not monsters. We'll hang them from the bowsprit. A fall from that height… death should be instant. Nor do we need to make a spectacle of it. Please carry a message to Mossé and Umberto. I want it carried out after dark."

"I will, Captain," I say.

An almost blinding blue sky greets me outside the captain's quarters. I shield my eyes. Grasping my blood-stained jerkin, I head back to the Spanish ship. Exhaustion drains any remaining vigor. An invisible weight slows my gait. At the gunwale atop the forecastle, I stare out at the endless blue.

Yonatan often told me I'm full of arrogance. But today I am truly humbled and chastened. With my own hands, I killed at least four men, and maimed many others. Never would I have imagined doing such things. But it would be justified by the Torah, as *Pikuah Nefesh*, for the sake of a life. Such horrible bloodshed. Now, I have sat in deliberation like a judge, and condemned two Catholic priests to death. I believe it is the right thing to do. However, it gives me no solace, no satisfaction. It only makes me sad that the world is this way. Yonatan and I are out here on this ship with a group of men seeking justice and restitution. But is it? Or are we just robbing and murdering other robbers and murderers? The line between right and wrong has become blurry. I understand now what Coron meant when he talked about struggling for years to make peace with his ghosts and sins; because now I have my own.

CHAPTER 22

Spanish Carrack, San Clemente

Aaron Déulocresca

Doctor Alamosa and I stand beneath the after castle on the Spanish ship, summoned there by Captain Coron. I stare at the two bodies, covered with a tarpaulin. How will I get through this gruesome task? My shoulders curl forward and chest caves. Rocking, I try to muster the grit to face it. Nine buckets of water will be required for each one.

"With no Holy League aboard this ship," Coron tells us. "Preparing the bodies of our fallen rests with the crew. But they know nothing about such matters. They've just been consigning them to the sea."

"But that isn't considered burial at all," I say, shaking my head. "From dust you came and unto dust you shall return."

"Yes, I know. And unfortunately, it will be another day or two until we reach land and can inter them."

My stomach roils. "I didn't bring a copy of the scriptures or prayers we need for this."

"Nonetheless, this is the *Ḥesed shel Emet*, the act of greatest kindness you could do."

I sigh and drop my head. "Very well, I will do the best I can."

Jewish law requires us to bury our dead within a day of passing, or as soon as possible. I've attended a few funerals in my life. But the details for ritual washing and dressing the bodies are something I've only read about; never actually saw or did. There's a brick on my chest and I want to run away.

Doctor Alamosa looks at me and smiles. "Don't worry, Aaron. I'm accustomed to seeing and touching the wounded and the dead. I'll conduct the washing, if you'll handle the liturgy."

"Alright. Hopefully, my memory will serve," I say. I take a deep breath. "Let's begin with a plea for strength." Everyone bows their head and I chant in Hebrew. "Angels of Mercy encircle us and give us the strength to do what is required of us."

Everyone says Amen. Then I turn to Captain Coron.

"Do you know their Hebrew names?"

He takes a piece of paper out of his doublet and then reads it. "Elazar ben Itzhak, he went by Eli. And Nathan ben..." His voice catches and he squeezes his eyes closed a moment. "Reuven. I was so fond of him. We called him Nato." He releases a long sigh and reins in his emotions again.

I speak in a reverent tone. "The Talmud says that the soul lingers near the body for three days before returning to God. So, we will address them as if standing here with us." I step forward and picture the souls of Eli and Nato beside their bodies. A chill snakes down my back.

"We ask for your forgiveness and mean no offense. We will do our best to prepare you for your final journey." Then, I rock as I chant in Hebrew, "Elazar ben Itzhak and Natan ben Reuven, may your souls rest with the righteous, and may you be gathered to your fathers in peace. Blessed is the Lord who pardons and forgives the sins of the dead."

Doctor Alamosa steps forward and lifts the corner of the canvas from the first man. He reaches down and closes the man's eyes. Nico, who's kept watch over the bodies this entire time, helps him. They carefully cut away his clothing while I recite a passage from Zechariah, as best as I can recall it.

"The angel of the Lord spoke, saying remove the filthy garments from him. And the High Priest replied, behold, I have removed your guilt from you and clothed you in robes."

Starting with his right shoulder, they sponge the blood and dirt from his body. I gaze at his face. I didn't know him, but he appears to be about my age or a little younger. This could have been me or Yonatan. The huge gash in his ribs is probably what took him. It's the very same thing I did to another man. I swallow hard. A sensation I've never felt before descends through my chest and stomach, as if a stream of icy water flows through me. I wince through closed lips. Captain Coron turns and glances at me for a moment with a pained brow.

"During the washing, we're supposed to read a certain part of the Song of Songs," I say. "It praises the wonder of the human body. But we have no copy of it, and I don't know the specific verses by heart. Perhaps we could hum the folk melody version," I say. "The important thing is his honor and dignity." I begin swaying and humming the tune. Everyone seems to know it and they join in. A sort of trance settles over us like a mother's lullaby and the chill in my chest wanes.

They finish cleansing each quadrant of his body. It's now the time for purification. One at a time, they pour the buckets of water over his entire body in a stream. I chant the words, *he is pure, he is pure, he is pure*. The water flows onto the floor, out of the after castle, and drains through the openings at the gunwale. Then the doctor covers him. That wasn't as horrible as I expected. I really can do this.

We turn our attention to the second young man. Nico takes the buckets to draw more water, while the doctor trims away the deceased's clothing. I recite the scripture about dressing him in robes.

When we finally complete the ritual purification, it is nearly twilight. I recite a final saying about purity from the Mishna by Rabbi Akiva. Then, Doctor Alamosa and Nico stitch each body inside a shroud, made from a large piece of new sail cloth. To ensure they will not be left alone, per tradition, Coron directs Umberto to assign one crewman to remain with the bodies on each watch. We won't be able to bring them to their rest until we reach the island of Djerba.

Their faces will haunt me for a long time. "I hope our labors honored you," I whisper to the invisible spirits. Turning away from the deceased, I walk to where we tethered the skiff to the San Clemente. I was the only person among the crew who knew how the ritual went. Now both Coron and Dr. Alamosa share that knowledge and can better prepare for future voyages. What good is all my Talmud study if it's not used in the service of others? A smile crosses my lips and I can finally breathe freely.

The sun is setting as we row together back to La Represalia. I gaze at the captain and the doctor with admiration. This was our second collaboration. I'm not even an actual member of this crew, but I've found unique ways to contribute. With their faith in me, I faced an onerous task that seemed impossible at first. But I found the fortitude to overcome my revulsion. I have looked death in the face. It's no longer a shadowy unknown, but a tangible inevitability. I was raised in a tradition that prizes life above all things. But this experience has magnified how precious life is, even more. Life can be taken so easily and pointlessly wasted.

Sunset glitters on the water, and my vision and mind glow with new clarity. Inside me, a hunger and an urgency grow stronger; a yearning to grab onto life and love people more, while we still can. When I reach La Represalia and climb aboard, my brother sprawls out on the deck beside his new found companions, laughing together. The lively gleam in their eyes and their smiles make my chest fill to bursting. Tears well in my eyes.

The darkening sky sparkles in the east with uncountable points of light. Warm night air fills with the mysterious spell of Manoa's *balaban*. He blows on the plum wood instrument while his fingers flutter over the holes. The strain has a touch of melancholy and a cadence that matches the gentle rocking of the ship. My eyelids grow heavy and I yawn. I find my blanket and straw pillow and drag them over beside them.

"Where were you?" asks Yonatan. "You missed supper."

I slouch on the deck against my pillow. "Captain asked me to help with the *taharah* of our two crewmen who were killed."

Manoa stops playing and they all three grow quiet, staring at me wide-eyed.

"Oh, I didn't touch the bodies," I say, shaking my head. "Just led the prayers."

"What a noble act, Aaron," Saadia says. "You probably never imagined you'd be caring for the dead when you came on this voyage."

I shake my head. "No, but someone had to."

"And it's honorable that you did," says Manoa.

Saadia looks at Yonatan and then at me. "And you're not exactly practiced sailors, either. So, why did you two come on this voyage?"

I hesitate a moment, uncertain how much I should reveal about our true purpose. At the start, these men seemed like merciless cutthroats. I even feared them a little. But fighting together, protecting each other, and sharing our laughter; I've come to see them more like brothers. But if they learned of our hidden cache of family assets, what might happen? Could they turn against us, rob us? I take a deep breath. "Since you asked, we came on this voyage hoping to raise a ransom for our own father's freedom."

Yonatan stares at me with raised brows. Then he turns to Saadia. "He's being held by a clan of marauders near Jerusalem."

Saadia's face clouds and he crosses his arms. "So, the Mamelukes don't enforce any laws or protect the people?"

"No, mostly there's a lot of corruption," Yonatan says.

"The courts are often unfair and arbitrary," I add.

"How so?" he asks.

"For instance, there was this Muslim man who got drunk and killed his mother-in-law," I tell them. "But the court blamed the Jews and Christians and ordered our communities to pay a hefty fine."

"What? Why?"

"Because we make and drink wine," I say. "Which is illegal for Muslims. So, he must have got it from one of us, right? We caused it."

"And they let him go," says Yonatan.

Saadia groans. "That's terrible."

Manoa leans in. "But since you've been working and fighting alongside us; I see no reason why you shouldn't receive a share of the spoils like everyone else."

"That would certainly help," Yonatan says, and meets my uneasy stare.

"And what about you, Saadia?" I ask. "How did you end up on a corsair ship?"

"Oh, I love the taste of gunpowder and the smell of steel. No, wait. It's the smell of gunpowder and the taste of steel."

Manoa elbows him. "The taste of blood, you dolt."

"Ah, yes, the taste of blood. But that would not be kosher."

I laugh, but then sit up. "Seriously, brother. What of your family, your home?"

His face grows solemn, his eyes staring off at the night sky. "Like you, they forced my parents to flee Spain when I was only three. I grew up on the island of Tétouan. My father is a metal craftsman." He draws out a tether from his shirt. Dangling from it is a silver hamsa with a blue stone in the center.

"But you chose sailoring over learning his craft?"

"When you work with precious metals and jewels, people like to take them from you."

"Ohhh! He was robbed?"

"Many times. He nearly died. So, when I reached bar mitzvah, I chose to get myself killed a different way. Tétouan being an island, there was no shortage of ships looking for a page they could mistreat. Toughens you up."

"So, you've been doing this a long time," I say.

"More like, endured it. Probably long enough, too."

"Are you thinking of giving it up?" Yonatan asks.

"All the time. But the older I get, the more I understand what is really at stake here; our people's survival and destiny. I've been saving my shares of the spoils for years. And when I find the right place or enterprise, I plan to invest in it. Maybe."

"I see. And what about you, Manoa?"

"My family fled to Salonica," he says.

"That's how he knows Greek, Turkish, and Spanish," says Saadia. "And he knows the right way to cook fish."

Manoa snickers and shakes his head. "My father was a fisherman in Spain."

Saadia rolls his eyes. "He is more than a fisherman. Manoa comes from wealth. His father owns a small fleet of fishing vessels."

"So how did you wind up here?" asks Yonatan.

"It's how I met Captain Coron and was drawn to his mission. Not every exiled family has done as well as mine. It seemed like a sacred obligation."

"That's most honorable of you, too," I say.

He lifts his *balaban* and starts playing again. With the sleepy melody, we all seem to drift into silent contemplation. I slump down into my blanket and gaze up at the myriad of stars. Knowing the motivation behind their passion inspires and reassures me. Both Saadia and Manoa seem financially well off. So, neither one would have a reason to go after our family inheritance. At least I can rest knowing I have found friends I can trust. But that doesn't mean it's safe to reveal the details about the journal, the sea cave, or the hidden cache of riches. It's best to keep that confidential until it becomes necessary.

CHAPTER 23

La Represalia

Yonatan Déulocresca

THE BELL AT the binnacle wakes me from a sound sleep. Khizr's page calls out the hour and the start of the forenoon watch. As temporary boatswain, Mossé is already shouting orders, and the crew jumps into action. When I stand, the first thing I notice is the color of the sea. It's changed from deep blue to brilliant aquamarine over the white sand.

Next to me, Saadia peers over the side. "We're nearly there, *Nuevo*," he says. "Captain will give us shore leave once we've finished our duties. You'll be glad to know there's a Turkish bath and a laundry in the port. I'll be happy to show you where they are."

"You'll be happy? Are you trying to tell me something?" I say, grinning.

He laughs. "Listen, after all that fun we had, everyone smells like piss and alquitrán. Bathing will be a well-earned luxury."

Mossé comes over to us. "Captain wants you to report to his cabin, Yonatan."

"Right away, sir." I hurry across the deck and up the stairs to the forecastle. When I reach Captain Coron's quarters, his door stands open. He looks up from his desk and rises.

"Come in, Yonatan."

I step inside and stand in front of his desk.

"First, I want to say what an admirable job you've been doing. When we first spoke on the veranda at my estate, I had my doubts about your readiness for this voyage. You've fought well, even when wounded. And I'm told you eliminated a sniper that might have killed me."

I lower my eyes, but nod my head. "Yes, sir."

"You've shown yourself to be brave and trustworthy. I commend you."

No one has ever told me that. Warmth grows in my chest and I smile. "Thank you, sir."

"Accordingly, we're about to drop anchor. I have a special assignment for you. Because of your riding experience, I want you to escort the Medina family to the Sephardic village, Hara Seghira. It's only a short distance west of the town. You can take your brother or another sailor, whomever you wish. Also, you'll be transporting the bodies of our fallen crewman for burial in the Jewish cemetery there. Horses and a dray are available at the citadel stable. The rabbi at El Ghriba synagogue will help the family get re-established. Here are the funds you'll need."

Bending over, he lifts a small wooden coffer onto the desk. He opens it, revealing a cache of silver Spanish reales. My stomach flips.

"The San Clemente's crew won't be collecting their wages. Use what you need to gain transport, and pay for Eli's and Nato's graves. Give the rest to the Medinas to compensate for their losses." He hands me a small key.

"Very well, sir. I'd be honored. May I ask, is this a dangerous journey? Do we need to be concerned about thieves?"

"There's always a possibility on remote desert roads. But the penalty for thievery is being hung or having your hand cut off. And it's a small island. Not many places to run. So, take your firearms and blades, just to be prepared."

"I will, sir." But as I say that, there's a sinking feeling in my gut and the hair rises on the back of my neck. No one has ever entrusted me with such an enormous responsibility before. And this one comes with lethal hazards. His trust and confidence in me are so uplifting. I can't disappoint him or fail in this assignment.

"One other thing," Coron says. "It's best to avoid lethal action. You don't want to start a blood vengeance vendetta with the tribesmen here."

"I understand, sir," I say. This warning only adds to the weight on my shoulders.

When I return to the deck, I explain the captain's instructions to Mossé and my aim to bring Saadia with me on this assignment. He looks up into the shrouds.

"I'll tell him when he finishes," he says.

From the crow's nest, a sailor calls out the sight of land. I climb the stairs to the poop deck. On the horizon, domes and pinnacles of a massive white citadel come into view. It appears as if the castle is floating on the water. But as we draw nearer, a sandy bay sweeps in an arch in both directions like welcoming arms. There is no harbor or wharf; only a pristine beach.

Several other ships sit at anchor along the coastline. Landing boats ferry people and cargo to shore. On the eastern arm of the bay, fishing boats, nets, and heaps of ceramic pots for catching octopus crowd the beach. A hand claps me from behind on the shoulder.

"You got me released from duty?" Saadia asks.

"Not exactly. I hope you know how to ride a horse."

"What?"

"We're taking the family to their new home and our crewmen to be buried."

"We have shore duty? Alright, I'll be happy to help," he says. "I know the area."

We stare out at the landscape, which appears flat all the way to the southern horizon. The giant fortress commands the shoreline. It's bordered with date palms and enclosed by notched walls and corner towers. Canopies of a bazaar and a caravanserai spread out beyond it. Camels and horses huddle, tethered around the outside, not unlike Ramla. It calls to mind memories of home and my father's captivity, still weighing on me. But today, I must focus all my efforts on meeting Coron's expectations and returning safely.

Saadia points to the fortress. "That is the Borj El Kabir," he says. "It's the Ottoman naval base under the command of Arūj and Khizr Aga. The Spanish and Italians call them the Barbarossa Brothers. Some say it is because of Arūj's very red beard. But Baba just means Papa. Papa Arūj is a kind of grandfather of corsairs."

That makes me chuckle. "Grandfather? Have you met them?" I ask.

"No, but we might see them. Every corsair I've met who's sailed in their ranks can recount their legendary battles and victories."

We watch a short time as two of our prisoner-filled skiffs row toward the beach.

"What will happen to them?" I ask, pointing.

"That will be up to the Ottomans to decide. They won't execute them, but they might press them into service as galley slaves. Although, they're using fewer galleys and more gunships these days. Most likely, they will keep them here until the Spanish crown pays for their release."

I grow silent; struck by the irony. They will hold these prisoners for ransom at the same time I'm trying to raise a ransom for my father. I stroke my beard and stare at my friend. Saadia studies my face, tips his head, and then his mouth drops open.

"Forgive me, *Nuevo*. My stupidity must have made you think of your father. I'm sorry. But those men there… they will get what they deserve."

I shake my head. "It's alright, Saadia."

"We could have killed them, but we were nice enough to let them live."

"We're far more merciful than they would be to us," I say.

"Exactly. But that's what I like about you and Aaron. You have a heart and conscience. You care about people; even the most despicable ones."

I blink several times. His estimation of me is so different from everything I've been told my entire life; he may as well be describing someone else.

Saadia and I join one skiff transporting prisoners to shore. We arrange for a dray with a driver to convey the dead crewmen, and four horses. Then we send word back to the ship that we're ready to receive them at the shoreline. Secured to biers, they lower the bodies into the long boats and row them ashore. We load them on the dray and cover them with a tarpaulin. The steward uses a smaller skiff to ferry the Medina family and deliver the coffer of Spanish reales.

I would never have thought of myself as a guardian and protector before. But as I help young Sami and Rina mount the horses with their mother and father, I feel resolute that as long as I'm on this journey, no harm will come to any of them. Saadia carries an arcubus across his lap with a smoldering match. I bear a cutlass at my hip and a pistol in my waistband. We protect the family in the middle, with the dray at the rear.

When we go out onto the road, it makes me realize father gave me this same role of honor and trust in his pilgrimage business. But I never saw it as such. In my mind, I was just a lowly donkey-boy doing menial tasks. Had I known what I know now, perhaps al-Dabaa would have thought twice about taking father hostage. But then again, I wouldn't have learned all these things.

As our small company treks through the marketplace to the main route west, I enjoy a feast for the senses. My ears fill with the shouts of venders and the screech of exotic birds in cages. The smell of roasting meats mixes with spices and aromatic café. Light gleams off brass bangles and bolts of cloth stacked in a bright array of colors. There are even shops selling pistols, arcubuses, and black powder. Gradually the number of shops decreases and we find ourselves outside the town. We ignite the wicks on our firearms to ensure our protection for the duration of the journey. I've tucked the coffer with the silver reales between the bodies of our fallen crewmen behind the driver's seat.

Palms flank the hard sod road and provide shade from the punishing sun. We pass through open range dotted with pens for sheep and goats beside white-washed brick dwellings. The landscape reminds me of the Negev and the Sinai deserts, but without the mountains and plateaus. After a time, the road softens to sand and slows our progress with the dray. Up ahead, camels and horses gather beneath a stand of trees.

As we draw closer, it turns out to be an oasis. Goatherds water their flocks. A group of men turn their heads, watching us with narrowed eyes as we pass. They wear bright blue *keffiyot* wrapped Maghrebi style. On their faces, they have indigo tattoos. Swords and pistols bulge from their waistbands. These must be the tribesmen Coron spoke of. Three are on horseback. One rider gallops off in the direction we're traveling. My heartbeat races and I glance edge-wise at Saadia.

"They don't have one of these," he says, jostling the arcubus across his thigh. The driver of the dray carries another. "We have the advantage."

A short distance from the water station, two of the tribesmen ride up behind us. My mouth goes dry and my stomach drops. Ahead of us, the first rider has stationed himself in the middle of the road, blocking our path. We gradually come to a stop. Saadia raises the arcubus, aiming it at him. He reacts by taking out his pistol and pointing it at us. I glance behind us. The two other riders are inspecting the dray.

"What's in the wagon?" says one in Arabic.

I drop back to the rear. His request is so ridiculous it irritates me. What I want to say is, *fresh corpses, would you like some?* But I hold my tongue. Lifting the side of the tarpaulin, I show one of the shrouded crewmen. The odor of decay rises on the breeze, making everyone cover their faces. I'm hoping they don't look closely enough to notice the coffer tucked inside near the driver.

I say back in Arabic. "Two crewmen from our ship. We're taking them for burial."

One rider tosses his head with the click of his tongue. The other wrinkles his nose.

"There is nothing here you want." I narrow my eyes and place my hand on my pistol.

The two exchange glances, turn and gallop away. Covering the bodies again, I take a breath. Saadia keeps the arcubus trained on the other man. The marauder glares back at him. At first, he seems to be departing. He slowly rides until he reaches the family. But Señora Medina and Rina catch his interest, although they are veiled. He stops beside them, looking them up and down. I glare with heat behind my eyes. Señor Medina slowly slides the cutlass I gave him out of its scabbard. I meet Saadia's gaze and he gives me a nod. I pull my pistol and fire, intentionally aiming wide to miss the tribesman. Saadia swerves his horse around behind him, pointing the arcubus at the man's back.

"That was just a warning. The next one will blow your head from your shoulders," I say. "Make dust."

He growls but gallops away. We watch until none of the marauders are in visual range, and then I reload my pistol.

"All is well," says Señor Medina, who sheathes his sword and nods with a tense smile.

"Let's get out of here," says Saadia and returns to the lead. I take up the rear, and we continue our sojourn. But I can't help recalling the day al-Dhbaa's henchmen encircled us. One blast from an arcubus would have brought them to their knees. What a difference it would have made if father and I had been armed.

When we complete our assignment, Saadia and I return the way we came. But we don't encounter the tribesmen, or even see them at a distance. Bringing the horses to the stable at the fort, we find our way into the bazaar. I'm drawn to a jeweler selling all manner of pendants, rings, and cloak pins. Knowing what may lie on my horizon, I buy a hamsa, not unlike the one Saadia's father made for him. We also purchase fresh clothes and head to the Turkish baths. It's a welcome relief to soak in the fresh warm water after steeping in fishy salt water, piss, blood, and *alquitrán*. After an evening meal, Saadia and I return to the ship to get some sleep.

I report back to the captain on the successful resettlement of the Medinas and the final destiny of our crewmen. This includes the brief encounter with the marauders that ended without bloodshed.

"Well done," he says. "You should feel proud of your accomplishments. Once again, you've exceeded my expectations."

A smile takes over my face and I stand tall, despite my fatigue.

"Tomorrow, once we fully resupply, we'll turn our attention to the reason you came on this journey; to search for your family's assets. Umberto will inform the crew about the nature of our errand as *Pidyon Shevuiim* and instruct them to cooperate with you in whatever way you may need. The islands are about 12 hours' sail. Khizr is familiar with the area. However, should we encounter another Spanish ship; just be aware of our priorities. Whatever the outcome, we will bring you safely back here and determine the best way to get you home."

"I'm very grateful, Captain." I bid him goodnight and leave with a bow. Warmth radiates through my body and wakeful energy drums through my chest. I want to share the good news with my brother and friends, but Saadia has already curled up with his blanket on the main deck and is fast asleep. Aaron and Manoa lie nearby. Although I am bone tired, I can't shut my mind off. The images of the Maghrebi tribesmen flash in my head. I stood up to them and protected the family, despite the fear roiling in my gut. I never thought I was capable of that kind of courage.

Stars are scattered across the black velvet sky and the air is balmy. In the glow of the night watch's lantern, I admire the intricate patterns on the gleaming hamsa. By this time tomorrow, we might finally have the answer to the mystery. I picture the faded drawings in father's journal and imagine what these places might actually look like. Will we really be able to find this place? Is the family fortune still stashed in a sea cave? Or is it long gone? And if so, what will we do then? I squeeze the amulet in my palm.

CHAPTER 24

La Represalia

Aaron Déulocresca

When I awaken, I'm surprised to find grey skies and there is a chill in the air. After a bowl of morning porridge, I climb the stairs to the forecastle deck. Mossé studies a dark mass of clouds emerging on the western horizon.

"We're in for a rough start to our day," Mossé says.

The ship is beating with a north by northwest heading on the Ghibli.

"I've heard from several crewmen that the Straits of Sicily are risky," I reply.

"Always," says Mossé. "The colder winds of the north can make a dangerous mixture when they meet the warm winds from off the desert. It's unpredictable."

Light rain begins to fall. Umberto shouts orders to the crew to reef all sails but the mizzen. I watch Saadia and Manoa scurry up the shrouds to assist.

"Doesn't gathering the sails slow us down?" I ask.

"That is to prevent a gale from toppling us over," says Mossé. "When the sails get too wet and heavy, the wind can snap a mast, or pry it loose from the hull. Both are fatal catastrophes we must avoid."

"But you're leaving that triangular sail at the stern," I say.

"To keep the ship pointed in the right direction. But it may be necessary to heave-to."

"What does that mean?"

"We fix the helm and sail positions, go below, seal the hatches, and wait out the storm. The force of the wind on the masts and rigging can still push a ship along, hopefully ahead of dangerous waves."

Rain is falling in sheets. The air prickles with an eerie aura, making the hair on my arms stand on end. There's a metallic taste on my tongue. A blinding flash cracks open the sky. Thunder rolls across the water, louder than the crashing waves.

"Hold on," shouts Mossé.

I grip the gunwale. The ship rises and dives from prow to stern. The bow plunges into a huge swell. White spray explodes in every direction, drenching my head and shoulders. When it recedes, I can see the cloud bank is coming closer.

Within moments, Umberto orders the yardarms lowered. With a dozen other crewmen, Yonatan gets on the lines, struggling to haul them down on the slick deck.

"Come with me to the gun deck," says Mossé. "We need to double-check the ropes on the cannons. We don't want them breaking loose, damaging the ship, or crushing anyone to death."

I climb down the ladder behind Mossé and plant my feet in a few inches of water, sloshing back and forth on the gun deck. With the undulations of the ship, water on the deck above is leaking through the covering to the hatch and down into the decks below. It's also seeping between the planks. We test each of the lines securing the four cannons. Nothing has shifted, despite the heaving of the ship. But the squeak of straining timber and rope puts me on edge.

"We fastened them as good as can be," Mossé says. "Go below and help the men on the bilge pump. They most surely need relief. If they stand in that cold water too long, they can get the shivers, become confused, and even die. Everyone needs a turn to get warm again."

I descend to the orlop deck. Here the water reaches me mid-calf. It takes little to figure out that if we do not pump the water out fast enough, the ship will sink lower. More waves will flood the deck and it could sink us.

Two men furiously wind the handles on a mechanism that draws water up and out through ports on each side of the hull.

"Can I help? Let me take a turn," I say.

My crewmate is happy to have a respite and moves aside, allowing me to take his position. The crank is difficult to rotate and requires more effort than I expected. After a time, another crewman relieves my fatigued partner and the two of us crank away hard and fast. As we labor away, this continuous movement makes the muscles in my shoulders and arms burn, and then weaken and nearly fail. Other sailors notice our teeth chattering. They step in to take their turns, while we warm ourselves in blankets. With a constant trickle seeping in from above, the water level doesn't seem to change much.

The rise and fall of the vessel worsen. I find myself again in the grips of nausea and vertigo like the first time I sailed. But I'm not the only one feeling queasy. Even the most seasoned among us falls ill. But they all seem to take this in stride and pass a bucket to the next man in need, including me. The stench down here is almost more than I can bear. But, despite the stink of vomit, sweat, and mold, the four of us work as a team to pump the foul brine from the bowels of La Represalia. I lose all awareness of how long we're laboring until finally a dim shaft of light falls from the upper decks. They've opened the hatch. It must be safe to go topside. Someone rings the bells, signaling the end of the watch. It's been hours. I finish my turn at the crank handle and then take my leave and go up for some air.

It's still blustery, and light grey clouds are making their transit across the sky, but the rain has stopped and the sun is high overhead.

The violent rolling of the ship has diminished. Crewmen are scrambling around the deck, assessing the condition of the masts and rigging.

Navigator Khizr is taking a reading with the astrolabe. He goes into the chart room, returns a short time later, and approaches the boatswain. Umberto then calls out commands for setting the sails and rudder; and the crewmen again raise the yards and unfurl the sails. It's a wondrous thing to see all this unfold. I have such respect and admiration for this crew and their skill, and this amazing craft we are riding on.

I peel loose the damp robe clinging to my skin to let the air dry me. The fresh sea breeze feels good against my skin. My head aches, but the nausea has diminished with the calming of the waves.

A weight pulls on one side of my hem and I'm suddenly aware of what is still sewn inside my clothes; my father's journal. I'd not given it much thought, knowing I safely hid it from the eyes of others. But as I slide my hand down my thigh, my alarm grows. The bottom of my robe got soaked. Father's journal could also be wet. My heart sinks.

Where can I go to even take it out and evaluate? There is no private place on this deck, save the gardens. But the longer it remains wet, the greater the damage that might be done. I walk from one end of the deck to the other, searching for a safe corner. Everyone seems quite occupied getting the ship back in motion toward the coast of Sicily and the islands. But if the journal is damaged, how will we ever find the islands, or the caves? Maybe there is a place secluded enough on the gun deck. No one should be at the cannons right now.

I climb down to the lower deck. They sealed the magazine at the prow tight as a drum. There are shelves holding replacement sails and rigging. At the stern end, the whipstaff comes down through the deck and below to the rudder. Another locked storage vault and galley are just beyond that. Squeezing in between shelves of canvas and thick hemp rope, I sit on a crate, turn back the hem of my robe and examine the inner pocket. Carefully, I pluck out the stitching on the top edge and slide out the journal. To make sure no one is watching me, I check my surroundings. Then I open the cover. My heart falls. Water got inside the cover and made the ink bleed along the lower half of the pages. I cautiously peel the pages apart, one after another, with growing horror and alarm. The damage is throughout. Some illustrations in the top portion remain. But the navigational description and mathematical calculations are blurred and almost impossible to read. I don't know what to do.

Blood pounds at my temples and the room spins. It takes several deep breaths for the vertigo to subside. I need to find a way to dry the pages without smearing them worse. Where is a warm dry place? I wander over to the galley where the *cocinerillo* is building a fire in the brick firebox to cook a cauldron of beans for the evening meal.

He looks up at me. "There's nothing but *galleta* until evening," he says. "Perhaps a bit of cheese."

"I don't want food, Señor. I need the heat of your oven."

"What for?"

"My book got soaked in the storm and will be ruined if I don't get it dry. I was hoping I might sit here and dry the pages."

"I don't see any harm in that. Just keep out of the way or I'll put you to work."

I draw a halting breath. At least I've found a possible remedy. "Gracias," I say. I hold the book upright, fanning the pages so the hot dry air can circulate between them. If it takes me day and night, I'm going to stay here and save this book. Only time will tell if it's going to work.

We've been through so much and come so far. If this expedition is in vain because of my carelessness, it would be terrible. I should have known better. I failed to protect it. How will Yonatan take it when I tell him?

∽

Yonatan Déulocresca

This was quite a day. I'm aching from top to bottom and all I want right now is a hot meal, a cup of wine and a hunk of that bread we brought from Djerba.

"I've been through far worse storms than this one," says Saadia.

"Try sailing the Aegean, if you want to know about storms," says Manoa.

"I, for one, am ready for a game of cards," Saadia replies.

I shake my head. "Me, I'm ready for a long sleep."

We clamber down the ladder to the gun deck and stand in line to be served a bowl of *adafina*, the savory stew of beans and lamb with garlic and onions. While it does not even come close to what mother would make for the Sabbath, just the aroma alone makes my belly rumble.

When I reach the head of the line, I notice Aaron standing elbow to elbow with our *cocinerillo*, ladling bowls of hardy stew with a slab of *galleta*.

"What are you doing? Is this your new assignment?" I ask.

He stops mid-task and stares at me with red eyes. "Not exactly. I must talk to you."

"What's wrong?"

"Eat first. I'll come find you."

"Alright." I take my food and walk over to the usual spot among the crates with my friends. Saadia has already filled our cups and I bring out the loaf of bread we purchased in the bazaar in Djerba. The deck is noisy and crowded as the crewmen finish their tasks and attend to the call of their bellies. We make a blessing of thanks for having survived the day of dangerous hard work, and drink our wine.

After finishing our meal, we return our crockery to the galley. Saadia has brought out the cards when Aaron comes toward us. He's holding something against his chest and motions me over with his other hand.

"I'll be right back," I say to my friends and sidle out from the arrangement of crates. "What's gotten under your skin?" I ask.

"Let's talk in private," he says, and leads me to an area with tall shelves where we store extra lines and sheets. In the soft glow of the lantern on the overhead beam, I see his eyes grow glassy, and he clears his throat.

"Something bad happened today."

I cock my head at an angle as my stomach clenches. "What do you mean by bad?"

"It's the journal," he says, just above a whisper.

I gape. "THE journal?"

He nods and holds out father's leather-bound navigation journal. I take it from him and can immediately feel the dampness in the book's spine. A groan escapes my lips. "No."

"A lot has been smeared. Only a few parts are still readable."

I huff. "Shit!" I shake my head. "How?"

Aaron draws a breath. "They sent me to the bilge pumps and in the urgency of trying to prevent us from sinking, it didn't even cross my mind."

I rub my forehead. My heart thuds and the meal I just ate is like a stone in my gut. Opening the journal, I hold it up to the light. With my thumb, I try to fan through the pages, but they are too soggy.

"In the galley, I tried my best to dry the pages in the hot air. But as you can see, the damage is considerable."

"On the most important pages?" I ask.

"Those pages are faint and blurry," he says. He squints to hold back tears.

I sigh. "We'll figure it out, Aaron. These sailors know these waters well. I'd be surprised if they haven't been to the islands many times already. I trust them. We'll find the place, one way or another."

"I thought you'd beat me senseless," he says.

"None of us planned for this storm. It's a good thing our captain and crew are well-practiced and smart. Let's have hope, brother. We may still find the sea cave. All is not lost yet."

CHAPTER 25

La Represalia

Yonatan Déulocresca

My brother just finished helping Khizr take a sounding. The two cross the deck to me.

"We're getting closer," says Khizr. "Fortunately, the storm did not send us too far off course. Let's hope we have fair weather the rest of this voyage." He turns and walks toward the after castle to note the measurements in his log.

I was already annoyed after the storm delayed us by a day. But now I'm like a horse kicking to get out of its stall. We need to find this place as soon as possible so we can get back home before it's too late. Anything that slows our progress now will just add to my frustration.

"Look what I discovered," Aaron says. He's holding father's journal, slanting it at an angle in the sunlight.

I grumble. "What is it now?"

He flinches and then tilts his head. "What's wrong with you? I thought you'd be pleased. I just wanted to show this to you. You know how the ink on the lower portion of the pages was washed away?"

I nod my head. "And?"

"Once the pages dried, I noticed that the tip of father's quill etched the parchment. So, I tried brushing a little charcoal over it, blowing off the residue. See."

I study the pages for a moment. "Look at that. It settled into the scratch marks."

"Exactly. It's not likely to last. But I can transcribe the parts that are legible. At least we'll have that. Most of the drawings on the tops of the pages are faint, but they survived. I feel more reassured it can help us find the cave."

"That's a relief. I thought for sure it was ruined."

"But there is something else we should talk about," he says.

"Such as?" I lean against the gunwale and fold my arms.

"They're going to an awful lot of trouble just for us." His brows pinch into a knot. "Aren't you the least bit worried? Coron's gone deep into his pocket for this risk. They expect something in return."

I shake my head, not quite grasping what he's getting at. "We've gone to a lot of trouble for them, too, risking our lives. I think we've lived up to our side of the *Hezchem*. You think they're going to double-cross us?"

He drops his gaze, pressing his hand to his chest. "It's not that at all. But my stomach is doing flips. My heart is in my throat. I'm not sure I should say it aloud so as not to jinx things."

"Jinx things." That stops me cold. It takes a moment to recover. "Then don't say it."

I know why Aaron is so on edge. He fears the same thing that gnaws at the back of my mind. I should have known. When I get annoyed or angry for no obvious reason, something is brewing underneath. What if there is no cache of family riches? What if thieves have already found them? Not only will there be no ransom money to save our father; but Coron will be out his investment. And every crewman with a stake in this will feel cheated and robbed. What will we do then?

"I want to believe we can count on them," I say.

"Me too. They claim they're doing all this for justice, to restore what was lost, and for *Pidyon Shevuiim*. In some ways, we are no different than the Medinas. We might have pitched in as members of the crew, but we are their mission, too."

"I hope they see it that way. Let's focus on trying to find it."

He waves the journal. "Then I'll get to it." He turns, walking toward the chart room.

My gut feels like I swallowed a cannon ball.

෴

Manoa calls out the first sighting of an island from the crow's nest just after four bells in the afternoon watch. From this distance, the island appears like a giant shard of layered limestone tilted at an angle. We drift on the cool wind in waters the color of lapis lazuli. As we draw closer, the sea floor turns white and the water changes to luminous aqua. Irregular indigo patches cluster around the perimeter. These must be the shoals.

A fever spreads over me and my legs grow restless. Inside, my stomach is churning. I hurry around the deck hunting for my brother. The page at the binnacle tells me he last saw Aaron with navigator Khizr. They must be in the chartroom. When I approach the door, it stands ajar. I knock against the doorframe and Khizr bids me to enter. He and Aaron lean over a map spread across the table.

"This is where we are," Aaron says, pointing to a spot on the map. His face beams and he bites on his lower lip.

I lean in. My breath bottles up in my chest for a moment as I gaze at the map.

"Seems there are three tiny islands isolated out here in the middle of nowhere," says Aaron. "Looks like we've found the general area." He smooths the front of his clothing and raises his eyebrows at me. My belly flutters.

"The island that just came into view is the largest and is called the

Isle of Torches," says Khizr. "Legend tells of a torch-lit signal tower on it. The Saracens probably built it to warn ships of the rocky shoals."

Aaron gasps. "A lighthouse? Our father wrote about finding some ruins on a parapet that overlooked a crescent bay." He waves his hand in an arch. "That's where the caravel Jubilee went aground, on some reef."

Khizr tips his head. "Well then, perhaps you should begin by searching the perimeter for this parapet."

My chest expands like our wind-filled billowing sails. Please, let it be the place. When we emerge from the chartroom, Umberto has ordered the crewmen to furl sails and drop anchor. He comes over and clasps me on the shoulder. "Gather what you need. Then, report to the Guardián. We'll have the longboat ready for you to go ashore. Everyone's hoping you find what you're looking for."

"Thank you," I say. I request that Saadia and Manoa accompany us.

The crew loads the long boat with drinking water, galleta, weapons, and a lantern. We each take a pistol, check the powder and insure it's loaded with a ball and wadding. We then lower the boat into the water alongside the ship.

"Let's make a circuit around the island. Hopefully, we'll find the landmark."

"And what exactly would that be?" asks Saadia.

"We're looking for an old signal tower on top of a high plateau," says Aaron.

The four of us descend the ladder to the longboat. Manoa sits at the stern and clasps the rudder to steer us. The three of us sit facing him and begin to row. My pulse pounds hard in my throat. As we get closer to shore, Manoa tells us to row only on one side and he veers the longboat to parallel the coastline. The boat rocks gently as small waves splash against it. Chalky cliffs rise from the sea floor, cleft by deep gorges. At their roots, the ocean has carved out a grotto, but there is no beach. Seagulls and cormorants swoop and wheel around the rock face. We continue rowing west and swing wide around a more pronounced rocky barrier. I'm huffing and covered in sweat when we reach the farthest point west. There amid the craggy rocks, the large skeleton of a ship's hull angles up from the reef against the sky.

"Father wrote about finding a shipwreck. Not much remains of it," says Aaron. Everyone stares at the carcass in ominous silence as we paddle past, knowing sailors probably met their end here. We come around to the south face of the island. The cliffs gradually melt away to a lagoon, surrounded by a rocky shore and a massive reef. The water here has a greenish tint from plant life and is teeming with fish. I glance over my shoulder at Aaron.

"Can I look at the drawings?" I ask.

Aaron stops rowing for a moment to take out the journal. He hands it to me and I start pawing through the pages, searching for anything that resembles what we see in front of us. But no drawings look like this. The afternoon is slipping away and we've still not found it.

"A lot of good this is," I mutter, handing the journal back to Aaron. "Let's hurry past this area. We're wasting time." I take up oars again and throw my strength into rowing harder.

We make a sweep around several enormous freestanding columns of rugged stone. Beyond them, we discover a broad arching cove. Brilliant aqua surf laps onto the white sand beach. A few large seals sprawl just beyond the water's edge. I notice several cavities in the rocks above the tidal markings.

"Look there, those would be good hiding places," I say.

Aaron and our shipmates point and comment. I grab the journal again and scour the smeared pages.

"But I don't see any cliffs here," says Manoa.

"There's no watch tower, either," says Saadia. "Let's keep going."

We round the far end of the cove that juts out to a cape. There's another cluster of stone pillars studding the shoreline. Beyond them, a second, broader bay comes into view. I straighten. Craning my neck, my eyes rake over the landscape. This bay has a sloping escarpment rising to a bluff. My mouth goes dry and my heart pounds hard in my throat. As we come around to the other side of the pillars, a vast patch of indigo spreads out beneath the water to our right. A sandy land bridge links the cove to a tiny island. I raise my eyes to the top of the ridge. There on the crest stands a tumbled down Ashlar block structure.

"Aaron, look," I say. "There it is!" A tingle surges down the back of my neck.

"It sure looks like it." He pivots in his seat the other way and points. "That area in the reef would have been where the ship might have gone aground. And over there, that looks like where they could have stowed the cargo."

"Shall we steer ashore and explore?" Manoa asks.

We heartily agree, and Manoa turns the rudder toward the shallows. We glide into the sand, which alarms a handful of seals. They immediately hobble to the water and swim away. We haul the boat out of the surf onto the beach. Aaron opens the journal and charges off, jabbering and pointing.

"Don't get too far away," Saadia calls. "Let's scout out the safety first. We don't want any unpleasant surprises."

Aaron hikes back and holds out the journal, displaying an illustration for all to see. In the corner at the top is a trace of a compass rose designating this vista as looking west. He points skyward, tracing the sun's course.

"See, we're here. Ampoletta Shoals, father called it," says Aaron, "There's the hourglass shape of the terra firma with a sandbar connecting it."

My stomach clenches. "I think we've really found it," I say.

"Alright, then," says Saadia. "Aaron and Manoa, you survey the far side of the cove; and Yonatan and I will take this near side."

We take out our pistols and ignite the wicks from the lantern. Saadia brings the lantern along, in case we discover the cave. The two of us slog through soft sand toward the near side of the cove, studying the landscape. The sandy shore gives way to packed ground and fine grit.

Bushes and shrubs cluster around large rocks and crevices. Tall wild grasses wave in the breeze. It's silent here, except for the sound of gulls and the gentle splash of water lapping against the sand. There are no people, structures, or other seacraft anywhere in sight. From here, La Represalia looks like a child's plaything that could fit in my hand. We find the foot of the precipice, but there is no way to climb up from here.

My brother's voice calls from the distance and we jerk our heads toward them. He's waving both of his arms over his head. My heart thumps in my throat. Saadia and I scramble over the soft terrain toward Aaron and Manoa. I can see a strange formation made of sandstone. Bands of white and yellow layers span the face of the palisade like bread and butter. But the cliff face looks like someone has chipped away at it, forming stairs or terraces about knee height. Aaron shakes the journal.

"It's El Teatro, I just know it." He points to another blurry illustration. "We're close. The sea cave has got to be right here." He holds out his hands and pivots.

"It looks like an ancient Greek amphitheater or colosseum," says Manoa.

My insides go watery. Everyone is smiling and buoyant. I follow the lower edge of the rock formation until it butts up against a jagged stone pillar. The foaming tide laps against my feet as I sidle around it. On the other side, boulders jut from the wet sand, encrusted with barnacles. Pinkish gray shore crabs skitter everywhere. I squeeze in between the boulders to the mound of dry sand beyond. That's where I notice what appears to be a crevice or recess on the cliff. I gasp.

"Brothers, I may have found something," I shout.

The other three come swerving around the jagged column, splashing through the surf. Aaron arrives first and stares up at it with his mouth agape. We look at each other, eyes ablaze. He edges in between the boulders to me and we clamber to the opening. Saadia and Manoa follow behind us. It's not quite the height of a man. We have to hunch over, but the two of us easily fit through. Crabs scuttle out of the way. As we enter, the air is musty with a tang of salt.

"You think this is the cave?" asks Aaron. His voice echoes. That is the first telltale sign. My heart sinks.

It's dark inside, but after a few moments, my eyes adjust. Then Saadia brings the lantern. The candlelight reveals how the space widens and the ceiling is jagged and uneven. There's a flat stone surface beneath drifts of sand, almost as if a floor had been laid. It's hard to tell how large the cavern really is.

"This can't be it," I say. "It looks empty."

Aaron and Saadia walk around the perimeter, searching with the lantern for hidden clefts or recesses. Saadia bends down and grabs hold of something, a dark amorphous shape.

"What is that?" I ask.

"Cloth, it seems. Perhaps canvas." Saadia drags it toward me and it frays apart.

"Maybe it's an old sail or tarpaulin," says Manoa.

Aaron's brow furrows. He shakes his head and backs up against the wall of the cave. His hands go limp and his dark eyes stare into nothingness.

Shuffling around, I brush aside the accumulated sand with my feet. One foot collides with a hidden object. I bend down. It's something cold and metallic, like a sword. Bringing it toward the light, it looks like a rusted barrel hoop. I know what this means. I grit my teeth and fling it aside. Pointing at the journal in my brother's hand, I hiss through my teeth.

"But he said the Janissaries couldn't find it." I feel cold all over, and shudder.

Manoa comes over and grabs me by the forearm. "I found this in the sand, over there," he says and places a single tarnished coin in my hand. I close my fingers around it, and a lump swells in my throat.

The four of us make a final close search of the cave's floor and crevices, but all we recover is another barrel hoop and planks of splintered rotted wood. My body goes numb and I stumble toward the opening. Aaron is right behind me, frantically scouring the pages of father's journal.

"No, no, no, this can't be it," he says, panting. His face twists and chin trembles.

Standing between the shoreline boulders, I stare at him. He drops the journal and takes his head in his hands, keening and trembling. I lift my eyes to see Saadia and Manoa at the cave opening. Their heads are bowed and faces somber. My chest heaves to hold back a cry and my eyes grow glassy. I reach for my brother and embrace him as a groan escapes my lips. The sound that erupts from Aaron's mouth is like the death cry of a man pierced in the belly by a sword. I squeeze Aaron in my arms, bobbing as if in prayer. The tide splashes in between the rocks at our feet and then recedes again, leaving a haze of spindrift. Our rocking movement gradually slows, melding into the sea's gentle rhythm.

It's really gone. Taken. We've come all this way for nothing.

CHAPTER 26

LA REPRESALIA

Yonatan Déulocresca

THE PROW CUTS through the water effortlessly, on a return course to Djerba. We're sailing against the wind, tacking back and forth in a sawtooth pattern. As we prepare to change the direction of the bow again, Umberto calls loudly.

"Ready about!"

We scramble to prepare the lines and carry out the tacking maneuver. "Ready," we holler back. My head is pounding so hard; it feels like the veins at my temples could burst at any moment. I grit my teeth.

"Thieves, marauders, whoever they were, I could strangle them with my bare hands," I say to Saadia.

"With the force you're hauling that line, it's easy to tell. Don't over tighten," he says.

"I want to shoot someone, stab them in the fucking guts."

"No one's trying to talk you out of it. We're all angry right along with you."

"But there's no way of ever finding them, which makes me even more mad." I growl through my teeth.

A few moments pass and Umberto shouts again. "*Helm to lee.*"

The ship gradually steers to starboard. Finally, we hear the order, lee ho. We watch and listen as Manoa and the other teams trim the jib and adjust the halyard. Once complete, the wind is blowing on the other side, and we can adjust the lines to trim the mainsail. We're both panting when we finish. I hunch over to catch my breath. Then straightening, I stare at Saadia with a clenched jaw. He studies my face.

"I don't blame you," he says, breathless. "Your rage is justified, *Nuevo*. But ultimately, the Inquisition and the Spanish crown are responsible for your losses." His voice darkens. "That's where you should direct your wrath. Your family should never have been forced to flee, transport their assets, or hide them in a cave."

My tone deepens to match his. "Now I understand the bitterness and drive for justice and reparations. After all our time and effort, I'm furious that we have to go home empty-handed."

"I'm sorry, *Nuevo*."

"Meanwhile, my father is still in captivity. I don't know what to tell my mother. She was counting on us."

"Perhaps Coron will cut you in on a portion of the spoils from the San Clemente," Saadia replies.

"I doubt that. We probably owe him now for the wages and provisions of this voyage. We signed the *Hezchem*, promising a portion of the family assets."

"But there was nothing to get. That's not your fault, *Nuevo*. And it wouldn't be the first time Coron led us on a fruitless mission."

"Really?"

"One time we traveled seven days to stake out the Costa de la Luz for incoming vessels laden with riches returning from the New World. But there was absolutely nothing of value, and the poor bastards were starving and sick. Over half the crew had died. Some were *conversos* who ended up joining us."

"That's beyond belief. So, he just absorbed the loss?"

"It's the nature of being a corsair, *Nuevo*. It's feast or famine."

"I'm just afraid that by the time I get home, I'll be reduced to poverty. Then I'll end up washing dishes, pouring coffee, and catering to ill-mannered patrons at a caravanserai."

Saadia bunches his nose. "You'll what?"

"A family friend offered us jobs to raise the ransom, if we failed. That damn crime lord!

"A crime lord?" His eyes widen.

"Yes, there's a tyrannical clan leader who has been threatening local businesses if they don't pay protection money. He runs a brothel, traffics in stolen goods, and secretly sells wine to Muslims. After I won a fair wager, he tried to bully me out of my winnings. When I refused to surrender the money, he wanted revenge. So, he took my father hostage, and demanded triple the amount."

"I knew your father was being held for ransom. But I didn't grasp that a *Jefe del crimen* was involved."

"He deserves to be in jail for extortion. Add to that kidnapping, assault, and horse thievery. But everyone is afraid of al-Dabaa and would never dare oppose him. The only recourse is to pay the ransom. How will I ever do that?" I punch the air.

"Perhaps you've been asking the wrong question," says Saadia.

I pinch my brows together. "What do you mean? What question would you ask?"

"You're not thinking like a corsair. The question is not, how will I raise the ransom? The better question is, how do I free my father from his captors?"

I go completely still.

"And *Nuevo*, you already have the answer. If the rings fall off, the fingers still remain. But you've grown up in a land that so squashes your spirit that you got used to this lowly status, being treated like dirt. The very thought of standing up for yourself never enters your mind."

My mouth drops open. He's right. I've been going about this all wrong; chasing after a fantasy of riches and hoping to buy father's freedom. When what I should have focused on is bringing the judgment of Sinai to these criminals.

"Justice," I blurt out.

Saadia gives a sly smile and nods his head. "You don't need a stinking ransom. Just go get him, liberate your father. You said you wanted to shoot or stab someone."

"Why didn't anyone say this before?"

"I suppose we all had a stake in your finding the cache of riches. But would you have been able to hear it before now?"

"Probably not. But there is a whole band of cutthroats. I don't know if I can do it alone."

"Maybe not. But it's no different than taking over a ship of armed Spanish sailors."

I look aside, reflecting for a moment on the battle for the San Clemente. Our fire power, smoke bombs, and incendiaries gave us an advantage. I clasp my forehead. Aaron had mentioned using firearms before, but I didn't catch his meaning at the time.

"These marauders have no experience with such things as matchlock pistols, arcubuses, or grenados," I say. "We'd easily overpower them. And the Mamelukes would know these weapons came from outside the land. So perhaps they would suspect outsiders, and not us."

"Could be. Even in small numbers, you have a distinct advantage."

"Come with me Saadia. You and Manoa, both. Come to Jerusalem."

He glances away. "I had always dreamed of one day visiting the Holy City. But I didn't know anyone there, not to mention I'm a wanted man."

"You'd be welcome in my home. And now, the Spanish would label me a criminal, too."

"I might consider helping you. You see, I'm well acquainted with this type of brute. When I told you my father had been robbed several times and nearly died, that was the reason. Make no mistake. This al-Dabaa won't stop, even if you pay him. He'll just come back for more. In my case, the bastard was a government official, demanding the *jizya*."

"What is a *jizya*?" I ask.

"In Islamic law, the government is allowed to levy a tax on every person of *dhimmi* status, just because they are Jews or Christians. The problem is, the Quran doesn't specify how much, leaving room for impossible extremes and personal grift. And that is why I can never go home to Tétouan, because I put an end to him."

I stare at Saadia wordlessly for a few moments. "That's justice," I finally say.

"Yes, but what he was doing was technically legal. What al-Dabaa is doing is not. There are probably more than a few who'd welcome his passing."

"So come with me. You said you wanted to build a new life, start a business. You could even bring your father to the Holy Land to live out his days."

Saadia sighs and stares off in the distance. "He's grown so frail. He'd love that."

"What about Manoa?"

"Manoa will have to speak for himself, but he might agree. He has a sister in the port city of Acre he's not seen for many years."

"Won't Coron be upset if you leave?"

"Sure, he'll miss my lovely smile. But I've given him ten years. That's enough time. He'll find another sailor, and I'll find another venture."

My mood brightens. "Fantastic. Let me go tell Aaron. You know how devastated he is," I say, and turn to scurry over to the forecastle. "I'll be right back."

"Oh sure. Go right ahead. These sails will simply adjust themselves."

⚜

Aaron Déulocresca

This post on the forecastle as dawn watch makes a good retreat, as I don't really want to talk to anyone right now. Sleep evaded me all night, and I've lost any appetite. The heaviness in my body anchors me to this spot. All strength has drained away and all I want to do is stare out at the blue horizon.

How could I have been so stupid? There must really be some defect in my mind to have believed the family assets would just be sitting there, waiting for us to walk in and pick them up. Weeks have been wasted on this fool's errand that has proved to be an illusion. The only solution I see is to remain a corsair with Coron, and take more spoils and more lives. But I can't accept the idea of becoming a professional killer. I'm at the end of my tether.

So, what is there for me to go back to? There is Rehm? Can we eke out a living together in Safed without my stipend? We can never marry or have children, because she is a Christian. And to continue residing under the same roof as before diminishes her. I know she cares deeply for me and I don't want to hurt her. But I think she would be better off without me. I'm no good for anyone.

I stare at the matchlock pistol in my hand and blow on the wick to make it glow. I know this is not the answer. It would exclude me from traditional mourning rituals and burial in a Jewish cemetery. And throwing myself overboard would mean my soul would wander for eternity. I guess I'm just cursed.

I hear footsteps from behind me. I turn to see Yonatan approaching.

His brows pinch together. "You look terrible," he says.

I slowly shake my head, staring at his face. "Everything is hopeless. When mother handed me the journal, I felt an obligation to take up this hunt, despite my misgivings. How can I go back and face her now? I failed her!" My eyes well with tears and I look away. "However critical and scornful she was before; now she will surely disown me entirely. And if he's still alive, father will languish in the hands of his captors because there is nothing we can do to help him. Without his business, all means of support will disappear. You, mother, and I will all become beggars."

"You are really in a dark place, brother." Yonatan glances down at the pistol in my hand. "What are you doing with that?" His eyes widen and he grimaces. "Give that to me, this instant," he says and places his hand on mine. I hesitate at first, but then release the pistol from my grasp.

"And you didn't fail her. We did exactly as she asked us to do," says Yonatan.

I search his eyes as the power of those words registers. Then I shake my head. "But there's no way to pay the ransom now," I say.

"It doesn't matter, Aaron."

"What?" I bunch my fists. "How does it not matter? Father will die."

Yonatan grasps my shoulder. "It was always the wrong answer. We just didn't see it. Even if we'd found the treasure, and paid off al-Dabaa; he'd just learn his extortion works. He'll become even more emboldened, and do it again, to us, to others. And he'll keep getting away with it until someone stops him."

"I suppose you're right. We're just doing what al-Dabaa wants."

"What we need to do is bring him to justice, liberate father, and take the Urbān down."

My stomach flutters like the pennants in the wind overhead. "Are you out of your mind?"

"No. We have the skills and means to do it. I'm trying to persuade Saadia and Manoa to come with us to help. We have pistols, arcubuses, grenades, and smoke bombs. The Urbān don't. And they are completely legal for us to have. You said so yourself."

"I guess I did."

"We have the advantage. I need you, Aaron; your strategic mind. Father needs you."

"Coron might have a large supply of those weapons. But how on earth would we get our hands on such things?"

"Right there in the Djerba marketplace. I saw merchants peddling them when I escorted the Medina family. They're plentiful and cheap. Think of all the weapons we just collected from the San Clemente. They're probably being sold as we speak."

"But how will we smuggle them through the port?" I ask.

"That's one of the many things we'll have to figure out," Yonatan says.

I rub a stray tear from my cheek. "Slow down. Give me a moment to reason this out. You're proposing we take the law into our own hands. It's so illegal. The authorities may not be eager to go after al-Dabaa, but they wouldn't hesitate going after a handful of Jews. We'd face execution."

"Only if they can identify and capture us," Yonatan says. "There's no question we'd need stealth to catch the Urbān unprepared and disguises to avoid getting caught. It would need to be a lightning strike."

Frozen in place, I gape at him. He's really been thinking this through. The gloom pressing down on me starts to lift. I take a breath. "I don't know. I have a lot of doubts. We were wrong about so many things. What makes you think this is the right course, now?"

"Aaron, can you just trust me for once?" he says. "We have to do this for the sake of our father's life. *Pikuah Nefesh.*"

I clasp my forehead. "*Pikuah Nefesh*? Listen to you. So, you're a Talmud scholar, now."

He shoves me, grinning.

"But you're right, Yonatan. We have to do something. I need to get my head on straight, stop worrying about all the reasons we shouldn't do this, and start figuring out how to make it happen. You really think Saadia and Manoa will come?"

"Maybe."

"That might be the edge we need. Keep talking to them about it. It could really tip the scale, with the four of us together." I stare aimlessly at the deck for a few moments. "Or maybe it's the most insane thing we've ever tried to date."

"You may be right. You usually are. But what's the alternative?" Yonatan asks.

∾

Yonatan Déulocresca

From a large coffer atop the table, Captain Coron counts Spanish silver reales of different values into piles. The scrivener sits on his right to record payments. I've never seen so much silver in my life. I turn a coin over and over in my palm, studying it. It's not quite round. Each coin is irregular except in weight, and the image stamped on it. One side displays a sheaf of arrows beside a flourish of ribbons. The other bears a heraldic crest with lions and castles, encircled by the sovereign's names: Ferdinand and Isabel, may their names be blotted out.

Coron pushes a mound toward me.

"Count those again and make sure you have 132 reales," he says.

"This may be a stupid question," I say, holding up the four-piece, "but how much are these worth?"

"That would be the ordinary wage for a day laborer in a week's time."

"Four reales?"

"That's right. An artisan would earn six, and sailors in the royal Armada earn 35 per month or roughly eight per week."

"So, is that the sum of wages we agreed to in the *Hezchem*?" Aaron asks.

"Yes. That's what you each would have earned for our time at sea. If you do the math, you'll see it barely covered the cost for two days' wages to the island and back. However, you are both entitled to an equal share of the spoils from the San Clemente."

"That's fair," I say.

A twenty-seventh share turns out to be far more than I expected. In silence, I count the value of my coins, in pieces of two, four, and eight reales, with growing excitement. I feed them into a leather drawstring pouch. Coron begins a new tally for Aaron's share. When he finishes, he slides the pile across the tabletop to my brother. Aaron pinches a few coins at a time, dropping them into a kidney-shaped bag, and whispering the count to himself. Then he pauses.

"What is the relative value of reales to the Venetian ducat or gold Sultani?" he asks.

"Thirteen reales are equal to one ducat or one gold Sultani."

Aaron and I look at each other wide-eyed. He weighs the kidney bag in one hand. "This is a little over 10 Sultani," he says. That means we now hold two-thirds of the ransom, nearly all, if we include what the Iman held for us. But I can think of far better uses for this silver than lining the pocket of a corrupt clan leader.

"Is that a lot to earn from one mission?" I ask.

"A moderate profit, after costs. But we were lucky," says Coron. "And speaking of lucky, I again want to acknowledge my gratitude to you, Yonatan, for your hasty interception of that sniper's arrow. You saved my life. I wish we could have recovered your lost inheritance. But at least these spoils are something."

"We're very grateful, Captain Coron, for everything you've done for us," says Aaron. "This voyage has changed me in ways I never expected."

He grins. "I don't appreciate you stealing my crewmen, but I understand the challenge that stands before you. They are fine fighters and honest men. I sincerely hope your mission is successful and you walk away in one piece. I know a certain young lady that would be most distressed if anything happened to you, Yonatan."

My mouth falls open, but I instantly close it into a smile. "Really?"

"I hope you'll be returning to Crete before too long. We'd welcome you."

That makes my insides tingle and my heart dance.

"However, there is something you should know," says Coron. "I'm being promoted to the rank of admiral. So, the days of La Represalia may be behind me, although Umberto may take the helm. But war is coming to the Holy Land. The Ottoman army will invade in less than a year. You, your family, and friends should prepare."

This sends a chill through my blood.

"Thank you for warning us," says Aaron.

"I wish you a safe journey home," Coron says, "and every success in your endeavor. Peace be with you."

"Farewell until we meet again," I say.

"I wish you success in your new role," says Aaron. "May God protect and keep you."

Aaron and I leave the captain's quarters and hurry to the gunwale where shore craft ferry crewmen to the beach. While we await our turn, we exchange farewells with the members of this remarkable crew of Sephardic corsairs.

"So, first order of business," says Aaron. "We'll have to find a ship heading east. Let's get a room at the caravanserai, since we don't know how long that may take."

"Right," I reply. "And Mossé said he'd meet us at midday to take us to the best place to purchase weaponry and ammunition."

"With this windfall, we should be well supplied," says Aaron.

"Saadia and Manoa want to rendezvous later, for supper, backgammon, and Arak."

"I'm looking forward to celebrating," my brother says. "I think we've earned it."

"Me too. We're headed home."

CHAPTER 27

Jaffa, Filastin District

Aaron Déulocresca

It took us nearly a week to reach the port of Jaffa. We sailored two uneventful voyages on cargo ships. The first skirted along the Maghreb coast, eastward from Djerba. We stopped in Benghazi for water, and finally docked in Alexandria after four days. The lateen rigged dhow carried fine cloth, ingots of iron, copper, and glass beads. In Egypt, we found work on this Greek trade vessel, which had Jaffa, Acre, and Beirut as ports of call. The small, flat-bottomed pinque is laden with ivory, spices, and aromatic woods. It was necessary to learn the boatswain commands in Greek, for which Manoa was enormously helpful.

This kind of sailoring is hard work. But despite our exhaustion at the end of our duties, after filling our bellies, we filled our evenings with discussion. In previous seasons of sail, Captain Coron led the crew on missions to plunder Spanish ports. Saadia and Manoa shared their knowledge of tactics and pitfalls to avoid. We sketched out possible scenarios for how to stage an attack on al-Dabaa's base. But we will need to find it first.

This morning, golden ripples of light dance on the deep green waters. A bank of purple clouds with brilliant orange underbellies is drifting across the northern horizon. Rising over the bluff from the east, a hazy opalescent sun radiates. Its warmth reaches inside me and spreads through my chest and limbs as I complete morning prayers. My brother and our companions stand at the gunwale nearby, listening in reverence and gazing in awe.

"Are we really here?" Manoa whispers.

"The land of our forefathers," Saadia says, turning to look at me. His eyes are glassy. I pat his upper arm and smile.

"Yes. We're finally home." But as I stand there gazing across the water toward land, the shadowy outline of a flock of pelicans soars along the beach in chevron formation. A chill shoots down my spine. I know they're harmless creatures. But their appearance at this moment seems like a gathering of *shedim*, the ominous black winged harbingers of evil. By the 70 names of God's angels, may we be protected as we face this danger.

When the ship drops anchor, the four of us take our wages, offload our belongings into a shore bound dinghy, and head for land. Two other vessels sit in the bay, a caravel and a galliot, likely bringing pilgrims. It is midsummer, the height of pilgrimage season. How sad that the Déulocresca family of guides is not here to serve them. Competitors have stepped into the void of our absence. But we can rebuild the business, if we so choose.

As we near the water's edge, I notice two Catholic monks waiting with donkeys.

"I recognize those two," says Yonatan. He growls. "I had an unpleasant encounter with them just before the Urbān took father and the pilgrims hostage. It makes me retch to think we have to hire them now."

"Unless you have a better plan, this is the fastest way to Ramla. We are paying customers and they'll be happy to take our silver," I reply.

"I know. But I wonder just how much they've profited, with us out of the way," he says.

His comment jars me, as if I'm being shaken from a deep sleep. Could there be some link between the monks and al-Dabaa? "Perhaps they intended to eliminate the competition all along," I say.

"That's the way these grifters work," says Saadia. "If they can't squeeze you for your silver, they make sure your business goes to competitors who are willing to pay."

He just answered my question, but raises another in my mind. How large is this web of grift and double-dealing? A shudder rattles through my core.

We clamber out of the dinghy and unload our bundles and bags onto the sand. Yonatan scrambles up the beach toward the port authority to get visitor permits for our friends. The silhouette of the watchtower looms over the port in a veil of mist atop the ridge. Manoa gapes at the old Crusader citadel against the early morning light. Saadia stoops down and takes a handful of sand. He glances at me with wilted brows.

"Eretz Israel," he whispers.

I nod and smile. In my haste to get our plan in motion, I overlooked the magnitude of this moment for them. I gather Saadia and Manoa together and quietly recite the blessing for milestone occasions. "We will toast later," I say. Then, I leave them with our gear while I approach the monks, waiting with their donkey coffle.

"Good morning, padres. We need passage for four with our cargo to Ramla today."

"Four? That will cost four *hatichot* to Ramla, in advance."

Opening my money pouch, I draw out a silver real. His eyes widen. It's far more than he asked for, as *baksheesh*. When the monk holds out his hand and breaks into a yellowy grin, it feels vile, like some slithering thing just crawled up my leg.

"Spanish silver? Thank you," he says. "You look familiar. Have we met?"

"I don't believe so," I say. "But I'm also seeking information and hope you might help."

"If I can, young man."

"Do you know of a group of Genoese pilgrims who were taken hostage by Urbān tribesmen not long ago?"

He looks down his nose with narrow eyes. "By God's grace and our intervention, we were able to get those men released. We guided them on to Jerusalem and they just departed these shores two weeks ago."

I stiffen, "Then, perhaps you know the fate of my father, Maestro Déulocresca."

His face reddens and his eyebrows knot. "As far as we've heard, Maestro Déulocresca is still in captivity. But, as I say, it's been weeks. We can make an inquiry for you."

Yonatan appears alongside me and mutters. "I'm sure they can, for a price."

My stomach sinks. I'd already guessed their captain would supply the funds and the priests would negotiate their release. I can only hope the Imam was able to stave off any harm directed at father until we returned. Perhaps Shuli knows more.

Yonatan and I approach our two friends. "I've arranged our passage. But according to this monk, they got the Christians released, but not our father."

"I pray he is safe, that they haven't abused him," says Yonatan.

"Well then, there is no time to lose," says Manoa. "Let's load up."

We secure our bags and bundles onto the donkeys and then mount their crude saddles. The summer heat quickly rises on the journey inland from the sea. I'm grateful Saadia showed me how to tie this *keffiyeh*. The open weave fabric lets the air cool my sweat. Yonatan jabbers away to our friends. He's actually laughing and grinning as he recites the facts about the territory, as if he is giving a tour. It's just the way our father would do. The irony of this makes me smile.

After two hours, we arrive at the monastery close to the caravanserai. The air is steamy as we haul our bundles and bags the short distance to the inn and obtain lodging. We stow everything in our rooms, including our weapons and black powder. The Turkish baths are our next stop. We purchased loose-fitting cotton *jalabiyas* in Alexandria. Knowing that our color choices would again be limited here; I suggested rich shades of goldenrod and ochre, with brass and bronze embroidery down the front. When everyone is dressed, we take Saadia and Manoa into Edna's establishment.

The enticing aroma of café and savory meals is inescapable. Friendly diners' voices and the clink of pottery fill my ears. From the bank of open portico doors, a cheer rises from a table where a game of Mancala is underway. My shoulders relax and calm spreads over me like a warm blanket. This place and these women have always nourished me, body and soul, since I was a boy.

"This is quite a place," says Manoa, surveying the colorful wall hangings.

"I could get used to spending time in here," says Saadia as he studies the gaming tables.

Across the room, Shuli is serving full plates to customers, draped in her honey-colored veil. When she turns, her eyes catch on us standing at the threshold.

"*Baruchim ha-bayim*," Shuli calls, and gives a short celebratory ululation, which alerts her mother. Edna stops what she's doing, and the two rush over and embrace us.

"We've been so worried about you," Edna says.

"Praise God. I'm so glad to see you," Shuli says. She takes a step back. With bunched brows, she looks me up and down, then meets my gaze. "You've grown as brawny as Samson."

I don't know how to respond at first. I finally say, "It was hard work."

Then she eyes Yonatan. She instantly notices the scar on his cheekbone, reaches up to touch it. But my brother pulls back, covering his cheek with his hand. "And dangerous," he adds.

I introduce Saadia and Manoa and explain how we sailed together and became friends.

"Welcome," Edna says. "Looks like you've had quite a journey.

Come and relax." She escorts us to a quiet corner. "I have a few things I must take care of, but I'll return, shortly," Edna says and goes to attend another table.

Shuli brings coffee, sliced melon and fried cheese and spinach bourekas. She joins us at the table and speaks in a hushed but urgent tone.

"Waiting for you to come home has been a torture; not knowing if you were alive or dead. I hope your journey was worth it."

I gaze into her expectant face and reach across the table, taking my sister's hand. "I believe it was. There's a lot to tell. But first, what news do you have about father? We weren't sure what we'd find upon our return."

"The monks who transported us said that they got the Christian pilgrims released," Yonatan says.

"Yes. They passed through here again before they departed. Mother asked them about where they had been held and what it was like. She can tell you what she learned."

"That'll be helpful," says Yonatan.

"And the Imam?" I ask. "Do you know if he paid al-Dabaa the good faith money, or is he still holding it?"

"I couldn't say," Shuli says. "Being women, we couldn't talk to him."

"But do you know if father is still alive?" Yonatan asks.

"As far as we know. Those tribesmen have come back here several times since you sailed, looking for you and threatening us. Were you able to find the island?" she asks.

Yonatan lowers his head as he speaks. "We found the island, alright, and the cave. But someone else beat us to the cache long ago."

"All that remained were barrel hoops, decaying wood, and an old tarpaulin," I tell her. "And this Spanish silver eight piece." I hold out the coin, polished and turned into a pendant on a thin silver chain. I had it made before we left Djerba.

She slowly shakes her head. "That is terrible news."

"It was devastating at first," I say. "But Captain Coron gave us a share of the spoils from a Spanish vessel we helped to capture."

Her posture straightens. "Spanish vessel? So, you may still be able to pay the ransom? Why not have the Imam make the arrangements?"

I exchange glances with Yonatan and our friends. Then I turn to Shuli. "Slow down. We must carefully plan our next move," I say.

Shuli's eyes shift back and forth, searching our faces. Raising one brow, she stares at me. "What do you mean by next move?"

"We don't know the specifics yet," says Yonatan.

She clucks disapprovingly. "What are you two going to do? Or should I say, four?"

I lower my voice. "We're putting an end to al-Dabaa's operation and restoring justice."

Rearing back, she grabs a hold of my forearm. She yells in a whisper. "That's impossible. You're going to get yourselves and our father killed."

Saadia leans toward her. "I doubt that, Señorita."

"After sailing with Coron, we're well prepared," says Yonatan. "We just need to do some reconnaissance and work out a coordinated plan of attack."

Shuli's mouth drops open. "I've never heard you talk like that before." She shakes her head. "Coordinated plan of attack?" With pursed lips and narrowed eyes, she studies each of us. Gradually, her face softens and brows rise. She draws a deep breath. "Alright, is there anything I can do to help?"

As I look into her eyes, an idea jumps into my head. I point to the corner of my eye. "That kohl you wear; let me borrow it."

She tips her head to one side. "What for?"

"To make us look like we're from the Maghreb," I say.

She rears back. "Maghrebi? *Wau!*" She blinks several times. "Do you need the brush?"

I nod. "Please. All of mine are in Safed."

At that moment, Edna returns with the cezve and refills our cups. Her forehead is rippled, and she clutches the sides of her veil at her chest.

"Thank you, Edna," Yonatan says. "Please sit with us for a few moments? There are some things we want to talk with you about."

"If Shuli will see to the other patrons," she says. Shuli rises from the table and goes toward the larger dining area. Then, Edna sets down the pot and pulls out a chair. There's a pained watery look in her eyes.

"Are you still planning to pay the ransom?"

Yonatan shakes his head. "No. That would be like pouring water down a rathole," he says. Saadia covers his grin and Manoa stifles a snicker. I shade my brow. My brother.

Edna glares in horror and then squeezes her eyes shut, shaking her head. "If you don't pay that ransom, they will murder him. You don't know these kinds of men."

"Ruthless cutthroats? Actually, we've met quite a few," I say. "They want you to believe they are more powerful than they really are."

Yonatan leans forward on his forearms. "You have every reason to doubt, Edna. But because our survival and the safety on that ship depended on it, this journey forced me to become far more focused and strategic. I learned to work together with my crewmates." He gestures to Saadia and Manoa.

She sits listening with a sullen expression, and finally speaks. "So, you think you've changed now, and that's going to make everything alright?"

"I can't change past mistakes," he says. "But I can tell you this. Growing up in this land made me a weakling. I accepted ill treatment, as if it's all I deserved." He glances at Saadia and the two nod with a shared understanding. "But no more."

She rolls her eyes with a cynical smirk, holding back an urge to laugh.

Leaning in, I speak in a respectful tone. "It's no joke, Edna. Yonatan saved the life of the captain and helped free a family destined to be burned at the stake by the Inquisition."

Manoa points at me. "Aaron prevented a sneak attack. I'd trust him to fight alongside us anytime."

Yonatan shakes his head. "I can't get the picture out of my mind. My brother Aaron is covered in blood, holding a sword and shield in his hands, as powerful as Gideon or Jephthah."

His comparison surprises me and I gawp. But when I look at Edna, she presses one fist to her lips and closes her eyes. Her hands tremble and beads of sweat glisten on her brow. This is not the same gutsy titan of a woman I've always known. From the moment we walked in here, I've had a weird sense. A looming threat hangs over the place. There is something she cannot say aloud. She's frightened and desperate.

"I don't think you doubt us," I say. "But because the Urbān keep coming back and are making threats toward you, you must be feeling trapped and afraid." I extend my hand and take hers. "How long have they been demanding you pay them *baksheesh* to stay in business?"

Her eyes widen and mouth falls open. "How could you know that? I've tried in every way to shield you all from that knowledge."

"Just a logical guess," I say. "The Urbān don't work. They have to be extorting *baksheesh* from everyone else who does."

"All except your father. He refused to play their game."

I close my eyes a moment as I take in that revelation.

Yonatan leans in. "Are you saying his kidnapping is retribution? That I didn't cause it?"

She drops her head. "Your gambling win was just a provocation."

This new awareness fans the embers of anger already smoldering inside me, and solidifies my resolve to bring them to justice.

"How broad is al-Dabaa's reach?" Yonatan asks.

"Everywhere."

"The mosque, the church?" I ask.

She nods her head.

"And let me guess," I say. "The Mameluke authorities take a cut to turn a blind eye."

Her eyes turn glassy. "Everything in this land operates on *baksheesh*."

I lean back, reeling with this new disclosure. "Does everyone have a stake in it? What about the Kahal and the synagogues?"

"No one speaks about it, but they all must pay."

"This sounds all too familiar," says Saadia.

"Shuli said you know where they're holding father," says Yonatan.

Edna looks around the café and then leans closer, lowering her voice. "The pilgrims spoke of being locked in a cistern of a Crusader Church on the outskirts of Abu Ghosh. It's well guarded. They could see a vineyard from a small window."

"We'll find it. But we're going to need donkeys, and not from those backstabbing monks," says Yonatan.

"Is there someone you trust, Edna?" I ask.

She rubs her lips with her fingertips and stares off into the distance. "I know of two people, Jewish friends. They're not the kind to say anything."

I take a deep breath and straighten. "Then, brothers, our task is clear."

"That's right," says Saadia. "When you find a rat's nest, there's only one thing to do."

CHAPTER 28

Ramla, Filastin District

Yonatan Déulocresca

While Edna works on finding donkeys to transport us to Abu Ghosh, we move our operation to our *gedayrah*, the family stable from which father conducts business. We heft our bundles of weaponry through the orchard in the muggy late afternoon. When the four of us arrive at the now empty pen, it makes my stomach pang. I picture this paddock as it once was; filled with our ten donkeys. We climb the stone stairs to the upper floor. I unlock and open the door. The stale and musty air is smothering. Hurrying to the window, I draw back the shutters to let in both light and fresh air. The walls and wood cabinets glow orange in the last of the daylight. A thick coating of dust covers the large central table. Dozens of rolled parchments extend from a bank of compartments underneath. Saadia and Manoa wander the room, tilting their heads and studying the contents.

"This collection embodies 20 years of knowledge and expertise," Aaron says.

"Our father mapped the whole country from north to south, even east to the Dead Sea. No one knows the land as well as he does." A lump grows in my throat as I say this. It's been two months since I last stood here with him.

Aaron brushes his palm across a shelf of leather-bound journals. "He chronicled his travels, describing the landscape and the history, too. We should be able to find out about this Crusader church near Abu Ghosh right here."

"Aaron, why don't you search through the journals while I review the maps? Saadia and Manoa, if you would, please unpack our weaponry and lay out supplies."

I paw through the rolls of parchment in partitions labeled inland, coastal, north, and south. It doesn't take long to locate a map of the region. I unroll it on the map table. Aaron thumbs through father's journals until he finds a description of churches and other buildings in the Judean Hills.

"It shouldn't be that hard to find," I say. "I know the road fairly well, but not the village."

The four of us stand over the map and trace the route from Ramla to Abu Ghosh. Aaron reads a passage aloud and shows us father's illustrations of Kiryat-el-Inab.

"Al-Dabaa had scouts on horseback stationed right about here," I say, pointing to a spot west of the village.

"They'll be hard to see in the dark," says Saadia. "But so will we. It's best to keep as quiet as we can. Speak only if it's necessary, and in a whisper."

"Should we go now or wait until later?" Aaron asks.

"I would say the dog watch," says Saadia, "before the muezzin calls for the Fajr prayer before sunrise. Most people will be asleep. We want to limit the number of civilians and witnesses."

"That also makes it safer to scout out the place and weigh what we're up against," says Manoa. "Then we can decide the best way to proceed."

There's a startling knock on the door. When I open it a crack and peer out, I see Shuli standing at the threshold.

"We've brought the donkeys," she says. I open the door wide and she comes inside. She holds out a small velvet drawstring bag to Aaron. "And here's the kohl you asked for."

"I'd nearly forgotten about it," Aaron says. "Much appreciated."

When I step outside, there's old farmer Bensusan and a boy who have brought four donkeys, riding tack, and a cart full of fodder. Hurrying downstairs with Manoa, we get the animals settled inside the stable. When we finish, I'm sweaty and out of breath. For his silence and the use of the animals, I pay Bensusan two reales. Shuli and Aaron descend from the map room. She reaches inside the cart and hands me a small bundle.

"Knowing swords are illegal for us, I thought you might need these," she says, smiling. I open it to find several large kitchen knives.

"Actually, they'll come in handy."

Aaron helps her climb back onto the cart beside the old man.

"Is there anything more I can do to help?" she asks.

"I don't think so," says Aaron. "But you and your mother keep your heads down, and your eyes and ears open."

"God protect you all," she says, and they ride away.

By the lantern's glow, we divide up the weapons and supplies, saddle the donkeys, and make everything ready to carry out this operation. Aaron has each of us sit beside the lantern to paint our faces to resemble the inky tattoos of the Maghrebi raiders. I study how he paints triangles between the brows, on the upper cheeks, and lines from the lips into the beard. While my hand may not be as skilled as my brother's, I carefully daub kohl on his face in similar manner. We all put on the brilliant blue *keffiyot* the Berber tribesmen wear, which we found in the Djerba bazaar. A warm feeling expands in my chest as I look around the circle of conspirators. I feel confident we're well prepared to ride to Abu Ghosh.

It's well past midnight when we travel east astride our sturdy donkeys toward the Judean Hills. The one I'm riding is Giboor. He used to belong to us, but I was forced to sell him to Bensusan to raise the ransom. His mate, Malka, was taken by the Urbān. When we've finished our mission, I hope the pair can be re-united.

A pale moon is rising in front of us, casting its silvery glow across the treetops. I keep an eye on adjacent knolls for possible watchmen. I estimate we've been traveling a couple of hours. We continue in silence with only the rustle of the breeze through the trees, the thud of hooves against the packed earth, and the occasional yipping of wild dogs. Soon enough, the dark grove of olive trees stands ahead. I slow Giboor as we approach.

"This is where they ambushed us," I whisper. I stop at the edge of the clearing, surveying the moonlit patch of ground. Then I lead the group single file around the perimeter beneath the shadow of the olive trees until we meet the trail on the other side. Seems no one is guarding it at this hour.

By the time we reach the outskirts of Kiryat-el-Inab, the moon has climbed midway across the sky in its transit. Steep hills rise in terraces planted with grape vines from which the village gets its name. I raise one hand and signal to the others to stop. We all dismount.

I wave them into a huddle, and whisper. "Look for the footpath father described. It should be right around here. Right Aaron?"

"Yes. It will transect the terraces and come out at the edge of the village."

Now on foot, we lead the donkeys along the trail until we reach a wide path curving up through the terraces at a gentle grade. Manoa and I take the reins of Aaron and Saadia's donkeys, and tie them into a coffle. Saadia and Aaron creep out ahead, checking for anyone standing watch. I pause to take out one of my pistols to light the wick. Manoa notices and shakes his head and waves one hand vigorously. Coming over, he whispers.

"Not yet. The wind direction will carry the sulphury smell. Anyone guarding that church will get suspicious. We'll lose the element of surprise."

"Ahh! Got it," I whisper back, nodding.

There's a faint glow above us from the hillcrest village. But the terraces are too steep to see the buildings as yet. Manoa and I ease the four donkeys onward. We finally reach level ground between rows of shoulder height grape arbors. Over the moonlit sea of leaves, the village comes into view. There are staggered points of light rising upward to the top of a peak. Reaching the edge of the vineyard, my gut tells me to wait, not to venture out and be exposed. I stroke Giboor, all the while listening. Manoa taps my arm and points. I see a shadow skulking past a stone wall and hear footfalls. It's Aaron. He tip-toes over to me and whispers.

"I think we've found the Crusader church. Come have a look."

"Alright, where's Saadia?"

"He's scouting their defenses."

Manoa and I secure the donkeys' reins to the grape arbor. Aaron leads us back along the cut stone fence. Then he pauses and points. I peer over the top course of blocks and see two men with swords standing guard on a stone-paved porch in front of a large but simple edifice. The church has huge, thick walls with an arched door flanked by two oil lanterns. The only visible windows are high above on the second floor. So, it would be difficult to sneak inside. Arches crest the top structure in the center of an upper terrace, but the walls have eroded over the centuries and there is no roof covering it. I recognize the place from one of father's sketches.

Saadia rejoins us. "There are two other guards standing on the upper terrace. No telling how many are inside."

"Alright," I say, "let's draw them out. Saadia, you toss a grenado on that porch. Maybe they'll open that door and I can lob a smoke bomb inside."

"That should bring the two on the upper terrace out front," he whispers. "Aaron and Manoa, you pick them off."

"Between us, we've only got eight shots to subdue them without reloading," Aaron reminds us. "Let's hope there aren't more than that inside."

"Oh, for an arcubus with scattershot," I say.

"But we can relieve them of their swords, too," says Saadia.

"Now's the time to light wicks and be ready to go," says Manoa.

We each ensure our matchlock pistols are ready to fire. Aaron and Manoa take a position beside the wall, aiming at the upper deck. I touch the hamsa through the cloth of my shirt and take a breath. Saadia and I creep up beside the block wall within throwing range. I light the fuse on one of the *alquitrán* grenados and Saadia hurls it over the wall. Splinters of glass and sticky flaming tar explode in all directions. Screams of pain and panic fill the smoky air. We run toward the church, each firing a pistol, hitting the two distracted guards. They fall to the ground, writhing and groaning.

The commotion brings the sentries on the upper terrace to the front as predicted. Aaron and Manoa are ready for them and open fire. One round strikes a guard in the shoulder, the other man is hit in the throat and he collapses. The huge double doors open and three more men come through the threshold. I throw a second grenado at their feet and then lob the smoke bomb through the open door. Saadia points his pistol at the first guard through the doorway and shoots him point blank. Seeing this, the other two guards in the entrance throw down their swords and raise their hands.

Manoa and Aaron vault over the wall and join us. Saadia grabs the scimitars from the two guards. Plumes of smoke are now wafting out of the door.

"Lay down on your bellies," I shout. They quickly comply, despite the fuming pitch and glass strewn everywhere. Aaron and Manoa tie the hands of the surviving guards, while Saadia reloads his pistols. I distribute the swords, and then we approach the entrance. While there is still a wounded man on the upper terrace, no others come out. I peer into the smoke-filled interior of the church.

"I'll stay and guard the prisoners," says Manoa. "And keep a lookout."

I cover my face with my *keffiyah*. Running inside, I locate the fuming globe and kick it outside. Oil lamps hanging from the ceiling make the interior visible through the yellow cloud of smoke. Skulking carefully around the pillared expanse, the three of us search the alcoves and niches. But we find no one. At the far end of the church, there is a lighted archway leading to a hall. We follow the passageway to the right and notice a staircase downward to a lower level.

"Maybe this leads to the cistern Edna talked about," I say.

We descend to the next floor. Smoke hasn't made its way down here. At the bottom of the stairs is a massive wooden door with a thick iron stave barring it closed. My heart is racing. Could my father be behind this door? We draw back the stave and open it. I peer into the dark space.

"Abba, are you in here?"

Saadia comes from behind me carrying a wall sconce from upstairs. The light penetrates the shadowy space revealing row after row of clay amphorae, braced in wooden frames. Wine.

"This must be where al-Dabaa stores his supply," I say.

"Look at all this," Saadia says, wandering around the cavern.

I walk over to an enormous square bale wrapped in burlap and twine. The odor coming from it is unmistakable. I peel back the edge of the burlap, revealing the brown waxy contents.

"What is that smell?" Aaron asks.

"It's *kaif*, and plenty of it," I say. "Al-Dabaa must be the biggest supplier in the district."

"And it's worth a fortune," says Saadia.

I notice a large stone plate covering an opening in the floor. Could they have thrown him in some cavern down here?

"Help me move this, I say. Aaron and I fit our fingers under the edges of the stone plate and slide it aside. Saadia holds the light over the opening. There, beside a pool of water, are several blankets.

"Looks like they had someone imprisoned here, but no longer," says Aaron.

"One of these guards must know something," I say. "Let's get that fallen guard from the upper terrace and start asking questions."

We scale the stairs, continuing to the upper terrace. There are numerous tumbled down stone pillars here. The wounded guard sprawls on the tile, covered in blood. I point my pistol at him.

"Where is he? Where did they take him?"

"I don't know what you're talking about," he gasps.

"The man you were holding here," I growl.

Saadia kicks him in his wounded shoulder and he wails.

"Where is he?" I shout, again.

Aaron puts the edge of his scimitar at the man's throat.

The man quails. "They just moved a prisoner to Jerusalem, earlier this evening."

"Where in Jerusalem?" I demand.

"Al-Dabaa has a brothel, at a caravanserai in the Valley of Gehinnom."

"Gehinnom?" I know the caravanserai he's talking about, but never realized that is where his brothel is. "Tie his hands," I say. Aaron pulls the man's *keffiyeh* off. With one of Edna's knives, he cuts and tears a strip to bind him. We make him stand and then force him downstairs. Gathering the other surviving sentries Manoa is guarding, we march them all down into the room with the cistern.

Manoa shoves one of the captives in the shoulder. "This one said they knew we might be coming. They just didn't know when, and didn't expect us to be so well armed."

"What? How did you know? Who told you?" I ask.

"Someone had to inform you," says Saadia. "But who?"

I slam one of the men up against the wall. "Who told you?"

At first, he doesn't reply. So, I raise my fuming pistol at his temple. "Tell me now or I'll blow a hole in your scull!"

He swallows hard. "The Catholic monks. They're al-Dabaa's eyes and ears."

I meet Aaron's angry stare and shake my head.

"I knew it," Aaron says. "They're in league with him."

"The damned monks we rented donkeys from in Jaffa, no doubt."

We exit the cistern and bolt the door, sealing them inside, and then leave the church. The moon has made its arc to the western horizon, when we reunite with our donkeys. I'm surprised the village people never ventured out after all the noise. They must know who inhabits this building and what occurs here. No one would dare come near. We all stare at each other.

"Well done brothers," I say. "Well done. Unfortunately, we will need to do it again."

"There's one huge problem we must consider now," says Manoa. We all turn to focus on our usually quiet, astute friend. "Because we did this, you can be assured that when word gets to al-Dabaa, he will seek revenge. None of your family or friends are safe anymore."

I rub my forehead and groan. I had assumed we would kill him in this attack. But all I've managed to do is endanger those I love all the more. A shudder sweeps over me. "There's no time to waste. Aaron, you and Manoa go on to Jerusalem and get mother to safety. Then scout out the brothel."

He nods. "Alright."

"Saadia and I will return to Ramla to warn Edna and Shuli. We'll re-supply and meet you around midday at the edge of hell, the Valley of Gehinnom."

CHAPTER 29

RAMLA, FILASTIN DISTRICT

Yonatan Déulocresca

As we descend through the olive groves, the first glow of sunrise behind us blankets the Judean Hills in orange. I have but one objective, one purpose; to resupply our weaponry and get back to Jerusalem with all speed. We continue our descent down the sloping plain where sheep and goats crowd together in folds. In the distance, outlines of Ramla's stone buildings, domes and minarets glow pink. At this hour, there are usually wispy spirals of smoke from the bake ovens, cook fires and roasting spits. But when my gaze falls on the northwest part of town, my belly twinges. A huge black pillar rises from the area of the caravanserai. My heartbeat hammers at my collarbone.

"What wicked curse is this?" I ask.

Saadia perks up and rises in his stirrups. "What could be burning?"

As we draw closer, smoke permeates the air and stings my eyes. I kick my heels into Giboor's sides to quicken his pace. We weave between merchant stalls in Ramla's bazaar where the awnings are still lowered. While it's too early for business, villagers mill around the caravanserai in the roadway, babbling with urgent voices. They stare and point toward the source of the smoke. My heart sinks and I clench my jaw.

Saadia and I dismount and tie our donkeys to the metal rings on the stone tethering pillar. I ask him to stay with our mounts while I search for Edna and Shuli. I hope nothing's happened to them. A red glow is visible above the roofline as I walk toward the caravanserai. When I reach it, flames are shooting upward from the top of the café. I cover my stinging eyes and groan.

Continuing my search, I thread between onlookers. Peering inside the walled yard, there are now charred black ruins where the storage shed and bake oven once stood. Just beyond the wall, Shuli and Edna are side-by-side, watching the fire. Several other women encircle them with comforting arms. A handful of men haul buckets of water up to the roof of the inn, dousing it to prevent the fire from spreading to the caravanserai.

"There you are! I'm so glad you are both safe," I say.

"Yonatan, you're back," Shuli says and reaches out to me. I embrace her, and then Edna. We turn again to face the destruction.

"There was nothing we could do," says Edna. "The light from the burning outbuildings awakened me and I ran for help. But it spread too quickly, and the café's roof caught fire."

"How did this happen?" I ask.

"We don't know," says Shuli, wiping tears from her cheek.

Blackened rafters collapse inside the café walls with a crash, shooting sparks and embers outward. Shuli gasps and Edna covers her face, muttering.

"We grabbed everything we could from inside until the smoke got too thick," Edna says.

"But how could the outbuildings just catch fire? What do you keep in there?"

"Only bags of beans, grain, and coffee; nothing that would ignite on its own."

My chest aches. "Then someone set it alight intentionally," I say.

Edna shakes her head with grim lips. "I suppose the threat was always there."

"But why?" says Shuli. "Everyone draws benefits from this café and inn, the travelers, merchants, transporters, and craftsmen. Why would anyone want to destroy it?"

"Al-Dabaa probably ordered it as retribution," I say, "when you didn't bother to tell him we'd returned. Last night we confirmed what I'd always suspected. The monks are his spies and messenger boys. They're in league with him. Your lives are in danger. Let's get you away from here until we can settle things."

I take a last glance as smoke pours out of all the windows and doors. Fallen rafters have ignited the tables and furnishings. I shake my head. We used to drink café, share sumptuous meals, and play backgammon here. So many joy-filled times. It's now destroyed and they've robbed these good women of their livelihood. It makes my gut burn. If I was angry and determined before; this cruelty just magnifies my outrage. I snort and narrow my eyes.

Taking Shuli by the elbow, I lead the women to where Saadia waits. We help the two climb onto the donkeys. They cover themselves completely with their veils. Then, we guide them away from the crowd, out through the orchard toward our *gedayrah*. As we trek between rows of almond trees, I recount how we killed and captured seven of al-Dabaa's henchmen, but learned they had transferred father to Jerusalem.

"We only came back here to resupply," I say.

"So, it's not finished," says Shuli.

"No. We're going back to meet-up with Aaron and Manoa."

"Lord God, where will it end?" mumbles Edna.

"When al-Dabaa gets what he really deserves," I say.

The sun is well above the horizon when we reach the paddock. I've never been quite sure whether the monks or al-Dabaa knew this isolated stable was ours. There seems to be no one around, not even a flock of sheep or goats. All activity ended here, when they stole our donkeys and took father prisoner. And with us traveling for nearly two months, our *gedayrah* would seem deserted to most observers. However, they know we've come back. Malevolent eyes could follow us anywhere along the road. They could be watching this place now. The hair on the back of my neck rises, as I consider the possibility that our precious collection of maps and journals could go up in flames, too.

We bring the women quickly upstairs and go inside. Saadia begins assembling the ammunition and incendiaries we need for our rescue mission. I go back down to feed and water the donkeys. After I finish piling hay into the mangers, I again take a moment to survey our surroundings, the orchard and scrub. I hear only birdsong. The wild dogs and deer that roam before dawn have already ducked back into the brush. I study the branches of nearby almond trees for anyone hiding in them. We're alone. But we should take nothing for granted.

I return to the upstairs map room. Saadia is using one of the kitchen knives to sharpen the ends of several wooden splicing fids. Ordinarily, they're used for loosening knots and separating strands of thick rope. He's also laid out a handful of metal marling spikes. My eyes widen.

"What are you doing with those?" I ask.

Saadia takes a marling spike by the end and flings it toward the wooden door. It flies silently, almost invisibly, and imbeds into the wood with ease. "We can bring pistols and incendiaries. But taking this brothel won't be the same as a hoard of corsairs taking a ship. It's going to require different tactics; stealth and speed, like the sting of a bee."

"I agree. But the place will be full of civilians who could identify us. We'll need to get them out of the way somehow." I pick up a smoke bomb, feeling its weight in my palm.

"Being that close to Jerusalem, the last thing we want is to draw the attention of the Mameluke militia," he says. "So, these are perfect weapons if you need stealth for a sneak attack."

Shuli is watching all this with great interest. She comes over and picks up three marling spikes. Saadia stares at her with raised brows and he folds his arms.

"And what are *you* doing?" he asks.

"She's a woman of hidden talents," I say. "And so is Edna."

Shuli smirks as she tosses the spikes, one at a time. They each implant with precision beside Saadia's.

He shifts his stance. "That's impressive," he says.

"And she is better with a sword than I am," I add.

Shuli puts her hands on her hips. "After what they've done to us, I'm coming with you this time."

Edna gasps. "I forbid it. The danger is too great."

"It would be terribly risky, sister. Deadly combat," I say. "I don't…"

"Hold on," says Saadia, raising one hand. "Given this new setting in a brothel and our need for stealth; a woman with her skills could be quite an asset. Let's think this through."

Shuli juts out her chin. I shake my head and groan.

"Listen. She can go places and do things we can't easily get away with. Having her with us provides a good cover," Saadia says. "She doesn't have to be in a combat role. But she could do reconnaissance and with the right timing be a stealthy assassin." He grabs another marling spike. "One of these through the eye or temple drops a man in moments from a safe distance."

I lower my gaze, pace around the room, and stroke my beard. She really is skilled. But I can't bear the thought of her being harmed. They could take her hostage or, God knows what else. But she is also clever, sharp-eyed, and aware. I know how much she wants to help. I meet Shuli's penetrating stare. "We'd have to plan this flawlessly. Timing, position. And anticipate what could go wrong."

"Of course," Saadia replies.

Shuli breaks into a grin and rushes over, hugging me.

"Oh no, don't do this. Please," says Edna, growing tearful again. "You're all I have left."

Shuli turns to face her mother. "These monsters have demolished everything we've built. Unless they're stopped, they'll go on destroying more people's lives. We have to put an end to it." She stomps her foot. "I have to do this. *Eema*, you've taught me well. I'm going with them."

Edna closes her eyes and shakes her head. Shuli goes over and embraces her.

"I'm sorry," I say. "But we have no more time to waste. It's probably safer for you not to remain here alone, Edna. What about Bensusan? Can you stay with him? We will need another donkey now, anyway."

She inhales deeply and nods.

I reload my pistols, grab the grenados, a smoke bomb, and a handful of marling spikes. We also take a supply for Aaron and Manoa. Shuli and Edna gather their personal belongings and wait at the door. Descending to the paddock, we help the women remount the saddles, cross through several almond orchards, and reach Bensusan's farm on the east side of Ramla. After a brief explanation, the three of us canter away on the donkeys toward Jerusalem.

I gaze out across the tall grasses yellowing the rolling hills dotted with oak and carob trees. We each silently scan the countryside for watchmen. My thoughts now shift to the mission that lies ahead. I instigated all this, convinced my friends to sign on to the mission. Is it really going to work? We certainly won't catch al-Dabaa unprepared this time; nor overwhelm his defenses, as we did at Abu Ghosh. If he moved father to Jerusalem, he is expecting us to come after him. He's not stupid. We don't know how many men he has, or how well-armed they'll be. My chest tightens like a double carrack bend is cinching around it. Burning bile gurgles in my belly.

This will be a far more dangerous attack. Do I really have what it takes to be victorious? I could die today. Any one of us could be killed. The weight of their lives is on my shoulders along with father's life. We're taking an enormous risk. I used to believe I was lucky, and never could resist a good wager. That seems laughable now by comparison. But one thing is true. Back in spring, when I sat on the deck of the caravanserai, watching the Qabaq contenders, I was certain of my judgment. I made my best assessment. That won me the bet, because I'm not stupid, either.

Before all this, I never even had friends, let alone led anyone. Now I have the good counsel of trusted partners like Saadia and Manoa, and Aaron's sharp insight. We won the first battle against al-Dabaa's men; and we have the weaponry, the skills and the cunning to do so again. As Giboor continues to plod up the slow grade toward the highlands, my eyes scour the bushes, trees, and shadowy outcroppings for scouts. But having Shuli with us, we look like ordinary travelers, not worth anyone's time or attention.

Shuli has every reason to seek justice for her losses. Recovering *our* lost family assets is what drove me to take a voyage two months ago. I believed a cache of riches could save my father's life. But after seeing that hollow echoing sea cave and our now empty corral, I realize that the true family assets are not these material things. Those can all be replaced with time, just like Edna's café can. My mother and father lost everything once before, when they fled Spain. But they built a new life, despite everything that happened to them, because of who they are. And they will again. I come from a long line of people who are dogged, unwavering, even in the face of fear. We just bounce back and keep going. Those are the real family assets; who we are. And knowing this gives me the courage to lead this little band of intrepid fighters. Today, I'm going up against my own Goliath. If the shepherd boy David with only a slingshot could be victorious over a giant, why can't a donkey-boy?

Jewish Quarter, Jerusalem

Aaron Déulocresca

In early light, we travel along the ridge overlooking the valley to the southernmost entrance to the city. The sunrise over the Mount of Olives paints the crests of the buildings in rosy light, leaving the corridors and footpaths in long indigo shadow. We leave the donkeys in a stable near the Tanner's Gate and go on foot.

This is the moment I have long dreaded, and do not know the response I will receive. The last time I spoke to my mother was when she placed my father's journal in my hands, entrusting me to recover the hidden inheritance. But when I stared into the emptiness of the sea cave, I thought I had failed her. But the truth is, I fulfilled her request, at the risk of my life and Yonatan's. There were no wine barrels full of gold and jewels to find.

However, I found something else at the bottom of my misery. Rather than give up or avoid, as I would have in the past, I found the courage to go on. Wisdom and discernment followed. I could not only face my future, but shape it. That is the inheritance from my father, which is his ability to persevere even in the face of despair. He taught me to use my intellect, to find a path forward; to map out that next step and the next. Even if it means starting again from nothing.

When Manoa and I arrive at my Jerusalem home, we find the iron gate to the courtyard barred. At this early hour, mother is likely awake, but won't be expecting us. I also realize my appearance will startle her. I pull off my Berber headdress and use a little spittle to rub the kohl off my face. Manoa sees this and quickly does the same.

I gently tug on the cable that jars the string of little bells, their delicate chime breaking the morning silence. The inside shutters on the courtyard window open an eye-width, but then shut. The door opens, and she rushes across the square.

"Aaron? God be praised, you've come back." She slides the stave aside and opens the heavy gate. We enter and my mother wraps her arms around me. "I'm so grateful you're safe," she says in my ear. At first, it takes me so off guard, I freeze. Then awkwardly, slowly, I return her embrace. The fragrance of rosewater fills my nostrils, transporting me back to a time long past. The sad longings of a little boy bubble up from deep in my gut.

"Where's your brother?" she asks, pulling back. She closes the gate and bolts it.

"Yonatan is on his way here. We have little time. Let's go inside," I say, and hurry across the tiled courtyard, around the small fountain to the entrance. Mother and Manoa follow me inside and I bolt the door. She stares up at our tall friend, Manoa and then looks at me.

"*Eema*, this is my friend Manoa Falcon, from Salonica, where many Jewish exiles from Spain now live. Manoa, this is my mother, Señora Aularia Déulocresca. We met on a ship that carried us to where father hid the family assets."

"You found them?" Her face brightens.

"I gesture for her to sit and I slide onto the bench across from her. Manoa stands at the window, keeping watch through the gap between the shutters.

Her eyes fill with alarm and worry creases her brow. "What's happened?" she asks.

"It's been a long and difficult journey, for which neither of us was prepared. But we learned immeasurably," I say, as my throat tightens. "Yonatan and I found the island and even found the cave described in father's journal." I pause and peer deeply into her eyes, as months of welled-up emotions flood mine. "But the wine barrels holding grandfather's estate…" My voice catches. I clear my throat and take a breath. "Others discovered them long ago." I hold out the solitary coin pendant. "This is all that remained."

She gasps and starts to cry. I wipe my eyes, but my chest feels lighter. She now knows I fulfilled my obligation to her. There's nothing to feel guilty about anymore.

Mother covers her face in her hands. "Lord God. How will we pay the ransom?"

I raise my chin. "We aren't going to pay al-Dabaa so much as a *haticha*. We have come with our corsair friends and powerful weaponry and skills to liberate father and bring justice."

"Corsairs?" she whispers.

"Dâvi Salmonis introduced us to Captain Gabriel Coron and his crew of Sephardic Jews. These are principled and just men who have been collecting restitution from Spain and the Inquisition, and restoring it to our people all around the Mediterranean. What an honor it's been to serve on his ship. It changed us both."

"Dâvi Salmonis?"

"We learned how to use sophisticated weapons with explosive black powder. And when our ship came under attack by a Spanish vessel, we fought to save the lives of our fellow crewmen and our own. We rescued a *converso* family from being burned at the stake. And we delivered justice to the two inquisitors who were taking them back to Spain."

Her mouth drops open, and her eyes widen. "Aaron? This is beyond belief."

"It's true. But right now, your life is at risk. Let's go to Rabbi Bertinoro, so he can find the best place to keep you safe."

She gasps and sits back. Her forehead creases. "Alright, I'll get my cloak."

We step outside into the courtyard. I glance around at the beautiful tiled square and fountain in the morning light and wonder if this is the last time I will see it, or my mother. Then, Rehm's face comes into my mind. I close my eyes a moment as an ache grows in my chest. We hurry out of the gate and along the Cardo to the synagogue. The cantor is already leading morning prayers when we enter. But Rabbi Bertinoro notices us and his face brightens. He leaves the *bimah* and comes toward us.

"May God be praised," he says. "Come join us. We can speak of your travels afterward."

"I cannot stay," I say. "*Pikuah Nefesh*. There is something I must do. Please look after my mother until I return."

The rabbi's eyes bulge and he nervously nods. "Then, may God protect you, Aaron, and your friend, here."

As I escort my mother to the screened-in women's section of the sanctuary, I'm seized by a compelling urge to say what's on my heart. "Before I go, there is something very important that I must not leave unsaid. Because I don't know if I will have the chance to, again."

Mother's face contorts, and she squeezes my hand.

"I never knew that the Inquisition still hunted you, *Eema*, until I went on this journey. Having that dark cloud of fear hanging over your head all these years explains a lot. I didn't understand your reasons or what happened to you that caused you to…" I falter, hunting for the right words. "It must have been something so terrible that it scarred your soul. But I now know I was just the recipient of your pain. I am not the cause of it. After all the things I've seen and the stories I've heard from other exiles from Spain, I cannot judge you."

She is trembling, and tears pour down her cheeks. She reaches out and caresses my arm, a touch I've not felt since I was a young child.

A whisper is all that comes out. "*Eema,* I forgive you."

She gasps. "Aaron, my sweet, precious son. I love you."

My gut wrenches. It takes a few moments to collect myself. I take a deep breath.

"I have to go."

CHAPTER 30

Jerusalem

Yonatan Déulocresca

"Here we are," I say, to Saadia, "the Valley of Gehinnom."

Saadia and Shuli lean to peer over the bluff toward the parched valley floor.

"It sweeps around Jerusalem from west to southeast like the blade of a scimitar," I say, making an arch with my hand.

"Who'd want to live there?" asks Saadia. "There's nothing but a barren, rocky rift."

"No one," says Shuli. "They say the place is cursed."

"Aaron told me it was because when the kings of Judah turned to worshiping pagan gods, they offered their children as sacrifices in the fire there."

Saadia shakes his head. "And what's that golden dome, way over there?" he asks.

"It's a mosque, built atop the Temple Mount. The last remains of the *Kotel* for the Temple are right there, below it."

"Can we go there?"

I shake my head. "You wouldn't want to. The Mamelukes use it to dispose of their refuse. But maybe one day."

We slow the donkeys as we pass the caravanserai. I make a subtle gesture toward the inn.

"This *khan* has been here as far back as I can remember. Al-Dabaa must have taken it over at some point, which he no doubt would like to do in Ramla. My father would never bring pilgrims to stay there, or even take a meal. I assumed it was because we were so near Jerusalem. But now I know the real reason is because he refused to give-in to al-Dabaa in any way."

"Well, with all those camels, horses, and donkeys outside, it has no shortage of patrons. We'll have to factor that in."

"There are probably gaming tables and gambling, too."

When we reach the northern edge of the city, it's the start of *taaseela*, the rest period after the midday meal, when it's too hot to work and people often nap. We bring the donkeys to the public stable near the northern gate of the city. A large donkey pace huddles under the shade of several olive trees. Giboor brays, lurching toward the pen. Studying the animals, I realize many of them are ours. Giboor trots over and immediately begins grooming Malka on the withers. The sight of this lifts my spirit. We can restore everything we lost. We just need to take this next perilous step.

As we walk back toward the *khan*, I spy my brother and Manoa crouching in the shade of an olive tree away from the road. They've removed their Maghrebi disguises and dress as common laborers. Aaron waves. In the distance, a solitary doorman in a cuirass keeps guard in the caravanserai's portico. The front door stands open.

Aaron's eyes widen. "Shuli, this is unexpected."

"Sorry for the delay," I say. "We got here as soon as we could."

Shuli narrows her eyes. "Those thugs set fire to our café. We saved some items, but it's destroyed."

Aaron groans and shades his eyes with one hand. "*Mamzayrim*! Demons take them," he says, and spits.

Manoa purses his lips and shakes his head. "We'll bring them to justice."

"How did things go with mother?" I ask.

"Better than I expected," Aaron says with a soft smile. "But she's shaken. I took her to the synagogue. Rabbi Bertinoro will keep her hidden."

"That's a relief," I reply.

I crouch down and sit cross-legged on the ground. Saadia joins me, while Shuli leans against the tree trunk.

"On our ride in, I was thinking through our strategy here. In a way, it's like changing direction on a ship, adjusting the sails. Everyone has a vital task to perform in coordinated timing."

Saadia and Manoa pin their eyes on me and nod in agreement.

"We'll start by infiltrating the place. Saadia and Manoa, you assess how many armed men they have in the main area and where they're posted. Notice any escape routes."

Manoa points toward the *khan*. "We scouted it briefly. There's a back exit that leads to their latrines. All the windows are small and close to the ceiling, too small to climb in or out."

"I'd like to get a good look in those back rooms, somehow," Aaron says, pointing to the left wing extending from the main entrance. "Surely that's where they're keeping father."

"Agreed. You and Shuli could pose as a married couple visiting the holy city," I say. "If you rent a room, that could get you down that corridor to have a look."

"Good idea."

Shuli stoops. "I don't suppose you brought your European garments with you?" she asks.

Aaron rubs his jaw. "No," he replies, "but I know where to find some fairly quickly; at home in father's armoire."

Saadia speaks up. "Manoa and I can start at the gaming tables, have some coffee, and see who crawls out of the chinks in the wall."

"That's a good start," I say. "These men will easily recognize me, so it's best if I come in last. I'll remain here as a lookout. That gives Aaron and Shuli time to get in and investigate the hallway. Then, I'll eliminate the doorkeeper and light the smoke bomb. When you see me inside the lobby, that's the cue. We'll remove key sentries, bodyguards, and search the rooms. Shuli, as soon as you see the smoke spreading into the hallway, you scream fire, and run out of the building. That should create a panic. Hopefully, it makes the innocent people flee."

"Some Urbān could also slip out," says Saadia. "Watch for them."

Aaron leans in. "So, in all that chaos, I'll search the rooms until I locate father."

"We'll join you as soon as we remove al-Dabaa's chief defenses."

"Alright. Let's get weapons ready." Aaron draws out his pistols and I give him and Manoa fresh powder and balls. Then I hand Aaron a striking flint.

Aaron looks at me. "You brought incendiaries?"

"Right here," I say, drawing back my *durra'ah*, revealing a leather pouch. "But remember, the more pistol fire and explosions, the more attention we'll draw. We want to avoid having the militia show up. We'll save grenados for the end to torch the place. Any other thoughts?"

We all exchange glances and then Aaron stands.

"It's a sound plan."

Saadia and Manoa nod in agreement, and we all rise. They saunter over to the caravanserai and go inside. Aaron and Shuli hurry back to the Jewish quarter, and I wait beneath the tree, observing the activity from a distance. A short time later my brother and sister return, dressed like Venetians in father's blue doublet and hose and mother's gray hooded cloak and gown. Both look a little frayed and discolored.

"You look completely out of place," I say.

"Good. I'll brandish some silver and demand the best room," Aaron says.

"Where are your pistols?"

He opens his doublet, showing one tucked inside beneath his elbow.

"God be with you two," I say. "I'll be in there shortly."

The two of them promenade across the road. The doorman bows when they reach the entrance and they go into the lobby. My stomach flutters. I draw out my pendant and stare at the blue stone in the center for a moment; then drop it back inside my collar. Folding my arms, I wait. I try to picture in my mind how things might be playing out inside, rocking restlessly. After watching the arc of the sun for a while, I guess it must be about four bells in the afternoon watch. Time to move.

Wearing my Maghrebi headdress and facial tattoos, I run across the hard-packed sod toward the paved entrance. The guard's eyes widen and he unsheathes his sword and shifts his stance to fend off the attack. But before he can engage me, I throw a marling spike at his face. It pierces him at the bridge of his nose, paralyzing him. He sways and drops like a stone.

I duck into the colonnade and ignite the fuses on my pistols and tuck them into my waistband, partially hidden by my *durra'ah*. Taking out the smoke bomb, I light the wick and casually stroll into the polished tile lobby, holding it behind my back. Seated at one of many gaming tables crowded with backgammon players, Saadia and Manoa meet my gaze. Saadia points to his eye and then holds four fingers at his collarbone. I nod my understanding and survey the room.

One guard holding a spear stands next to an enormous ceramic urn at the arched portal to the hallway. Two flank the back entrance, armed with scimitars. Beside them is a bank of lavish upholstered benches with pillows. A handful of guests lounges with half-naked women, drinking Arak. The fourth guard paces, monitoring the gaming area. With a tilt of the head toward the hallway guard, I signal my choice. Saadia and Manoa rise, and the three of us fan out. I toss the smoke bomb across the floor, igniting the *alquitrán*. It slows when it meets the thick carpet and lodges beneath an adjacent table. Saadia and Manoa dart toward the back entrance like birds of prey. As they dispatch the two rear sentries, the lounging guests babble with bulging eyes, and they scatter.

Dark sulfurous plumes billow from under the table and drift down the side passage. The sentry at the hallway calls for help and starts toward me. But as I grab another marling spike and raise my hand to throw it, he suddenly plummets to the carpet. Embedded in his temple is a splicing fid. Shuli skulks out of the hallway and meets my surprised stare.

"Well done," I say.

She smiles at me and then lets loose with a scream. "Fire, fire! Get out, get out!"

"Meet back at the stable," I say. Then she flits out the door.

Within moments, half-dressed, shrieking prostitutes and their patrons are rushing out of the rooms and down the hallway toward me. Another armed man comes rushing down the passage with a spear, but Manoa comes in from the side, stabbing him in the throat. He collapses, clutching his bleeding neck.

I look for Saadia. But with the upper windows now clouded by smoke, I can barely see. A shaft of light juts into the lobby when the back door bursts open and two more women flee outside. In the haze, I make out two figures in a struggle on the floor. I run over. Between the now empty gaming tables, the guard has Saadia pinned to the floor. With both hands, my friend strains to hold off a huge knife from stabbing him in the chest. I pull out one pistol and fire. But the wick has gone out. Snarling, I bash the man in the side of the head. This is enough to disrupt the struggle for a moment. Saadia wrestles himself free. I pull out my other pistol and fire a bullet at close range at the guard's head. He slumps to the side. I offer Saadia my hand to get up. We look at each other a moment.

"You alright?" I ask.

He nods. "Thank you."

I pat him on the shoulder. "Let's search the rooms," I say.

"Check wicks, first," he says.

I quickly reload, take out my striking flint and ignite a bit of fuzz stuffed into the end of both wicks. Saadia readies his pistols and squints through the smoke. "Let's go."

My eyes sting and I cough. We find Manoa already searching the bays and alcoves. Saadia speeds ahead. Most rooms stand empty, but a few stragglers pass by. I yank back a drape from across one doorway and point my pistol. Two naked male occupants stare at me, cowering.

"Get out, if you want to live," I shout. They grab their clothing and run bare-assed out of the room and up the hallway toward the exit.

There's a shot. I draw my second pistol and run through the smoke in the direction the sound came from. As I go farther down the hallway, the smoke thins. Unseen from the front, the corridor turns, extending even further. From high above, the afternoon sun pours through a window, illuminating the end of the passage. My brother is standing in profile. At his feet is another armed guard lying dead. Aaron is pointing his pistol and speaking to someone inside the room. Saadia and Manoa stand against the wall, ready with pistols drawn. My pulse is thundering in my throat as I creep toward them.

"No one else needs to die," Aaron says. "Just put the knife down and let him go."

The hair rises on the back of my neck. I blow on my wicks until they glow red.

"Those weren't the terms. Pay the ransom or I'll slit his throat." It's al-Dabaa's voice.

"Be reasonable. Think of all the *baksheesh* you would lose," Aaron says.

"*Baksheesh?*"

I step past my two friends into the doorway and fix my eyes on al-Dabaa. He holds father by the hair with a knife at his throat. Father is on his knees, bound and gagged. I don't hesitate. A round explodes from my pistol. Father dodges to the side, but loses his balance and falls. Al-Dabaa tumbles to the floor, wounded in the upper chest. His blood pulses onto the tile beside him. Aaron hurries to father, reaching down to help him get up. At the same moment, al-Dabaa raises himself and swipes awkwardly with the dagger toward Aaron. I rush in and squeeze the trigger of my other pistol. The round makes al-Dabaa's head jerk back, but not before the knife plunges into Aaron's right shoulder. My brother screams. He falls to his knees as the deep red stain spreads out, soaking through his shirt. Al-Dabaa collapses in a heap.

"Aaron, Aaron, my God," I gasp. My head is spinning as my heartbeat roars in my ears.

Saadia and Manoa rush in. Manoa uses his hand to put pressure on Aaron's wound, but blood seeps between his fingers. Saadia tears off al-Dabaa's *keffiyah* and slices off a long swath. Father's eyes are full of alarm and his brow furrows. He groans.

Aaron speaks with a breathy voice. "Yonatan, there's achillea in my bag there. Small vial." He looks down toward the leather pouch at his waist.

"Let me get it," I say. Stooping, my hands tremble as I hunt around inside the pouch. I find the little ampule and remove the stopper. Aaron astonishes me. He thinks of everything. Peeling back Aaron's doublet and linen chemise from his shoulder, I sprinkle the crushed yarrow onto the oozing stab wound to staunch the blood. Then Saadia binds it tight with a strip torn from al-Dabaa's *keffiyeh*. Grasping my hand, Aaron gets to his feet. I pull his clothing back over his shoulder.

Turning to father, I cut the rope around his wrists, remove his gag, and help him rise. His skin is ashen and he's emaciated. There's an odor of rotten onions. He takes a step back, blinking rapidly. His mouth opens to speak, but nothing comes out. Then he falters to the side into Manoa, who grabs him by one arm.

"Let me help you, sir," Manoa says.

Father starts panting. "Who are you? Where are you taking me?"

"Home, Abba, we're going home," I say. "These are our friends."

Tears well in his eyes and his forehead ripples. "Why are you dressed like that, Yonatan?"

My heart drums as father's dire condition becomes clearer. I clench my jaw. "It's just a disguise, Abba."

"Let's get out of here," says Saadia. "Out the back."

I grip Aaron by his uninjured arm, and the five of us make our way back through the passageway. It's deserted. Coughing through the smoke, we push open the doors to the exit.

Father cringes, shading his eyes from the bright light.

"No, no. Someone will see us."

"We'll be alright," says Aaron. "You're free now."

I take out two grenados, light the fuses and pitch them inside. They explode, catching the curtains, wall-hangings, and carpets on fire. I take off my *keffiyah* and rub the remnants of kohl from my face. Hiding our weapons, we carefully creep around to the side of the building. A sizeable crowd has gathered across from the *khan*, watching the smoke pour out. Now the building is really on fire.

Noticing how the blood seeps through his doublet, I strip off my *durra'ah* and drape it over Aaron's shoulders to hide it. Manoa guides father around the perimeter of the crowd. Aaron, Saadia, and I merge into the group of onlookers, weaving a path to the other side. Then we dart from the scene beneath the olive trees. Once we are some distance away, we slow our pace. Aaron is gasping with pain and looks pale.

Outside the stable, Shuli stands staring with pursed lips and a rippled brow. When father sees her, he squints and rubs his forehead.

"Shuli?" He stops, gaping.

"We need to get out of sight," says Saadia. "Let's keep going."

She comes over and wraps her arm around father, and with Manoa, they guide him onward. Aaron is losing strength and leans heavily on my arm.

We enter the city near the Church of the Holy Sepulchre. Taking the main thoroughfare, the Cardo, we head south, straight toward the Jewish quarter. The streets are still deserted and shop awnings are lowered. People have not yet roused from their afternoon rest. I can only hope that when the authorities question witnesses to the melee, and examine the bodies strewn around the *khan*, they will speak of a Maghrebi raider who attacked and disappeared. Few people got a good look at any of us and lived, except those two men. But I doubt they'd want their activities at the *khan* revealed. And while I don't know the full range of al-Dabaa's villainy, the Mamelukes might just believe he enraged some other crime lord who took revenge. Will they consider it a crime worth investigating, or celebrate his demise? But Goliath has fallen. How the landscape will look after the dust settles remains uncertain, because the control of the Mamelukes is about to end, as well.

My energy has drained away and my head aches. A day and a half without food, drink, or sleep must be catching up to me. I desperately need a simple meal, a cup of ale, and a quiet place to put my head down. Then, I have every intention of celebrating. We've earned it.

※

Aaron Déulocresca

A hot breeze off the desert rifles awnings of the closed market stalls. Dense stone arches in the Jewish quarter are cool to the touch. Our footfalls echo through the vacant corridor between the tall building facades. Beneath a painfully blue sky, the stark afternoon sun casts all things in a high contrast of shadow and light. Everything is laid bare in its brilliance. Father is alive and safe. But the light reveals patches of yellow and sepia; bruises in various stages of healing on his temples, neck, and limbs. The traces of a kick or a pounding will all fade with time, surrounded by a loving family. But the injury to his clarity of mind may take longer to heal.

My shoulder throbs with a pang so deep it hurts to breathe. I ball my fists and grit my teeth. Trying to keep my pistols covered, I pivot my arm. Mistake. A punishing twinge flares from my neck to wrist, making me wince. Yonatan glances at me with a concerned wrinkle in his brow. There's a shared understanding between us to hold our tongues until we're out of range of any eavesdroppers. The synagogue's staircase is just ahead on the left.

We descend to the huge oak doors. It's reassuring to find them bolted on the inside. Mother is safe. Yonatan pounds with his fist several times. I gaze up at the bank of arched windows on the right. After a few moments, white bearded Rabbi Bertinoro peers from the one nearest to us. He turns and recedes from the window. With a rasp, the staves draw back and the doors open. The rabbi gazes at us with teary eyes and a toothy grin. We all gather inside the vestibule and close the door.

"Praise God," he says. He surveys father from head to toe and then embraces him. Then he turns to us and offers his hand, first to Yonatan, and then to me.

"*Yashar Koach*," he says.

When I try to reach, the pain is crippling. A wave of vertigo makes me reel.

"He's injured," says Yonatan, steadying me.

"And Señor Déulocresca is not so well, either. We need a physician," says Manoa.

"Right away," says Bertinoro. "But first, let me tell your wife and mother that you've returned triumphantly." He turns and hurries to a hallway beside the Holy Ark and disappears into the door leading to the inner courtyard and *bet midrash*.

Father stares at Manoa and Saadia, his eyes shifting back and forth. "Do I know you?"

"Abba, these are our crewmates and friends, Manoa Falcon, from Salonica," says Yonatan. "And Saadia Benatar from Tétouan."

Father has a blank look, but offers his hand. "Crewmates?"

"Yes, sir," says Saadia. "We sailed together on La Represalia under the command of Captain Gabriel Coron. *Çiphut Sinai*."

Father's eyes grow large as lemons. "*Çiphut Sinai*? What is that?"

"Justice for our people," Yonatan says.

"It's a long story," I say.

Father slowly shakes his head, rubbing the base of his neck.

At that moment, the rabbi returns with our mother. She is tugging at the hair behind one ear and clutching the front of her robe. Her eyes are wrinkled with a strained expression. But when she sees the six of us, she gasps. Smiling, her eyes lift toward heaven.

"Thank God." She rushes over and reaches up, cupping father's face in her hands and carefully looks him over. Her face crumbles, and she draws him close. He lays his head on her shoulder and squeezes his eyes shut. "I thought I had lost you," she says. She pulls back and then kisses him several times.

I can't remember ever seeing my parents gaze at each other this way. Rabbi Bertinoro looks on, stroking his beard with a warm smile. I yearn for my own comforting embrace. My stomach twinges. With this searing pain and my utter exhaustion, if Rehm were here, I'd rest my head on her shoulder, too. Then, mother turns to me.

"You really did it. You saved him." Her tear-filled eyes survey each of our corsair company, one at a time. Finally, her gaze falls on Shuli for a moment. She smiles. "Thank you, every one of you."

Shuli softly winces and I give her hand a squeeze.

Mother tips her head, noticing my blood-stained shirt and gasps. "You're hurt." She wraps one arm around my waist. "Oh, *cariño*."

"I'm going for Doctor Abravanel, right now," says the rabbi. "Return home together, and I'll bring him to you." He rushes out the door behind us.

Father turns to Yonatan. "Hard for me to find my words." He stares off blankly for a few moments. "I thought I would die. Your courage and skill. You…" His eyes water and lips move as he struggles to speak. "Did what no one else dares. Saved my life. So proud."

My brother's lower lip trembles and his eyes fill with tears. He wraps his arms around father and draws him to his chest. I know how much he yearned for this. I sigh deeply.

Meeting Saadia's and Manoa's misty-eyed smiles, I place my hand at my heart and mouth the words thank you.

"You're welcome. It's finished, my friend." Manoa nods.

Saadia gives a satisfied grin. "We're all safe, now."

"Let's go home, Eema," says Yonatan.

"Come. Everyone is welcome to our home," she says and leads the way.

We file out of the door and climb up the stairs. When I reach the top, my empty stomach, light-headed fatigue, and my loss of blood overtake me. I nearly pass out. Then, Shuli comes alongside, takes my arm, and we walk together.

I peer down the stone corridor with its concentric arches. The tunnel-like passageway converges in a blinding radiance, pouring in through the distant gate, like a keyhole. I take a deep breath. My chest fills with new hope for the times to come. Warmth infuses my softening limbs, and my body seems lighter. Even the pain in my shoulder dulls as my mind quiets. A verse rises to my lips, recited at the close of every prayer service.

Don't fear sudden terror, nor destruction when the wicked come.
Take counsel together, and it will be brought to nothing.
Say the word, and it shall not stand; for God is with us.

CHAPTER 31

Two years later

Malevisi Valley, Crete

Yonatan Déulocresca

My dam, named Balada, lies on her side in a stall strewn with fresh straw. Her black velvet coat glistens with sweat and she strains in rhythmic motion. With a soft grunt, she puffs with each wave and a leak of birth waters spurts out. I rock back and forth, seeing her wrestle with such pain. A scrawny leg shrouded in white membrane inches outward from the birth canal.

"Good girl, *querida*," I say softly, standing nearby, but distant enough not to interfere.

I was wise to forsake my short career as a corsair, in favor of my first love and ambition. What better use for my share of the spoils from the last two seasons of sail? Combining my share with Aldonza's dowry allowed us to take a gamble. I'm proud of the enterprise we launched, breeding Messara horses.

Balada is growing more uncomfortable, shifting her legs restlessly. She rolls back and forth like she wants to get up. Then, with her energy spent, she slumps back down. My stomach tenses and I shuffle my feet, wishing there was something I could do. But this is the way of nature. Her ribs and belly visibly rise and fall with her breath. But when the pangs resume, she makes a tremulous grunt and continues pushing in pulses.

A little muzzle and nose appear through the opening. Through the stretched membrane, I can see a small eye. Blood-tinged liquid jets out around the angular head. But so far, the little one is not moving. I bite on my thumbnail. The little one will hopefully survive. Balada is awfully young to be a mother. Again, she tires, holding still to regain strength.

"You're doing so well, my princess," I say. "Keep going, your baby is almost here."

With her legs thrashing, Balada rolls up onto her chest and belly. This seems to expel the foal out a little more. I find myself crossing and uncrossing my arms as her discomfort continues. She strains and squirms. Pushing herself to her knees, the little one slides out further.

"The shoulders are the hardest part. Push, push."

As if she understands me, she bears down. Once, twice. On the third push the shoulders squeeze out. She sprawls exhausted and panting.

"Come on, *querida*. Two more strong pushes and it will be over."

The foal's front hooves rupture the birth sack. A crimson-tinged gush leaks out around the little one. Balada's body releases the hind quarters onto the ground. I stand completely still, my jaw goes slack, and my eyes fix on the foal. It begins to wiggle its legs. A wave of gooseflesh washes over me. Miraculous. The slash in the birth sack widens and the foal nudges it's face out to take its first breath.

"Hello there, little one," I say, softly. I take a deep breath.

A flood of draining birth waters spreads out on the floor at my feet. Balada rises from the knees to standing. I go to her, stroking her jaw and neck. My chest swells.

"Well done, my princess. Your little one is finally here."

She turns to the foal and begins chewing on the membranes, releasing it from inside the suffocating sac. Once free, she licks the newborn, which perks his movement. I can clearly see the foal is a male. Now,

I must watch and wait. The baby needs to suckle in the next hour, if he's going to be strong enough to survive.

This is not the only birth in recent days. Today marks the eighth day since my wife, Aldonza gave birth to our son. The uncanny timing of this leaves me no doubt that the two newborns will be bonded for life. For weeks, family and friends have been arriving on the island in anticipation of my advent into fatherhood. It is something I always dreamed about, but never believed was actually possible.

I yawn. I've been up all night with my closest male friends and family. We gathered for a vigil, a *shemirah,* to guard our son from what Aldonza calls the *danyadores.* In keeping with an old custom, we hung a sword on the wall of the nursery beside a parchment with verses from the Bible and the names of protective angels. Señora Coron also placed a bundle of rue in his cradle and a strand of blue beads.

"We must protect him from the Evil Eye," she told me, clutching my wrist. "And from Lillit, who tries to steal the breath of newborns before they're given a name and enter the covenant of Abraham."

I've heard the legend of Adam's jilted first wife. Although these are just superstitions to me, I see a kind of beauty and mystery in these long-held old wives' traditions.

Mother made marzipan and candied fruit, and Señora Coron baked a honey cake. We drank Malevisi wine, ate sweets, and Aaron read poems from the mystical Zohar. This morning, we will welcome my son into the covenant of Abraham with the *brit milah* ceremony. As it turns out, Dr. Alamosa was once a mohel, before the Alhambra Degree. I trust him to perform the actual circumcision.

The new foal clambers up onto his wobbly legs. He staggers toward his mother, pauses to gain balance, and then begins nursing. My weary heart warms and I smile. He's going to be fine. I sense the presence of someone behind me and turn. Aaron stands a short distance away watching in silence.

"I came to tell you we're about to begin morning prayers. But I didn't realize your horse was giving birth. A double *mazel tov,*" he says softly.

"I knew it would be any day now. But this sure seems like a heavenly coincidence."

We walk together back inside the Coron hacienda.

"I presume you'll be leaving later today," I say.

"I must. I've got numerous eager students waiting for me in Safed," he says. "It's amazing to watch the rebuilding of the great houses of learning."

"Rebuilding? I'm just grateful you're alive and safe."

"God works in mysterious ways. Had I not been living in the Maronite village with Rehm, I wouldn't be standing here," Aaron says. When the Ottomans finally came down from the north, the Mameluke army encamped at Safed to fight them. They slaughtered any Jew who couldn't escape, claiming they were traitors and collaborators.

Returning to my room, I bathe and don my celebratory clothes. The velvety nap of my dark blue doublet is smooth and luxurious to the touch. I fumble trying to fasten the buttons down the silver brocade placket. I'd had it tailored for my wedding day; and it's the finest thing I've ever owned.

My belly flutters when I enter the salon. The great hall is filled with the fragrance of abundant flowers, and the glow of candles warms my face. Aaron stands with our five dearest friends, Saadia, Manoa, Simon, Mossé, and Umberto. Unfortunately, Coron is in Istanbul, conducting wartime naval activities as an admiral. We hover around a tiered silver tray on the credenza devouring sweets. On one side sits a bottle a Raki and stemmed glasses. A large platter on the other side collects *tzedakah* for the poor.

A glittering stitched cloth of purple and gold catches my eye. It wafts on the air as mother and Señora Coron lift it by the corners and drape it over a chair intended to summon the presence of Elijah the Prophet. Beside it, stands a large velvet dining room chair for the *sandek*, the person who will hold my son during the circumcision. By our tradition, my father is given this honor.

With the addition of Aldonza's brother Olivar, we have enough for a minyan. We assemble in front of a bank of windows facing east.

Aaron leads us in prayer. At the close of the service, the time arrives for the *brit milah*. Father sits in the specially designated chair and I take my place at his right shoulder. My knees tremble and I shrug to loosen the tension in my neck and shoulders.

From the hallway, Señora Coron calls out. "Let the groom enter."

Everyone assembled chants in Hebrew, *we welcome him*. The women arrive at the threshold wearing shimmering fine silks and gold embroidered robes, escorting my infant son as if it were a wedding. I can't remember ever seeing my mother's face beam so bright, as she carries my son on a velvet embroidered pillow in slow procession. Aldonza and Señora Coron walk on each side of her. Shuli and Edna follow close behind. I smile when I see Shuli's bulging belly. She and Simon married last year, and expect their own baby in a few months. Edna opened a new café in Famagusta to be near them.

The women's high-pitched staccato ululation sends a quiver down my spine. They enter the salon singing, accompanied with a frame drum and rhythmic clapping. It's impossible not to bob to the cadence. They deliver the baby to Father's waiting arms and everyone's spirit rises, clapping in rhythm to the drumbeat and joining the song.

My hands are shaking as Aaron gives me the prayerbook. Everyone's eyes are on me. With Aaron's guidance, I recite two blessings with a tremor in my voice. One is for my son's fruitfulness, and the other to appoint Dr. Alamosa as *mohel* on my behalf. Aaron raises a cup of wine, blesses it, and passes it around along with a silver filigree spice box. When I recite the circumcision blessing, my voice catches and my eyes well with tears. Aaron takes over to lead the blessing for reaching this milestone event.

Doctor Alamosa comes forward and he places a sop with sugar water and wine in the baby's mouth, to soothe him. I stare down at the tiny little boy in my father's arms. My insides go watery and I'm dizzy. I shift my weight from side-to-side as we sing a welcome hymn to summon the presence of Elijah the Prophet. Strangely, it brings a calm to my middle.

Silence takes over the room, as if everyone is holding their breath, when Doctor Alamosa uncovers my son's genitals. How odd, with all the blood and violence I've seen, to be quaking and dizzy right now. But this is my son. He's so tiny. As I watch Dr. Alamosa take out his fine surgical tools to sever the foreskin from my infant son's penis, the room starts to spin. Saadia grips my arm. My son turns purple and shrieks in pain. Dr. Alamosa staunches the blood and wraps the wound in a bandage.

"Blessed is he who comes, Joachim ben Yonatan Déulocresca," Dr. Alamosa calls. "Always keep the covenant faithfully, for God has promised to preserve us." He then hands our crying infant to Aldonza, who nestles little Joachim in her arms, comforting him.

Señora Coron brings around a silver tray with small glasses of Raki. Saadia takes two, shoving one glass into my hand.

"A tonic to steady you," he says. Raising his glass, he calls out the blessing. Everyone says *Amen*, and tosses back the spirits in one gulp. A chorus of *mazel tov* and *horas buenas* follows. Manoa brings out his *balaban* and Shuli takes the frame drum. They play a stirring dance song. With lifted hands and swiveling hips we all sing a welcome to the newest little one to join our people. Warmth radiates out through my limbs. The melody stirs me inside.

I'm surrounded by loving family and friends with eyes aglow. Bouncing to the rhythm, I cradle my infant son in my arms and dance. I stare into his tiny face, glassy-eyed. Knowing how fragile life is, how at any moment it can be taken from us; it makes me appreciate my life all the more. And at this moment, life is even sweeter. For now, we're safe on this island. But the tides will always change. So, we must always keep our eyes on the horizon. Whatever may come next, we will be ready, because that's who we are.

THE END

I HOPE YOU ENJOYED THIS BOOK.
YOU CAN MAKE A BIG DIFFERENCE.

Reviews are the most powerful way to introduce new readers to my novels. Much as I'd like to, I don't have the influence of the New York publishers and can't take out a full-page ad in the New York Times.

(Not yet, anyway)

But I do have something that those publishers would love to get their hands on.

A loyal circle of readers who love my books.

Honest reviews help bring my work to the attention of others.

If you enjoyed this book, I would be very grateful if you could spend just five minutes leaving a review (it can be as short as you like) on the book's Amazon page.

You can be the first to know.

Building a relationship with my readers is the very best thing about writing. I occasionally send newsletters with details on new releases and giveaways. Sign up for my mailing list here: *Contact - Michelle Fogle, Author (michellefogle-author.com)* My most avid readers may be invited to join my VIP list and receive pre-release copies of my books FREE.

Thank you very much

GLOSSARY

Abba (Hebrew) Dad

al-arjwany- (Arabic) purple

alquitrán- (Spanish) foul smelling tar mixture used to seal the hull, and in explosives

anusim (Hebrew) Forced ones

awlād an-nās (Arabic) sons of the amir, gentry

bağlama (Turkish) stringed instrument in the lute family

baksheesh- (Persian) tip or bribe

baruchim ha bayim (Hebrew) Blessed are those who come

Benvenuto (Italian) welcome

beshaah tova- (Hebrew) a good hour, celebratory saying announcing a pregnancy

bet midrash (Hebrew) study center

bourekas- flaky fried pastry

brit milah (Hebrew) circumcision

buona sera- (Italian) good evening

buenos noches (Spanish) good night

cariño (Spanish) sweetie

cocinerillo (Spanish) cook

converso- (Spanish) convert, refers to Jews forced to become Catholic

danyadores (Ladino) demons

dhimmi- (Arabic) infidel

din rodef (Hebrew) law of the pursuer

despensero (Spanish) stores steward

durra'ah (Arabic) sleeveless long vest

Eema (Hebrew) Mom

faris- (Arabic) knight

ful- (Arabic) mashed fava beans

Furusiyya- (Arabic) horsemanship

Galleta- (Spanish) twice baked tasteless flat bread

gilui arayot (Hebrew) incest

giudecca (Italian) Jewish quarter

Halachah (Hebrew) Jewish law

hammam (Arabic) Turkish baths

hatichot- (Hebrew, pl. of haticha) pieces of silver

jalabah (Arabic) loose-fitting ankle-length robe

jefe del crimen (Spanish) crime boss

kaif (Arabic) 15th Cent. form of hashish

hamsa (Arabic) Hebrew hamesh, meaning five, refers to open palm protective amulet

khan (Arabic) inn or hotel

kame'ah (Hebrew) amulet

keffiyot- (Hebrew and Arabic) plural for keffiyah, a woven headscarf

khamsin- (Arabic) the name of a hot wind blowing north off the Sahara and Egypt

khassaki- (Turkish) member of the sultan's royal guard.

kisa (Arabic) a kind of shirt

kubbait- carob almond butter

madrich (Hebrew) professional guide

mamzayrim (Hebrew) bastards

mehitzah (Hebrew) divider separating women's worship seating

meshuga (Hebrew) crazy

metumtam (Hebrew) stupid

migdal-or (Hebrew) lighthouse

mikveh- (Hebrew) special ritual bath

mimtar- long loose-fitting robe

niddah- (Hebrew) menstrual cycle

nuevo (Spanish) newbie

pesukei dezimra (Hebrew) song passages

pidyon shevuiim (Hebrew) ransoming the captives

pikuach nefesh (Hebrew) preservation of life.

rachmanut (Hebrew) compassion

refuah shlayma (Hebrew) complete healing

ribono shel olam- (Hebrew) master of the universe

rida- (Arabic) long cloak

salam Alekim (Arabic) peace to you

sandek (Hebrew) man holding the infant to be circumcised

sayid (Arabic) sir

Señyor- (Catalan spelling of Spanish señor) mister

shochet (Hebrew) kosher butcher

shuk (Arabic, Hebrew) bazaar

taaseela (Arabic) afternoon rest

Tikkun Hatzot (Hebrew) all-night study event

tzaddiq (Hebrew) Jewish equivalent to a saint

Urbān- (Arabic) pl for Arab, but in 16th century literature was a marauding menace.

yashar koach (Hebrew) lit. straight strength, used to congratulate achievement

yeled-tov yerushalaim (Hebrew) goodie two shoes

zaragüelles (Spanish) coarse canvas sailor pants

zayin (Hebrew) profane name for penis

zhug (Arabic) Yemenite hot sauce

ACKNOWLEDGEMENTS

Historical research is essential to create the immersive experience of time and place in fiction. All of the resources I used in both print and online are far too numerous to list them here. But for readers interested in the era, the following works were indispensable. *Spain's Men of the Sea,* by Pablo E. Pérez-Mallaína. *The Spring Voyage: The Jerusalem Pilgrimage in 1458,* by R. J. Mitchell. *Pathway to Jerusalem: The Travel Letters of Rabbi Obadiah de Bertinoro,* edited by Avrohom Marmorstein. *Zion and Jerusalem: The itinerary of Rabbi Moses Besola,* edited by Abraham David. *Foundations of Sephardic Spirituality,* by Rabbi Marc D. Angel, PhD.

One key figure, Captain Gabriel Coron is a fictionalized composite drawn from actual Jewish pirates of the 16th Century. He is a combination of Çiphut Sinan, called the Great Jew, who was 2nd in command to Barbarossa; and Samuel Pallache, a Moroccan Sephardi who became a privateer for the Dutch Crown Prince and later co-founded the Amsterdam Sephardic community.

I'm also indebted to an intrepid group of writers, the Inkwells who provided critique, suggestions, and inspiration. These include authors Sarah Beauchemin, David Hoffer, Steve Nickell, Ruth Roberts, and Carol Pope.

ABOUT THE AUTHOR

Michelle Fogle is a former psychotherapist turned novelist, living in the Inland Northwest. Her passion for writing led her to coursework at the University of California, and finally to a Certificate in Novel Writing at San Diego Writers' Ink in 2016. She is a member of the Historical Novel Society. She makes her online home at Michelle Fogle, Author - Crafting the Odyssey of immersive Historical Fiction (michellefogle-author.com) Or on Facebook at www.facebook.com/MichelleFogle.Author.